THE LONG FORGOTTEN

David Whitehouse is an award-winning
novelist, journalist and screenwriter. His first
novel, *Bed*, won the 2012 Betty Trask Prize and
his second novel, *Mobile Library*, won the
2015 Jerwood Fiction Uncovered Prize.
Originally from Warwickshire,
he now lives in Margate.

DAVID WHITEHOUSE

THE LONG FORGOTTEN

PICADOR

First published 2018 by Picador
an imprint of Pan Macmillan
20 New Wharf Road, London N1 9RR
Associated companies throughout the world
www.panmacmillan.com

ISBN 978-1-5098-2753-4

1 3 5 7 9 8 6 4 2

A CIP catalogue record for this book is available from the British Library.

Printed and bound by CPI Group (UK) Ltd, Croydon, CR0 4YY

Visit www.picador.com to read more about all our books
and to buy them. You will also find features, author interviews and
news of any author events, and you can sign up for e-newsletters
so that you're always first to hear about our new releases.

For Douglas

ONE

Ten thousand feet deep, bones creak with solitude. Professor Cole feels it mounting in his sternum. Concentrating on the short canyon of light carved into blackness by the headlamps on his one-man submersible, he mutters to himself.

'Everything will be OK. Everything will be all right.' But it is over an hour since he heard from the research vessel on the surface. Cold with terror, he speaks into the radio receiver, winding the wire tight around his fingers, constricting blood so it bulbs beneath skin.

'This is Professor Jeremiah Cole. I repeat. Both engines are now down. Emergency buoyancy failed to deploy. Systems monitor says I have eighteen minutes of air left. Do you read me, over?' An inappropriate calm seeps into his voice, as though thrown there by a benevolent ventriloquist. 'Do you read me? Over.' He swipes a cuff across his brow, blotting pinprick diamonds of sweat on the cotton.

The luminous clock telling him approximately how much longer he'll be alive morphs to seventeen minutes, sixteen, fifteen. How apt, a life entrenched in the academia of oceanography, ending at the bottom of the sea. He punches the monitor until his knuckles split, lets a small blast of air slip his lungs and rues ever embarking on a mission with so many possible failures. Tech glitch. Bad weather. A cataclysmic power outage, like the one befalling him now. Shouldn't we be content to live in the smile of the sun instead of reaching out to touch it? He laughs, actually laughs – the oxygen his to waste. Don't we deserve our fingers burnt?

Wistfully caressing the grid of buttons on the console, he begins to grieve his own demise. This embarrasses him, as though he's anything other than alone. The blush has an intricate texture.

Twelve minutes of oxygen remaining. He spends the next three pressing the red emergency button, seriously contemplating whether to light the cigarette in his pocket. At the very least, it'd be a spectacular last action for a suffocating man. When he shuts his eyes he can almost hear the delightful piss-on-snow hiss of ash burning. He imagines smoke swirling around the top of the pod, almost able to convince himself he is lying on his back in the garden of their house, cigarette in mouth, clutching the sparrow weight of his wife's hand in his.

Then he sees it. Through the porthole above the navigation console, a brief glimpse of ghostly white bulk moving in the beam's golden glow. Death has come for him. Fear has given it form. His quickening breath thrums the limited air.

Without room enough to drop to his knees, he removes his shoes, folds his socks, brings both legs up beneath him on the seat and puts his hands together in prayer to a God he's never believed in. Plagued by visions of his skeleton found genuflecting, he flops back on the chair and fumbles through his pockets for a lighter. If he is ever found they'll understand: in his final moments, this sucker didn't bow to a higher being out of fear. Oh no. He smoked a deliciously woody cigarette instead. He was his own God.

No lighter. He murmurs a prayer half remembered from school, loathing himself more with each line.

A thud throws him against the panel to the left, smashing his head against the defunct power lights, then to the right, where he breaks a tooth on the hatch lever. The coppery taste of blood floods his gums.

Through the glass, another sight of the beast that has come to claim his soul. But now he sees; it is not death after all.

Instruments record that when Cole's craft chances on the goose-beaked whale, it is exactly two hundred miles west of Perth, Australia. Confused by the sonar's gentle whinny, the curious whale catches its tail in the elbow of the craft's mechanical arm, thrashes, then, distressed, its heart overwhelmed and in arrest, rises to the surface, taking with it the submersible and, inside that, the professor.

The whale is dead by the time the craft bursts out of the sea, and Cole's veins fizz, not with the bends, but with his good fortune. His wife of forty-four years will never read the words *I love you. I always have. I always will*, hastily scrawled on the back of a crumpled cigarette packet.

He opens the hatch and gulps down lungfuls of briny sea air. Beside him bobs the whale's carcass. Wave spray cools his face.

Peeling free his sweat-sodden overalls, he shoots a flare into the early evening sky, watches the sparks scatter a fly-past of gulls. Soon, on the endless horizon, where the blues of water and sky are hazily sewn, his ship comes into view. For twenty glorious minutes he observes the dish of a giant orange sun drop behind it, collapsed in ecstasy. He is alive.

The professor's team sling ropes from the side of the boat, averting their eyes as his near-naked body, chalky white, climbs the dull grey steel of the hull. A young woman drapes a towel over his shoulders. He forgets, though only for a moment, that they are professor and student, enough that he wants to kiss the fullness of her smile.

'You're safe, Professor Cole,' she says. A part of him he'd never let her see wants to cry, but he swallows it and snarls at nothing in particular. The young woman looks at her colleagues in confusion.

'Bring it aboard,' he says.

'Bring . . . *it* aboard?'

'That's what I said.'

'The whale?'

'Of course the whale! What else would I mean? The bloody ocean?'

So chains clank, cogs grind, a crane swings. Two hours pass and it's aboard. It's the longest and heaviest goose-beak he's ever seen, that much is clear from a cursory glance. While they dwell at depth – deeper and for longer than any other mammal – he's never heard tell of a goose-beak at 10,000 feet before. He is interested to know what it dives to eat. An observation of new behaviour may at least help assuage the guilt he feels for his role in its death. How much longer might it have lived if he'd been content with never knowing what's not ours to know?

He cuts its belly open with the blade of a crude machete. Thick crimson blood washes the deck. And there it is, amid the gore and the pungent swirls of steam somehow pretty. Battered shapeless, corroded by acids but intact; the black box recorder of flight PS570: a memory entombed in metal.

Nobody knows where or when the whale swallowed it, how far it travelled or whether it will still work, but it has long left behind the plane that carried it and 316 people into the water on a clear evening in May, three decades before.

Until this moment, flight PS570 had earned its place in folklore as the plane that simply vanished from the air. They call it 'The Long Forgotten'. Few but the bereaved and their children remember the actual facts of the case: the dead, the fruitless search and the many years it lasted. But Cole's endeavour has been rewarded with a quite unforeseeable prize, for when the handsome, silvering professor triumphantly lifts the flight recorder into the air, memories come flooding back.

TWO

Dove is walking to work along the canal when he remembers the bog violet. It just appears, however memories do, a glimmer of the past shining through the now.

The bog violet is the purplish of a ripening bruise. It is three inches high with small, kidney-shaped leaves, the lowest of five notch-tipped petals crowned by a storm-blue spur, and a carpel as fragile as freshly spun sugar.

Dove knows nothing of flowers. And there are few of his age (if his age is thirty, which is what he thinks it is) who know what he now knows of the bog violet; that's how vivid the memory is. He knows what it looks like, what it feels like – the intricacy of its structure, from the tip of the anther to the stalk. The memory is as lucid as his reflection, stilling in the black glass of the canal. But where had he seen it before, and why is he recalling it now? He scans through the flick-book version of his life from the beginning, getting all the way back to the present, still with no idea.

If he believed in reincarnation he might call it a vision from a past life. But reincarnation is a load of hocus, as made enjoyably plain by a documentary he'd recently found so compelling he watched it twice, in which four people laid claim to having once been Joan of Arc. Under the auspices of the producers they met to argue which of them had the stronger case, in the process revealing harsh glimpses of their day-to-day realities. One was an un-employed single father of two, another a waitress with tinnitus, the third a widowed failed inventor and the fourth a woman living in a remote Scottish bothy. But they all testified with a preacher's conviction to the truth of their previous existence as a tragic war heroine and Roman Catholic saint. Believing themselves to have been important in a past life helped them to navigate the lonely normality of the one they found themselves in now. If lonely normality is a qualifying factor, surely Dove – single, broke, orphaned – has as solid a claim as anyone. Though given his luck, it's far more likely he was the dung sweeper tasked with collecting dry grass to speed the fire. And it's either laughing at this thought, or the needling pain skittering across his scalp that he chases through his hair with a fingertip, that distracts him enough that the memory of the bog violet starts to fade, leaving Dove with nothing but a vague sense of déjà vu. Then it's gone. So that's all it is. A trick of the mind. A ghost in his thoughts.

The walk to work along the canal is pleasant. Bankside scents of mud and moss. Barges moving mournfully through locks. It is still early. Soon he will be at his desk again, answering the phones, listening to the problems of others. Today, it can wait. He sits on a bench, flattens a sprig of brown hair with his hands and runs the balls of his palms over the initials of young lovers scratched into the slats.

A funereal parade of litter floats past a cafe that has opened since he was last here. Buckets full of plump green olives crowd the window of what was, 140 years before, a spartan little eating house, designed to service the hardworking inhabitants of some of East London's first social housing. Its new proprietors have kept the letters adorning the glass, some scratched off but most still stuck, that read, *For Respectably Employed Working Men*. Beneath it a small group of people drink coffee, their faces framed by laptop screens in rectangles of glow-worm white light. In the distance, over the buildings, the spikes of a shifting cityscape are tended by an idling procession of cranes: this city, his city, quickly becoming a theme park for the monied. One of which he feels no part.

A young woman jogs along the towpath, her rust-red hair scraped into an untidy bun. She stops to take a photograph of herself. Unsatisfied with the first attempt, and annoyed by the second, she stoops to let a view she hasn't yet enjoyed fill the background. The third is more like it, just the right angle in her cheekbones' tilt, and the light that smoothes the bags beneath her eyes bouncing off the glass portholes of a passing riverboat. She pauses to upload the image to the Internet, where it will exist forever; an indelible memory of nothing in particular. And then she continues to run towards him, past the pigeons that examine cigarette butts like soldiers searching a battlefield for unspent ammunition.

'Dove!' she says, surprised enough to see him that she comes to a sudden stop halfway between the bench and the bank, where the grass performs a curtsy on the breeze.

Lara Caine is from Chicago, but her parents were both executives working in the derivatives market who travelled extensively around Europe. Her whole family moved to London before she was sixteen. Dove and Lara met while studying journalism at university, and from the very first day when she thrust her hand into the air and asked a question about libel law that temporarily flummoxed the lecturer, the other students widely accepted she'd excel. They were a notably international group – Norwegian, Japanese, Portuguese. To Dove, who had what suddenly seemed like all the life experience of a dust weevil, they were all unknowably exotic. But none more than Lara. She exuded the confidence bred by a good education and a happy family life as though it were a mineral stored within her she could mine at will, turn into an energy beamed as light through her eyes.

'Hi,' he says, and he's suddenly, perilously aware he can't think of a single question to ask to which he doesn't already know the answer. She's just turned thirty, a reporter for the London desk of an American financial news channel, working in the Square Mile. She has her own TV show, Saturdays and Sundays at 11 p.m., where she recaps the week's big news from the markets, with a catchy instrumental theme tune to which her name can be sung, and a generous wardrobe budget. She's engaged to be married to another American named Ross. He is tall and broad-shouldered in that rectangular, military-line style unique to well-bred Americans, as though their entire physique is a uniform and they'll be punished for any variation on muscle tone or posture. He works in property development, and together they own a miniature schnauzer Ross wanted to name 'Barky Bark Wahlberg' (his friends' comments underneath his Facebook photographs suggest they all think he's crazy, which suggests to Dove they don't know what crazy means), but who is now named 'Max', at Lara's insistence. Her whole story is extensively available online, carefully curated by her. On more than one occasion Dove has found himself scrolling through it, losing minutes and then hours on pictures of holidays he hasn't taken, featuring people he has never met. Has it really been a decade since he last saw her for real? Absences weren't absences any more.

'You look good,' he says, forehead flushing a pale maroon. She looks down at the expanding ellipses of sweat on her vest, a Venn diagram around her navel, both pretend they haven't noticed.

'Thanks,' she says, the swinging rhythms of her Chicago accent still intact. 'It's been so long. What, like, ten years?'

'Yeah. Ten years.'

'How are you doing?'

'Fine. And you?' He already knows. She's doing great. Is this what he thought seeing her would feel like? Cold.

Apart. Not like the version of her in his memory. Oh, the dizzying warmth that began in his gut when she walked into the lecture theatre, then rose until it reached his tongue and the moisture in his mouth turned to ash. That taste again now, but soured, clambering slowly up his throat. He should never have taken this route to work. But he'd seen her pictures. He knew there was a chance he'd bump into her here. This is why he did it.

'Things are good,' she says. 'I work in TV now. Y'know, print is dead and all that jazz.'

'Sure.'

'And I'm getting married next summer.'

'Great.' He nods a little too vigorously.

'What about you? What are you up to these days?' Dread of this question hardens inside him like a spear of cooling wax. He didn't graduate, she knows as much, and the facts of the matter still make him ashamed. Her expression remains generous, open, inquisitive. He reasons she's just being nice, which he isn't sure he deserves.

'Just working, really.'

'In journalism?'

He shrugs, a tightly engineered nonchalance. 'Ambulance chasing.'

'Hey, call it what you like. The world needs good reporters.'

He is heavy with memories of the aborted attempts he made to let her know how he felt. Binned letters. Unsent emails. In the student union bar, drunk, saying it, actually saying it aloud, underneath the speaker so the words were lost in the dirge of awful house music, and she shouted 'What?', and he replied 'Nothing', and the coolness of her spittle drizzled on his ear felt, for a second, perverse and fantastic, disgusting but right.

'Everyone's so busy these days,' she says, 'aren't they?'

'Yeah, seems that way.'

And that's when he's sure she starts to recall what happened all those years ago, because she begins to jog on the spot: short, tiny movements, as though time has slowed to make it hurt all the more.

'Anyway, I'd better go.'

'Me too,' he says, glancing at his wrist, the pale band around it enabling him to picture more vividly the watch on his bedside table, beeping and not being heard.

'Take care of yourself now, won't you, Dove,' she says. Then she runs in the direction he came from, back into his past.

Dove. Most people assume it's a nickname he has given himself. He has grown to loathe discussing it. To his mind there is nothing to discuss. As a teenager he briefly tried to assume the name John, revelling in its normality, its directness, its resilience to questioning. But it didn't suit him and wouldn't stick. The truth is, he doesn't know why he's named Dove. It's just the name he was given, by whoever gave it to him, whenever it was he was born.

Leaving the canal in Islington, Dove weaves through the backstreets of Angel into Farringdon via Exmouth Market, where road sweepers reset the scene of the day before; the stink of wetted pavements, dirty water. The grumble of their truck reminds him of the headache. Nothing he can't handle, just a twinge in his left temple that tugs when he turns into the wind. But he stops at a small supermarket close to his office to buy paracetamol regardless, because he still can't quite face work, not yet.

A man in his seventies operates the till. Pink scoops of skin underline his eyes and his mottled teeth are a sandy yellow. The subplots of age. There's an elephantine sadness to the movement of his hand across the scanner.

'The account is one point five,' the young man in front of Dove says to his colleague, his voice so loud it drowns out the tannoy, as he buys a pack of cigarette papers and stashes them in his breast pocket.

'Thou?'

'Mill. And that's just the digital side of the business.' He has a beard so black and thin and feeble that even up close it gives the effect it's drawn on with an eye pencil.

'That's branding for you,' his colleague says, hair gelled violently to the left in a way Dove thinks must remind *everyone but him* of Hitler. He is swiping through his mobile phone to show his friend a photograph of a young woman. Blonde, the pear-drop fullness of her lips pushed coquettishly towards the camera. 'This is the one I told you about. Meeting her again tonight.'

'Where are you going to take her?'

'Spent a hundred and fifty quid at that restaurant so

I'm hoping this time just a few drinks will be enough for a repeat performance.' He winks, his left eye closed a second too long, and they laugh. The one with the cigarette papers takes his handful of change without once looking at the old man giving it to him, as casually as he might pump a dollop of soap into his palm. He and his colleague are still chuckling as they exit the store. Dove buys the tablets and a bottle of water, head dipped by way of apology for anyone in the vicinity of his age group. The old man doesn't seem to notice.

Next door is a tall drab building, unremarkable yet malignant, for this is where Dove works, and where, on a bad night, his dreams take place to taunt him. They call it the Pit, which makes it sound as crowded and ferocious as the trading floor in a Wall Street bank, but the call centre for ambulance dispatch is remarkably muted, given the urgency of its business. An expanse of grey space is divided into booths by screens up to chest height, offering staff an illusory privacy. Dove's booth is at the rear, close to a vending machine that throws an unchanging season of light across the desks; an eternal, neon midwinter. There are no windows on this side of the building; a television is mounted in the far corner, set to a news channel with the sound off. Dove squints to half read the subtitles streaking across the bottom of the screen. *Black box flight recorder. Missing plane. Whale. Professor.*

There have been occasions in the past: the riots, disasters, bombings, terrorist attacks, when the pictures shared an eerie correspondence with the calls coming through, and he's imagined himself stationed at a listening post, far above an unravelling city.

'What time do you call this?'

Cliff is the office manager. His baldness bends reflections of the strip lights into haloes as he checks an imaginary pocket watch. Cliff smiles and sticks out his tongue – a friendly gesture that leaves Dove unmoved. The joke is always the same.

'Won't happen again,' Dove says, taking his seat and logging into the system, the screen immediately illuminated by a grid of pulsing lights. Each of these lights is a different call with a different emergency, and he answers whichever is next.

'London ambulance.'

'Hello?' a man says. His voice is hurried and reedy. 'I need help.' Dove takes the man's address. There are few scenarios he's yet to encounter. The most common calls regard choking, strokes, road traffic accidents or heart attacks, though almost every medical situation can be handled satisfactorily until the paramedic team arrives by referring to the corresponding diagnostic checklist that appears on screen at the click of a mouse. In that sense the role is automated, and the call is a series of cues for the next instruction. But the job cannot be done by a robot, for it also demands an essence of humanity. To maintain a tone both reassuring and authoritative, as on the other end of the line life's unnavigable map unfurls for some other poor soul to find themselves lost.

'My son,' the man says, 'his hand is stuck.'

'Where is it stuck?'

'Behind a radiator. I told him to get his sock from behind it and . . .' The man's breathing speeds.

'Try to stay calm,' Dove says. 'Now tell me. Is he in any pain?'

'Not yet.'

'Not yet?'

'The heating has only just switched on.'

'Can you switch it back off?'

'That's the thing. I can't. It's broken.'

Dove knows within seconds if a call will find foothold in his consciousness. He once spoke to a fifteen-year-old girl who'd abandoned her newborn daughter in a storm drain, for fear of her father finding out she'd had sex with a classmate then secretly carried his child to term. She begged Dove to save the infant's life. When he asked her to tell him *exactly* where the storm drain was, she couldn't give him an accurate answer, only that it was somewhere on Wanstead Flats. And so he had to piece together the fragments of her memory. She could see an electricity pylon. Behind that the silhouette of the Olympic Stadium to, she guessed, the south-west, because it was similar in angle to the view she always saw from the school bus. Directly to what must have been the east, street lights and traffic, which Dove figured could only have been Lake House Road, as it passed what she described as a circular muddy hollow a hundred or so metres away that he recognized from his walks there as Cat and Dog Pond (so named because it only exists when it's been 'raining cats and dogs'). An ambulance was dispatched, the baby found safe and well, but Dove stayed restless for weeks afterwards, his appetites for sleep and food frayed. This call, the hand behind the radiator, may linger for a shorter time, but remains for now a new and unwelcome guest in the hotel of his psyche.

Dove can hear the caller frantically pacing the room.

'It won't switch off!' the man says. 'Do you hear me? It won't switch off!' A pulsing orange blob moves across the grid on Dove's monitor – an ambulance passing slowly through rush-hour traffic. In the background, a boy sobbing, high-pitched and fearful. Perhaps eight, nine years old at most.

'What should I do?' the man asks. Dove scrolls through the checklist.

'It's important to remain calm for your son's sake as much as your own.' The boy shrieks again.

'He says it's burning!' The man shouts so loudly Dove's headphones vibrate. 'I can't get it out! What can I do!?'

Dove can't help but think of his own father, a man he has never met. Closing his eyes he sees a blank human shape, on which he superimposes his own gait and features. If they passed in the street would he recognize his own face, twisted by the years? Would there be magnets in the blood to pull them together? Are they the same man, timed to the same internal rhythm, written in the same infernal code?

'Daddy.' The boy's voice is both quiet and loud, fear pitching it at a frequency Dove can barely hear.

'They're coming,' the man says, and then again into the telephone, 'They are coming, aren't they?'

'They're almost there.' The orange blob moves a couple of millimetres – in real terms, the length of a bus, maybe two.

The walls of the Pit are lined with pictures of lakes, flowers and seascapes, and beneath them small signs read words like 'peace' and 'serenity'. Dove hasn't noticed before, but he sees now they've been scribbled out and replaced by words like 'anguish' and 'despair'. Gallows humour is a valuable currency when you've tried and failed to talk someone through a cardiopulmonary resuscitation.

On the telephone comes the sudden mechanical caterwaul of sirens. A door opening. Paramedics' boots beating on a stripped wooden floor.

'They're here,' the man says, and hangs up. Dove will never speak to him again, never know if the boy's hand is saved. And yet, despite the lack of resolution, the work proves cathartic. He imagines every call as a tiny hole in a wall, bleeding light into a dark room. When he puts his eye to the hole he can see outside. He can see life. He is illuminated.

Without warning, the headache reveals itself. What pain went before was a warning shot fired across the bows, but this is something tough, something solid. Dove squeezes the throbbing pupae of his temples just as Cliff passes, licking his thumbs to wet down his eyebrows, which he only does when he's thought of something funny to say.

'Dove, are you OK?' He scans the other booths, ensures his colleagues are listening. They dip their heads from his eyeline. 'Should I call an ambulance?' His joke told to little reaction, Cliff walks briskly back to his office, leaving Dove at his desk, rubbing his skull with both hands like a clairvoyant searching a crystal ball for visions of the future. He is almost never sick. Whoever his parents were, they apparently had strong immune systems; a thought that, on nights when he's particularly lonely, gives Dove hope they're alive, as though he wants to find them, as though they deserve to be found.

It happens so rarely that it's easy for him to imagine the headache as the baby steps of death. But this isn't how he imagined dying would feel. He imagined dying would be a draining. A move towards emptiness. But this is more as though he's being filled, packed with something new.

And then he remembers the bog violet again. But there is more. He remembers the bog violet and the hand that once picked it. He remembers it all and it hurts and is glorious. With searing clarity: a memory that isn't and has never been his.

THREE

Peter Manyweathers looked out of his third-storey window at the Brooklyn street below and the sweat dripping from the faces of the people passing by. He imagined the odours of their armpits and it made him doubly grateful for the zing of the lemon-fresh disinfectant he'd already cleaned the kitchen with once that morning.

He tossed the small book of instructions for the use of hazardous chemicals into his work bag and opened the fridge to the gleaming white teeth of near-empty shelves. An almost finished carton of orange juice, half a bottle of ketchup and two eggs a week past their use-by date – 8 June 1983. It was a balanced diet of sorts, he supposed. Clinging to that notion, he ate a bowl of dry cornflakes one by one, tossed the eggs in the garbage, leafed through his diary and considered the day ahead. Like most days, it was chiefly comprised of dirt.

He tried moulding his mousy-brown hair into present-able form, but it had grown disobedient, so he scooped it beneath a Yankees cap worn at a tilt unbecoming to his age. Raking the growth on his chin with his fingers, he twisted to glance at his profile in the mirror and knew there were middle-aged men looked far worse. Wobbling paunches. Thinning tops. False teeth. At least he had everything he was born with, and in roughly the shape it was at the start.

The kitchen was compact, no more than five steps between the oven on one wall and the door on the other; a collation of soft furnishings; sparse, dotted afterthoughts. There were fifteen minutes before he needed to leave for work. Loath to waste them, he buffed the metal sink, wiped down the countertops and mopped the floor until his reflection shone.

He left his apartment repeating the words 'buy some milk on the way home' and enjoyed the short walk to his lockup. The heat hadn't yet reached the point where it became unmanageable, but was certainly on its way there. Slipping keys from his pocket, Peter unlocked the huge door of a space far too big for his one-man band, but on which he'd landed an excellent rate some years before. The sign he'd had erected above the doorway – *Kingfisher Cleaning* (a cute painting of a kingfisher with a feather duster poised in its beak) – still pleased him every time he saw it. Smiling, he turned on the lights, the switches shifting with a gratifying clunk, and found the place satisfactorily immaculate. Changing into his blue overalls, he readied himself as best he could for another day of unsanitary extremes.

It was never an easy job, but especially not that summer. Iowa, Missouri, Illinois and a handful of other states were posting their hottest on record. New York was boiling over. Manhattan's mirrored walls trapped the heat inside the city: a giant greenhouse, its air shimmering with the funk of damp bodies. Tropical birds were reported nesting in Central Park. Even the kids that hung on the corner of his street were too hot to hassle anybody – not that they ever really hassled Peter, if they noticed him at all. The way they lay across the shaded steps, one on each, with their brightly coloured track tops off, made him think fondly of the bunk bed he'd once shared with his sister, Susan.

He drove to his appointment in a clapped-out sedan, its yellow shell zebra-striped with rust. According to his diary, he'd be spending much of the next week cleaning the Bronx apartment of a woman three years dead by the time anybody realized. It was impossible to know what to expect, his vast experience not equating to foresight. A number of regular contracts made up Peter's bottom line. More often than not, if neighbours noticed a strange smell coming from next door and called the police, who found a decomposing body or sometimes even a skeleton – people who had died alone – someone called Peter.

Above all else, this line of work meant Peter understood loneliness beyond its dictionary definition, or even the sad twinge he sometimes felt, lowering his aching back onto a chilled mattress late at night. Loneliness as he knew it – *in extremis* – was decay, subsuming not just the person, but everything around them: the walls, the carpet and the air. He saw it every day, in a thousand grotesque manifestations. Floors that heaved with pregnant rats and inch-deep shelves of scum. Cobwebs spun round towers of plates and piles of rotting shirts. The unrelenting sadness of a solitary life.

As summer went on, Peter decided to take on an assistant, kidding himself that it might be the beginning of the business's expansion, rather than a move born of his desire for company. He placed an advertisement in the local newspaper, half expecting it to come to nothing. The lady at the newspaper office laughed, rattling the earpiece of his telephone receiver.

'You want an apprentice?'

'I suppose.'

'To clean up dead people?'

'No, there are specialists who take care of that. I clean up whatever's left behind.'

'Don't sound too appealing,' the lady said. Peter imagined her grimace at the other end of the line and bristled.

'Well, a successful applicant is going to have to come to terms with that pretty fast. Probably before they apply.'

'Jeez. A lot of people want jobs, but . . .'

Placing the receiver back on the hook, he sat on the rug and conceded that the lady was right. It wasn't an alluring prospect for anybody, even with unemployment figures at their highest since the Great Depression. The few school friends he kept track of – good, honest guys who'd grafted in steel manufacturing or automobiles – couldn't get work holding half-price burger signs. The man on the street was being punished for the crimes of those with expensive cufflinks.

Maybe he wasn't cut out to have a colleague. The more he thought about it, the more cleaning seemed best kept a solitary pursuit. Isn't that what he enjoyed about it? This sense of it being him versus the task ahead. In front, the work to be done. Behind, the path of progress. There were so few signifiers of the route by which he'd stumbled through life – no marriage, no children – that the clean swathe through a grime-caked floor gave him a distinct high, or so he liked to tell himself. Lying awake at night, he wrestled with the notion of exposing another human being to the sights that regularly assailed him, least of all a young woman like Angelica Meek, the sole respondent to his advertisement.

Angelica met him outside a five-storey house on the Upper East Side of Manhattan early on a Monday morning. She watched him fumble with a bunch of keys, to find that the first seven he tried bore little relation to the shape of the hole in the door.

'I'd ask if you want me to try,' Angelica said, 'but seeing as you're my boss and this is my first morning on the job, I wouldn't want to find the right key immediately and undermine you.'

'I appreciate that. I think.'

Angelica was fresh out of beauty college. Her nails had tiny paintings of stars on them, her make-up was immaculate. She looked like Madonna, who, if Peter was perfectly honest, scared the shit out of him. Once he'd opened the door – *if* he could open the door – he reckoned on ten minutes before she quit.

'Look, like I told you on the phone, it's going to be horrible in there. I mean really grim. Mr Bertrecht died over two years ago and they didn't even discover his body until last week.'

'How can that even happen?'

'All that I'm saying is, this is going to be far removed from anything you're used to. So I'm still not sure why you applied.'

'I applied because I want the job.' She snapped on a pair of rubber gloves.

'You can be honest,' he said, smiling so she might relax. 'Is this one of those situations where your parents make you get a job to pay your way, and you just take anything you can find?' She shook her head like she'd just realized he was an asshole. He realized how patronizing he was being and wanted to start the entire day again.

'If you think it'll save time you can drop the concerned uncle thing and we can get started,' she said, with a smile crooked as lightning. He didn't know many young women. Maybe they were all this full of attitude these days. All he knew was that he liked her. He was glad she had shown up, and sorry for what she was about to see.

It was a bad one. Mr Bertrecht had lived a life of solitude, squalid and adrift. Rot. Damp. Piss. Shit. An unpalatable cocktail of odours. The mulch of an enormous newspaper collection that spanned back twenty years, smelling of eggs and grease. Old newspapers were a frequent fixture in the houses of the undiscovered. All these people had was a past of which they were barely a part.

Angelica was stoical, even when the mattress split, spewing cockroaches like coffee beans. They carried the bed outside, pulled up the carpet, then took a break. She didn't complain once.

'Mr Bertrecht had weeds growing up the plughole in the kitchen sink,' she said.

'You see that a lot. You'd be surprised how quickly nature takes back a building if you leave it untouched. Flowers. Plants. Those things are powerful. And they ain't like human beings either. They're forever.'

She ran a gloved finger through a thick patch of grease clinging to her plastic overalls.

'No, I wouldn't be surprised.'

He was delighted, and ashamed to feel shocked, when she lasted until the end of the day.

'You did well,' he said.

'Do I get the job?'

'Are you kidding me? Of course you get the job.' They shook hands, each as dirty as the other. 'Do you want me to talk to your parents or anything?'

'What?'

'Your parents. I can talk them through it.'

'Why?' she said. 'I'm old enough to have a job.'

'Well, if you were my daughter, and you got this kind of a job with a man old enough to be your father, I'd want to know a little about it. About him.' She put her hands on her hips, tilted her head to the side. It made her seem older than her years.

'Really, Mr Manyweathers, that isn't something you need to do.' He nodded and said goodbye. It was the eighties. Things had changed. He'd heard of fiercely independent teenagers. He just hadn't expected them to be so fierce.

Cleaning Mr Bertrecht's house took weeks, even with two of them at it all day every day. They'd scoured the floor until their backs locked in spasm. They'd lifted dust from ornate diamond chandeliers with a lightness of touch more commonly expected of archaeologists. Out of decay was emerging beauty unlike any that either of them had ever seen. Out of decay was emerging a home. Before long Peter couldn't remember how he'd ever done the job alone.

The upstairs bathroom was the last room to be cleaned. Nothing shocked Peter any more. Rarely did he see anything he hadn't already seen. But in that bathroom, black with grime from the floor to the ceiling, was something he'd truly never laid eyes on before. Behind the toilet cistern, in the foul crust that caked the porcelain, grew a flower so vivid that when he saw it, he jumped, as though it were a tropical spider with its front legs raised to strike.

A small flash of purple, white at the centre, shining in the blackness – it was its own source of light. There, where it was cold and dark and there was nothing else of life, it had survived. But more, it had grown. It was beautiful, irresistible. He plucked it and pressed it in the only book he had in the bottom of his bag – the book of hazardous chemicals used for cleaning.

'Peter?' Angelica said, lifting the muzzle-shaped plastic mask from her mouth and nestling it in her hair. He stopped where he was, sodden overalls sticking to his skin. 'Can I ask you something?'

'Sure.' He tossed the mangled scouring sponge he'd been using into a bucket. She opened her mouth but didn't say anything, as though she'd changed her mind. 'What is it?' he said.

'Nothing,' she said. 'It's just, kind of selfish, isn't it?'

'What?'

'To have a house this big and not share it with anyone.'

'I guess,' he said. It was a thought that hadn't occurred to him before.

'I think I'd like to live here,' she said. 'Maybe one day I will.'

'You have a home already,' he said, checking the watch he kept in a sealed plastic bag in his pocket. 'Let's go. It's Saturday. Half day. I'll buy you pizza.'

'Nah.' She flipped the mask back over her nose. He tried to argue, but couldn't make himself heard over the noise of her coarse brush on the tiles. At the end of the day she only downed tools when he threatened to lock her in. He got the distinct feeling, as he did most nights, that she didn't want to go home.

It was a stormy evening. The rain turned to steam as it hit the sidewalk. Peter insisted he drive her to where she needed to be.

'I can get the train,' she said.

'Don't be ridiculous. I go your way.' He divided his equipment into piles he could easily transport to the car.

'I don't mind getting wet.'

'I mind you getting wet.' They stared at one another for a while, before she sulkily helped him load the trunk.

They'd been stuck in traffic on Brooklyn Bridge for more than an hour. He honked the horn, sparking a chorus of others running both ways across the river. She'd asked him how he got into cleaning, and he told her it was all he'd ever been good at, which was a lie. In truth he was adept at most things he put his mind to. Most things that didn't involve other people, anyway.

'How old are you?' she said.

'Forty-four.' She whistled like he'd broken a record.

'Then why aren't you married?'

'I don't know. It just didn't happen.' Peter couldn't believe he was having this conversation with someone who'd just left school.

'Didn't happen *yet*,' she said, and smiled. Angelica opened the glove compartment, shot a pitying look at its only contents – a pair of Marigolds – then closed it again. 'I think you're a nice guy.'

'Nice?' he said, and laughed. 'What about your parents? How long they been married?'

'They're not.' She turned to look at the Manhattan skyline. 'Mom's not around. Dad's a total asshole. Drinks a lot. Gets mad.'

'I'm sorry about that.'

'Don't be. Just keep paying me so I can move out as soon as possible.'

'I've a spare room if you ever need it,' he said, only afterwards considering it might be a wildly inappropriate suggestion. She didn't respond and he didn't know what to say next.

They arrived at the lockup, the drains already flooded and the rain hitting the puddles with such force it seemed the ground was boiling.

'I can walk from here,' Angelica said.

'Don't be ridiculous,' Peter said. 'Let's unload the car and then I'll take you. Otherwise you'll catch pneumonia. What use will you be to me then?'

She clenched her fists, her knuckles nudging at her skin like carp at the surface of a pond.

'Seriously,' she said, 'it's fine. But thank you, Mr Manyweathers.'

'Peter,' he said, and watched her walk down the street. She paused briefly at the end, far enough away that he could only just see her grubby skin against the dirty concrete walls. She looked up at an ugly steel bridge as a train passed overhead and shook nesting pigeons from the stanchions, then disappeared round the corner as a snow-fall of feathers spun around her.

Instead of going back to his apartment, Peter went to Brooklyn Library, where in recent months he'd been trying to better himself. His mind whirred with thoughts of Angelica enough that he couldn't name a single book he wanted to read.

He approached the front desk, where the librarian, an old man with a full, reddish beard that appeared to contain slivers of brass, looked him over with a disapproving sigh. Peter opened his bag to return the four novels he'd borrowed last time, none of which he'd managed to finish, and to pay the fine for them being late.

'This isn't one of ours,' the librarian said, pushing a small black book back across the desk. Peter's instruction manual of cleaning chemicals. As he was putting it back in his bag, the delicate purple flower he'd found in Mr Bertrecht's bathroom slipped into his hand. His heart fluttered with excitement.

Peter took from the shelf a dusty encyclopedia of flowers that didn't appear to have been opened in many years. He retired to a quiet corner, where he usually went so he couldn't be spied upon by visiting schoolkids. Leafing through the pages, it wasn't long before he recognized that same vivid purple. The bog violet. As he did, a small slip of paper fell out of the book, onto the table in front of him. On it was a letter, in handwriting neater than he had ever seen. Minute and measured movements looped in ink about the page, lines that swooped and circled the point where they began, like petals themselves. This is what it said.

My darling,

As my studies take me far away, this time to the Pacific (how's that for adventure?), I write this letter for you to find in this book of yours. Feel free to tease me on my return with how dreadfully soppy I've become since we met. Every time you look at it, you will know I am thinking of you. This also applies when you're not looking at it, because I am thinking of you all the time. In fact, I'm starting to wish I'd never taken a course that would have me travel so much, and for so long. Perhaps if we had met before I had enrolled I never would have enrolled at all. Maybe we would be studying flowers together. Yes, yes, I know you think I give botany short shrift in favour of my own more lively pursuits . . . but you'd be wrong! I've done my research (you can stop laughing now) and found six flowers so unique, so fantastic that when I think of them, they could only ever remind me of you. Here to prove it is a list.

The Gibraltar Campion
Sheep-eating plant
Kadupul Flower
The living fossil
The Udumbara
The Death Flower

I already know what you're thinking. The sheep-eater! The death flower! How can these suggestions come from the mouth of a man who professes to adore me so much, to know so much about romance? And so when I come home I will tell you exactly how every last one of them is emblematic of our love. How you and I are the sum of them. How they make up a heart. I can't wait.

Oh I miss you. Oh I love you.

Jx

Peter stood in the library with the letter scrunched in his hand, rapt by the bliss of new obsession. Children stared down from the mezzanine, half convinced he was a mannequin, until he called over the librarian and asked him to retrieve the best reference book on flowers in the building. The librarian relished a challenge, and set about pursuing his prey with the tenacity of an expert marksman. The heavy tome he returned with made Peter's hands tremble. Sitting down in the quiet reading area, at a table well worn by scholars' elbows, he started with the last flower on the list.

The death flower was not its real name. Its real name was *Rafflesia arnoldii* – or, more commonly, the corpse flower. Though he hadn't seen the flower until now, instinct, or the mischievous fuzz in his gut he guessed was such, told Peter that 'death flower' was far more apt a moniker. Corpses were merely a by-product of death, the bones at the end of a meal. Death itself was the great unlockable. That's why he supposed the *Rafflesia arnoldii* took a place in the letter. Perhaps the writer of the note knew, even then when their love was fledging, that he wanted them to die together. Perhaps that was what he was trying to say. Peter had never heard of anything so romantic in his life. He had to stop reading for a second, just to breathe, just to be.

Rafflesia arnoldii, technically speaking at least, was the single largest individual flower in the world. It could reach up to six feet in height and three feet in diameter, bigger than a hippopotamus, and was endemic to the rainforests of Borneo and Sumatra, where it was especially difficult to find because the buds took many months to develop and the flower lasted for just a few days. There was more chance of playing midwife at the birth of a panda cub than there was of stumbling across the death flower in bloom. And yet it was unlike any other flower on the list. Most of them were scarce. But its scarcity was not what made it special.

The death flower was special because it defied everything a flower should be. Bodiless, stemless, leafless and rootless, its survival was dependent on the *Tetrastigma* vine, which it required for nourishment and support. Better still, it emitted the pungent funk of rotten flesh – hence the name – so that beetles and flies might mistake it for the carcass of a dead animal and land there long enough to pollinate. In fact, the death flower was not like a flower at all. It was free and precious and changing, without form or reason. It couldn't exist alone, and yet seemed to know the sadness of its own fate. It was almost human: beautiful, curious and brief.

Peter closed the book, overwhelmed, and headed home, forgetting to buy milk.

When he arrived, Angelica was waiting on his doorstep in the rain, her sodden bag a collapsed lung at her side.

'Can I stay here a while?' she asked.

'Your dad?' he said. She nodded.

He didn't know how to put his arms around her. They stood together until the time and the weather combined to mean nothing any more.

FOUR

Usually, Dove wakes to the squall of his alarm. Usually he picks splinters of a shattered dream from the supple flesh of a new day. Usually he showers, a part of him hoping that the water will wash away – as it does the grease from his hair or the dirt from his nails – an emptiness compounded by the fug of just waking. Usually he picks yesterday's clothes from the bedroom floor where they lie like a stranger vaporized in the night. Usually he puts them on again. Usually the day begins like all the days before, his passage through it little more than an act of muscle memory. Usually.

But today he can recall just as readily as he can the contours of his own face, or the route to work he shouldn't take, a memory that belongs not to him, but to Peter Manyweathers, a man he doesn't know. A fraction of another life entirely. He remembers Peter's excitement on finding the bog violet. He remembers the affection Peter felt for Angelica. He remembers the longing stirred in Peter by the love letter. He remembers it all with such startling clarity, it's as if it happened yesterday, and to him.

So this is how it feels to be someone else. Not blurred, like looking at the world through the wet window of a car in traffic. Explicit. In focus. Wonderful.

Where has it come from? He's never been to New York, his fear of flying almost as great as a hardwired phobia of the sea that cripples him with tension at the mere scent of briny air. He hasn't met or heard of anyone with the name Peter Manyweathers or Angelica Meek. In fact, he can count the people he interacts with on a regular basis on one hand.

He sits up in bed and opens his laptop. As he waits for it to load he's confronted with the transitory, infantilizing nature of his habitation. The table. The wardrobe. The sofa. Possessions that don't belong to him in a space he doesn't own, a studio flat, little roomier than a standard garage. But the rent is as cheap as it gets in the city, if it can be classed as such at the very north of London's sub-urbs. From the window at the front, a view of the capital receding. From the back, a splay of green fields, messily stitched by weathered hedgerows and the motorway's humming concrete seam.

He opens Google and searches for the name Peter Manyweathers. It returns 11,000 results. But there is no sign of a Peter Manyweathers who could possibly have been a cleaner in New York in 1983. He scrolls through the first page of links, then the second, the third and the fourth. How short a time ago it had been when the lives of ordinary people were not chronicled. No testament to their existence but the memories of others, which would die with them and be gone. How short a time ago there was nothing to know. A past where everyone was just like him.

About his own past, Dove knows only what he's been told.

Dove's earliest memory is of meeting Len and Maud. Many years later they would be the ones who'd explain to him that he'd been found as a baby in a Moses basket, written on which was the label 'Dove' (and so they presumed he was the abandoned child, or more likely grandchild, of a breeder or fancier of birds). Wrapped around the handle was a silver necklace with two tiny birds dangling from it and a silver ring threaded onto it. But when he first met Len and Maud he knew nothing of this. He was five years old and presumed this was how all children met their mothers and fathers, standing in the doorway of their home framed by a warm light that bled out into the evening. Len was taller and rounder and wider than Maud, his silhouette reminiscent of a snowman. He bent to greet Dove out of the car, squeezing the young boy's delicate chin between his fingers like he was plucking a berry from a bush. The man's breath smelled not unpleasantly of tobacco, which he'd tried and failed to disguise by sucking on a mint so strong the scent tingled in Dove's nostrils.

'You must be Dove,' he said. 'You're a big one, huh? Normally they're so scrawny when they get here.'

'Yes,' Maud said, a hand on her husband's shoulder,

'but never for long.' Dove's head was filled with fairy tales where children were fed until they were fat enough to be eaten. In other houses he'd lived in he turned to storybooks for escape – once from beatings but mostly from being ignored – and he always knew, somehow, this would be his fate: to be eaten, surely the fate of all orphans in the end. It's a scenario he must have imagined a thousand times. In the fantasized version he found the closest blunt object he could lift and hit his would-be eater over the head before running away so quickly that lightning exploded from his shoes. Now his grisly destiny was coming to pass, fear turned his leg bones to the consistency of treacle.

But because he'd been told to, and mesmerized by the pendulum of her hips as they swung to negotiate the gate, Dove followed Maud into the house. She had much softer features than Len, and an asthmatic wheeze he initially mistook for a cat hidden behind the threadbare velveteen curtains. This is what he pretended he was looking for when they eventually coaxed him out from behind the sofa with a cube of chocolate, impossible to resist for a child who'd known the bladed gnaw of hunger as often as he had.

In the intrepid glare of electric light he saw them properly for the first time. Maud's hair was grey and thin. Len's jowls slooped below his jawline like torn sails on a decommissioned boat. Dove's best guess was that they were a hundred years old or more. He'd heard about grandparents from a boy in a previous home. How they're older than real parents, slower and less able to play, but make up for it by always buying you presents. And now Dove was finally getting grandparents of his own it felt like a strange and brilliant dream, which is why he didn't trust it to last. He'd never been one for play. Even at this tender age he preferred his own company. But he imagined he'd enjoy receiving gifts.

'I'm Maud,' she said, 'and this is Len.' The man smiled to reveal a missing tooth through which his tongue was a fat, caged grub. 'And over there, that's Doggle.' Doggle was a basset hound that until that moment Dove hadn't noticed asleep and snoring in the corner. It had a wispy silver beard, and ears like the chewed soles of worn-out slippers. It made absolute sense to Dove that even the dog was old in a house where everything appeared ancient, ragged and warm.

'He likes walking and eating,' Len said, 'and so do I. I hope that you do too, because we do plenty of both around here.' Now they were indoors his voice filled the room, which was small and overloaded with trinkets and the scent of brass polish. On the far wall was a corkboard peppered with photographs, all identically posed: Len and Maud standing either side of various children roughly Dove's age, arms round their shoulders, grins on their faces so broad they almost split in two.

'Come on,' Maud said, 'you must be hungry.'

A vegetable soup simmered on the hob, the pan lid jigging on a stage of steam. Len served it up. He ran a finger around the rim of his bowl, tore a thick slice of bread in two and plunged it in, disappearing to the crust. He brought it to his mouth and swallowed it whole, the boy watching it slide down his throat.

'Nothing to be frightened of here,' Maud said, gesturing to mean the house but waving her hand across the view from the window, where the North Yorkshire Moors swooned into darkness. Dove held his butter knife so tightly his whole hand paled. 'Anything you can see is yours to use. Anything in the cupboards is yours to eat. You are one of us.'

'You don't speak much, do you?' Len said, with a wobble of his head rendering the nature of the question difficult to discern. No, he didn't. Was he supposed to? 'It's OK. They always speak in the end.'

'Len!' Maud said, tossing her spoon into the sink. 'You make it sound like he's here for a bloody interrogation.'

'Do I? Oh, well, that's not what I meant. I meant you'll relax soon enough, and then you'll want to speak or you won't, but either way is fine with us. Do whatever you like, as long as it makes you happy.'

In truth, Dove was already happy, and thus also afraid this was a giant trick, greater than any that had ever been played on him. That every time they went to the shops, or Maud took him to the library, or Len took him out to ride his bike, they would leave him on the corner of the street and drive away.

He wouldn't know until many years later how they'd suffered abandonments of their own. How Len had first suggested he and Maud become foster-parents in the bruising days after Maud miscarried for the third time, a moment of internal violence so barbarous their sanity demanded they consider it an unlucky twist of fate and not a bodily mutiny of which she was the cause.

Months later, when Maud was physically recovered, they began to take the suggestion seriously, eventually figuring – why not? The house seemed a third empty with just the two of them in it. The grass on the moors needed trampling by feet other than those of the goat they kept, roaming the outposts of their idyll with illusory freedom.

If it wasn't for them, if it salted the wound, they could end it whenever they liked. Each child would only be with them for a few weeks anyway, a couple of months at most. Just until they'd found a new and permanent home. If they decided against continuing, then, really, there was no harm done.

Eighty-two children passed through their doors before Dove arrived. They told themselves he would be the last of them, their swansong from a career of foster-parenting that rewarded and nourished them in ways they never thought possible, let dazzling fauna grow on stricken ground. They would then fully embrace their retirement, of which they'd long fantasized. They'd go to exhibitions and the theatre and watch so many films. Their love was forged over a shared appreciation of Humphrey Bogart and Katharine Hepburn. Though Maud disputed the fact while Len stood by it – their first kiss came after they'd rolled, literally rolled, around laughing at the scene in *The*

African Queen where Bogart's stomach rumbles loudly at dinner.

They were too old to be following young children around a field. Her knees ached, and Len's back was permanently sore: there was winter in their bones. And the parting got no easier with time. They might not be able to take it again. With eighty-two cracks in their hearts already, wasn't it inevitable they'd shatter soon? The eighty-third might just be the one.

'We should do the photograph now,' Maud said, digging a scuffed Polaroid camera from a shoebox on top of the fridge. Dove's face felt strange: aching, stretched, and he realized, lit white by a flash that bleached his vision, it was because he too was smiling, like the children in the other photographs. And now he knew why. When the three of them were together, the earth was a record spinning at the speed at which it should be played.

Dove is standing outside the building where he works, black cabs skulking by like a queue of kettled buffalo. A light rain is falling. He doesn't care. Today he has remembered his watch, and takes a perverse thrill from seeing the seconds pass. With each tick the day matters less, as does his existence in it. When he closes his eyes and remembers Peter Manyweathers – finding the bog violet, meeting Angelica Meek, chancing upon the love letter in the library book – his blood turns to warm gold.

So he is two hours late and counting when he opens

his eyes again to see, outside the supermarket, the old man who works the till is rolling a cigarette without once looking down at the component parts in his hand. He brings it to his lips with the care one might afford a rare and precious musical instrument. The cracks in his face fill with smoke. When it clears, Dove is entering the building, the door hinge's squeak so familiar he can imitate it with a whistle.

'What are you doing here?' Cliff waits by the vending machine, arms cocked at his hips, a physical manoeuvring of his limbs so ungainly it can only have misfired.

'I work here,' Dove says. 'Did you think I only came to buy snacks?' Cliff laughs a little too exuberantly – a man who loves to be in on a joke.

'That's not what I meant.'

'You meant me being late. I'm sorry.'

'I'm not talking about you being late either. I'm talking about the fact that it's only twenty-four hours since I sent you home because you were sick. You should be in bed.' Cliff follows Dove to his desk.

'I think it was a migraine, except it didn't really develop.'

'I didn't know you suffered from migraines.'

'I don't. Not really.'

'Listen.' Cliff's Adam's apple pumps like the forestock on a shotgun. 'I want you to think of me as a pal, rather than a supervisor.'

'I do,' Dove says, nodding awkwardly. It's not lost on him that Cliff is perhaps his only friend.

'Then you'll understand that sometimes I worry about you.'

'You worry about me?' Dove prods at his own chest in hope this might bring the conversation to an abrupt end. 'You worry about *me*?'

'Sometimes, yes.'

'Why?'

Cliff produces a coffee-stained napkin, dabs it at his palms. 'Well, it's not nice to go home to an empty house when you're sick. You should get out more. Maybe meet someone.' He lifts a mobile phone out of his pocket, a slug of lint hanging from the charger socket that he peels away with a slight air of shame. 'There's this new app . . .'

'Please, Cliff.'

'It's so easy to meet people through it. I've been on two dates in these last three weeks.'

'I'm happy for you, but . . .'

'All you have to do is input a little bit of information about yourself, upload a photo and you're away. A brave new world.' He holds the phone in front of Dove's face, close enough Dove has to make an effort to refocus, until he finds before him the photograph that welcomes new users to the app. A powerfully attractive man and woman hand in hand on a beach, their teeth a brilliant white. Neither appears ever to have worried about anything, or had sand in their shoes.

'Really, Cliff, I appreciate your concern, but it's not what I'm looking for right now.' The app seems so completely opposed to what Dove understands of romance or even lust that Cliff might as well be holding roadkill under the nose of a man to whom he's trying to sell a dog.

'You're not looking for fun times and nights out with like-minded single women?' Cliff waggles the phone from side to side.

'Not really, no.' Dove closes his eyes, desperate to slip quietly into the memories of Peter Manyweathers once more. It was the love letter that had piqued his interest most – just as it had Peter's – and he allows himself to fantasize about a world before apps, where that kind of thing – hidden notes, grand gestures, globe-trotting affairs of the heart – happened all the more frequently.

When he opens them again, Cliff, disheartened, slides the phone back into his pocket.

'There are other apps you might want to use.'

'Like what?'

'Like those that help you trace your family tree.' Dove spins a hundred and eighty degrees in his seat. He'd long regretted telling Cliff he was adopted – a brief discussion on one of the few occasions they'd socialized outside of work. Cliff, out of a misplaced kindness that on any other matter Dove would have found endearing, had made it a kind of personal mission to coax Dove into finding his parents when really he wasn't interested. Cliff thought this was the root of Dove's problem, and liked to allude to this hypothesis whenever he could.

'Might not be such a bad idea,' Cliff says with a wink that feels in no way apt.

'Seriously, Cliff,' Dove says. 'Not now, huh?'

Dove logs into his phone, which rings immediately. He swallows his fury, slides his headset into position in a way that suggests it's best they pretend this conversation never happened.

'London ambulance,' he says, guiltily watching a dejected Cliff zigzag across the Pit through a higgledy maze of half walls, head tilted to the floor.

The calls come thick and fast. Probable cardiac arrest. Possible broken femur. A woman in early labour somewhere in the back of a cab. By lunchtime he is exhausted, and keen to find a quiet corner where he can return to Peter's memories, remove himself from the humdrum of the office, of his life. He heads towards the staffroom with a badly made sandwich sliding around inside a plastic tub under his arm.

The staffroom is painted pastel green, with the dimensions of a shipping container. People pull the chairs from the wall into the centre of the floor, forming two smaller circles of conversation. Typically there is one circle for older staff and one for younger staff, and though plenty of people come and go, nobody notices Dove by the empty water cooler in the corner. There is no reason for anyone to bother him here, and it affords him the opportunity to listen, and, as best he can, distract himself from what he's increasingly convinced, and concerned, are symptoms of madness, or worse, a tumour pressing down on his frontal lobe. What other explanation could there be for Peter's memories than vivid hallucinations? Maybe Cliff was right. Maybe he does need to get out more. Find someone else. Maybe he is lost.

Two of the newer recruits are talking. Tania has copper-coloured hair, parted cleanly in the middle into two columns hanging over stark white skin. She'd friended Dove on social media – just as she had most of his colleagues – within days of starting work, but they'd never spoken in real life. This is how he knows she graduated in Women's Fashion Design and recently had a public spat with her ex-boyfriend after some pictures were posted of him with his arm around another young woman at a party. His attempts to remove the pictures from the Internet backfired spectacularly when he accidentally shared them with an even wider audience, at which she felt embarrassed and hurt. She is discussing this with Jed, another colleague with whom Dove is also friends on Facebook only. He is short and thin. He studied Business (Advertising and Marketing), and posts photographs – on a beach, in a club, at a supermarket – in which he's pulling a face (eyes narrowed, lips pinched) unrelated to any of the expressions he uses on a day-to-day basis. If he'd tried to explain this compulsion to a psychologist as little as twenty years ago, Dove doesn't doubt he'd have been institutionalized.

'So I'm getting my own back,' Tania says.

'How?' Jed asks.

She holds her phone in front of his face – the window to her soul. In the photographs she is at a party. Her mouth is wide open, fist raised in the air. 'Making him jealous.'

'You look great,' he says, an inflexibility to his tone that makes it impossible to discern between enthusiasm and sympathy. 'Was it a good party?'

'Terrible.'

'Oh, babe.'

'I think I'm not over him. I think I'm depressed.'

'The job doesn't help,' Jed says, glancing over his shoulder, a cowardly hush to his voice. 'If I get another pensioner that's fallen over I think I'm going to kill myself.' They laugh and finish the sandwiches they bought from the old man at the supermarket. They bin the packaging and head towards the door, footsteps in a perfect counter-time.

'If it wasn't for the drunks and nutcases I don't know what I'd do,' Tania says. Jed laughs again, louder this time, his hand on the small of her back. 'Had a woman yesterday who reckoned she was looking after some old guy who can barely move. Said he'd never even spoken a word.'

'Oh, that's sad. Poor man. Like a mute?'

'I don't know. But anyway she said she thought he had a headache.'

'How would she know?'

'Exactly.'

He laughs so hard he is unable to hold the door fully open as she approaches. 'And she was calling an ambulance *for that*? For a *headache*?'

'Oh no. It gets worse. The reason she was calling was

because she thought she caught him looking at something.'

'What?'

'Yeah, I know, right? Said she came into his room and swears he was focused on something outside his window.'

'Like what?'

'Some purple flower.' She pauses in the doorway, as though on the other side of it she'll instantly adhere to higher standards of professionalism. 'Hardly an emergency, right?'

Dove dashes through the door before it closes behind them, his tread so heavy they stop as they hear him coming. Tania's eyes move over his face, coming to rest on the background behind him, and just like that he doesn't exist.

'Yeah?' she asks. Jed snorts and returns to his desk, a grin cleaving open his lips that Dove suspects is finally a glimpse of his real smile.

'We haven't met,' Dove says. 'Well, not really. I sit over there.' She shifts her weight from her left foot to her right, indignantly enough that he rushes to end the silence. 'My name's Dove.'

'You're the one who went home sick yesterday.'

Suddenly aware of the phones ringing, people watching, the words repeated over and over again – What is your emergency? – Dove tries to concentrate on the pale blue of her eyes, but finds her so singularly cold he wants to walk away. 'It was a migraine. But it didn't really develop. Listen, about the call.'

'The call?'

'The one you were just talking about.'

'Oh, yeah.' She puts her hands on her hips and scans the room, and he understands immediately what she's thinking – can you believe this guy who sits here all day and never says anything was listening in on my private conversation? – as though she can broadcast her thoughts as well as she does her disdain.

'Do you remember his name?'

'No.'

'Not even his first name?'

'Why would I? It was a time-waster. And even if it wasn't, does anyone seriously remember the names of callers?'

'Then who was the woman?'

'How should I know?' Over Tania's left shoulder, Dove spots Cliff exiting the bathroom, tugging at the zip on his fly. 'Look,' she says, 'I have to get back to work.'

'Wait!' Dove grabs her forearm. For a second he is holding it, and she is pulling away, and he is stopping her, which he doesn't mean to do, but he is. People are looking, and suddenly he is angry, that familiar sensation of the cavity inside him filling with hot black smoke. He lets go, and she's gone, back to her desk. For a moment all is silent.

Then it comes again. This time he recognizes the tingle moving across his scalp, so that by the time the headache is forming he is ready. But more than that, he wants it. He wants to know what happened next.

It comes first as soft, warm light. Then the light becomes shape. A thin band of tension streaks across his shoulders as the shape gathers form, with edges, curves, corners, something almost complete. Pain worse than before. The form fills with colour. But this time it is different. This time Peter is not full of love and hope and excitement. This time he's angry. This time he's scared. Dove remembers. He remembers the man at the top of the cliff face, his silhouette blotting a blistering sun. He remembers Dr Hens Berg. And it fills a cold hollow inside him with fear.

FIVE

If Peter had known it would lead to him meeting Dr Hens Berg, would he even have picked up the newspaper in the first place? He'd been scanning the classified advertisements at the back for weeks, and was considering placing one himself (*Like flowers? Want to meet other people who like flowers?*). After all, the notice he placed to find Angelica had reaped greater results than he could ever have imagined. But on a quiet Sunday afternoon, when Peter entered the library to find the reference book fetched and ready for him to continue his studies, the librarian, who saw him scanning the classifieds and asked why, brought his attention to the communal noticeboard. *New club for enthusiasts of botanical etchings.* Peter didn't care much for etching. Art had always been his sister Susan's realm. But it was as good a place as any to start. If he managed to get even five minutes of meaningful conversation about flowers, or indeed anything, out of the experience, it would certainly improve the prospects for a balmy evening he'd otherwise have spent at home, nursing a cold beer, trying to stay out of his new housemate

Angelica's way to avoid cramping her style, and drowning out the sound his neighbours made when they argued by submerging himself in the bath.

And anyway, he hadn't been able to stop thinking about the love letter since he discovered it in the library. Yes, it was someone else's story, but he wanted to live it. He hoped learning more about flowers would draw him closer to the romance within the words, a romance he secretly desired in his own life. Until now, it had seemed unreachable, as though love was something that took place in another room. But something about the letter had left a door ajar.

It was a warm night. Moths amassed around street lamps. Peter, dressed in a thin white linen shirt already translucent on his back and a pair of jeans he'd cut at the knee with garden shears, walked from the station to a bar near Prospect Park, where he was one of three men and seven women who had congregated. Dr Hens Berg was the last to arrive.

Peter hoped it might be a good place to hear about some rare and interesting flowers, but in reality it was full of show-offs and bores, intent on proving to others how much more meaningful their experiences had been than those of the others present. He should have known better than to dismiss a theory he'd long held: in pastimes lie the best of men, but more frequently the worst.

After a lady with a plump bouffant delivered a tedious thirty-minute talk about how moisture affects bark (and thus how it's etched), which turned out to be little more than an excuse to show her holiday snaps, there was a short break. Peter found himself standing next to Hens. They introduced themselves and shook hands, Hens with such force that Peter thought his arm might be pumped out of its socket. Hens was broad-shouldered, reminded Peter of sturdy furniture, with a jaw square enough to absorb the gloved jab of a heavyweight. Atop that wide, muscular head, a light tuft of blond hair was cropped short. He worked at New York University and said he'd turned up for the same reasons as Peter – to see if a fledgling interest in botany might beget something bigger.

Once he had got to know him a little better over a sharp beer at the bar, Peter discovered that Hens was also single, and liked to sign up for groups where the women outnumbered the men by at least three to one. As a result he had become a proficient pastry chef, weaver of wicker baskets, folder of paper into the form of a swan, and, lastly, so he claimed, lover. He was also in his early forties and lived alone. That's why they got on, Peter supposed. Even though Hens was a doctor of psychology and he was a cleaner, they both worked with other people's shit.

'So you think you'll stick out the second half?' Hens asked.

'Absolutely,' Peter said, wiping a thin strip of froth from his top lip. 'I've come all this way.'

'But there aren't any women. No decent ones, anyway.'

'Believe it or not, I'm here to see the flowers.' It wasn't a lie. The second half promised a slide show of photographs taken by a man who had followed his love of

etching to South America, exotic-sounding enough to per-
suade Peter not to go home and run a bath. 'You're going
to leave?'

'Maybe,' Hens said. 'But if you're sticking around
afterwards, maybe I'll just prop up the bar.'

It wasn't until he sat back down that Peter realized
Hens had asked him no questions. In fact, he knew nothing beyond his name and the fact that he was interested in
flowers. Yet, despite his boorishness, Peter liked Hens. It
was a relief not to have to make small talk, and he was
happy to be with someone who'd tell stories while he
listened over a drink – anything that took his mind off
Angelica, at home in his apartment. A part of him was
convinced her father would turn up one day. But as the
days and weeks passed, the likelihood of this happening
seemed less and less. Angelica had grown more relaxed.
She was even starting to remove her coat and shoes, and
leave her few possessions lying around so it looked as
though she was actually resident there, rather than disappearing without a trace every time she left a room.
Maybe her father truly didn't care.

Peter sat watching the South American slide show,
which featured far fewer photographs of flowers than it
did pictures of the speaker sunbathing in his shorts, pretending he hadn't seen Hens feigning a yawn at the bar.
He almost yelped with joy when the man finally stopped
talking, and Hens had a cold beer waiting for him in a
small, otherwise empty garden, dotted with lit candles,
their flames bullied by a light breeze.

'You were right. That was tedious,' Peter said. They laughed together, the rambunctiousness of Hens's boom making Peter's voice sound like it hadn't broken.

'So you won't be coming back?'

'Probably not. I'm sure there are other groups. Maybe I should start one.'

'Maybe you should,' Hens said. 'You have the bug, huh?'

'I think so,' Peter said, showing Hens the love letter he found in the library, and recounting how it had captured his imagination, woken something in his soul. Hens's nose concertinaed in confusion.

'Why would anyone write a letter like that and put it in a book?' he said. His Danish accent kneaded the syllables in a way Peter found quite relaxing.

'Who knows why people do certain things? Makes for a good discovery, though, right?' As easily as Peter might recite the colours of the rainbow, Hens reeled off the Latin names for four or five of the flowers on the list.

'So you *do* know a thing or two about flowers,' Peter said. 'It's not all about the women after all.'

'I know a thing or two about everything,' Hens said, rolling a cigarette that seemed brittle and tiny against his fingertips. 'You should try to find one.'

'A woman?'

'Not a woman, for crying out loud. One of the flowers.' Hens took another sip, then licked white slugs of froth from his stubble.

'Oh, I don't know about that. They're mostly all but extinct.'

'Extinct just means they've not been found. And any-way, where's your spirit of adventure?'

This rankled Peter. His past was a litany of opportun-ities he feared he'd missed. Yet while he acknowledged he should act on impulse more often, something held him back, a dead weight of dread in his core. Another excuse tumbled from his lips.

'And they're all the way around the world.'

'Oh, come on, don't give me that.' Hens folded his arms and leant back in his chair, cheeks square as book-ends.

'Easy for you to say.'

'So instead you go to etching groups to hear boring botanical lectures and try to meet women?'

'I told you. I wasn't here to meet women. I was here to find out more about flowers from something other than a book.'

'If you're happy with that, fine. But a little airplane food won't kill you.' The air filled with the burning vanilla scent of extinguished candle wicks. Hens drank fast, and had already ordered another round before Peter was two-thirds of the way through his own. Regardless, he was more drunk than he had been in some time. The colours of Hens's clothes and skin blended into one another, a trick of intoxication not altogether displeasing, but one Peter wished would stop.

He went to the bathroom, washed his face with a sobering jet of cold water, and drunkenly rued the fact that he wasn't a man like he imagined Hens to be. Peter's reaction when he found the love letter in the library book was to get more library books. To join a club for botanical etching enthusiasts, for pity's sake! But Hens's first thought had been to track down a flower itself. Peter was in his mid-forties already. If his life was boring and lonely, did he really have anyone to blame but himself?

When he returned from the bathroom, Hens was trying to give his number to the barmaid. Uninterested, she went back to work and Peter pretended he hadn't noticed, launching back into the conversation as though he'd actually given the matter serious thought, rather than coming up with an excuse to save face.

'Anyway, I can't just disappear looking for a flower. I have a business to run. It'd be impossible.'

'What if I went with you?' Hens said. Peter knew that this was the alcohol talking, but he was having fun and so chose to indulge it.

'You came to a group for botanical etching enthusiasts to meet women and ended up planning a holiday with a cleaner from Brooklyn. That's the most tragic thing I ever heard.' Their laughter was so loud and obnoxious that the barman called time. They clinked glasses. Booze wet their fingers. Continuing up Peter's arm, the warmth found its way to his neck and face. It had been a long time since he'd made a new friend his own age. In fact, he wasn't sure whether men his age did make new friends. Ageing was the shedding of old bark, wasn't it? Not the time to grow it anew.

When Peter woke the next morning, he found the

words *Dr Hens Berg – finder of flowers and women*, and a phone number, written on a napkin folded into his breast pocket.

Peter and Hens met regularly over the next two months, and while Hens never mentioned the trip again, Peter started to think it might not be such a terrible idea. Despite his occasional arrogance, Hens was good company. And he knew far more about flowers than he let on. Peter enjoyed picking his brain about the rare blooms he'd read about in the library, testing Hens's knowledge, expanding his own. He spent fewer evenings at home, and, now that Angelica was proving herself more than capable of helping him run the business, less time consumed by thoughts of dirt and what to do with it. On Saturday evenings Hens encouraged Peter to try things he'd never done before, usually occasions he enjoyed only in retrospect, but which made him realize how small his breadth of experience actually was.

It was after an aborted attempt at a samba dancing class that Peter woke with the worst hangover he'd had since he was twenty-two. The phone rang, loud and shrill like a bird desperate to mate. It was Sunday, and because of a night-time heat so intense he could have argued the sun was still up, he'd barely slept at all. He ignored it, but the caller was persistent. After a few minutes his patience evaporated, and he picked up the receiver without saying hello.

'The Udumbara,' Hens said by way of greeting.

'Jesus, Hens, what the hell?' Peter said, his dry lips stuck together at the edges.

'You're hung-over, huh?'

'You mean you're not?'

'I don't really get hangovers.'

'But you drank all that tequila!' Peter could still taste it in the back of his throat.

'Forget about tequila. They found the Udumbara.'

The Udumbara flower, according to Buddhist legend, blooms once every three thousand years, when the Sage King of the future visits the present world. Peter had little time for tardy gods. All he knew was that the Udumbara was a flower from the list and a sketch in a Sanskrit book – the 'auspicious flower from heaven'.

'It's underneath a Chinese woman's washing machine.'

'What do you mean, "it's underneath a Chinese woman's washing machine"?'

'The Youtan Poluo.' Hens liked to refer to a bloom by its oldest, most unused name, a bad habit bestowed on him by academia. Peter didn't care for Latin or Greek. He loved a flower for what it meant, not what an understanding of its etymology said about him.

'Jeez, Hens, can you make this conversation a little easier to follow?'

'The Udumbara, you imbecile, it's been found underneath a Chinese woman's washing machine!'

'How do you know?'

'I have botanist friends at the university. They're a community. They share this stuff.' Peter doubted that news from China could ever reach him in New York City, but Hens's tone was serious and Peter's hangover didn't facilitate argument.

'You're going to China?' Angelica faced the wall of small drawers Peter had built inside the lockup, neatly folding and filing the company expenses. Peter had worried about telling her, and lay on a skateboard beneath the car pretending to fix it in the hope she wouldn't notice the tic that tremored in his neck when a matter was causing him stress.

'Yes. But not for long. You can stay at my place. I mean, I still think you should tell your father where you are . . .'

'My father doesn't care where I am. That's kinda why I'm staying at yours.'

'Right,' he said, realizing then his concern hadn't been the business, but her. 'And I've complete faith you can handle the work.' He looked down to see she was standing by his feet, and tapped a spanner against a pipe to make himself sound busy.

'I know I can. I was just saying, *you're* going to China.'

'Oh. I see.'

'You never do anything.'

'That's not true.' He wheeled himself out until he was on the ground looking up at her. She noticed the spanner in his hand, the size that might fix a radio-controlled car rather than an actual one.

'It's totally true. You never do anything. Except go to

the library and talk about flowers.' He raised a hand and she helped him to his feet.

'You'd do well to listen more often. Might be an education.'

'Have you met a woman?' she said. He couldn't help but be delighted by the mischievous kink in her tone.

'No. I'm going with a friend.'

'What friend?'

'He's a doctor,' Peter said. 'His name is Hens Berg.' She shook her head. 'You think I should stay?'

'You're kidding,' she said. 'I've never met anyone who needs to go do something exciting more. It's just that I'll miss you, is all.' He embraced her, and she clung to him in a way that made him feel needed for the first time in as long as he could remember. 'Don't go dying out there hunting flowers, OK? It feels like we only just met. And, obviously, I need a place to stay.'

Peter bought himself a new suitcase and breathed in the rich chestnut smell of leather. Packing almost all the clothes he owned, he was overcome with an anxiety that weighted his head to the pillow. What if a property needed urgent cleaning whilst he was gone? Then, the whisper of reason. There was nothing urgent about what he did. The moment for urgency had passed by the time he got there. They were already dead. But still he couldn't settle. What if someone needed him? Who? he asked himself. His brief relationship with the woman down the hall had collapsed long ago, after she decided she wanted horses in her life more than she did men and moved to snowy Colorado. Peter took deep breaths, the leather scent still a warm novelty in his lungs, and sat on the corner of the mattress looking at the wardrobe. Only his overalls hung there, a bodiless ghost imploring him to go.

The journey was long. Air hostesses served the aisle with a poise Peter couldn't help remark upon more than once. When they passed, their hairspray made him sneeze into his hands. His nervousness mounted as they bounced through turbulence, and he sought reassurance from whichever hostess was closest. Usually it was the one with the perfectly sculpted bun semi-visible beneath her hat, who'd taken a liking to Peter, and kept him topped up with free wine.

'Excuse me, ma'am?' he said, his voice leaping through the octaves.

'Sir?'

'I just wondered, to put my mind at rest, if you'd ever been in a plane crash?' The hostess laughed, her immaculate red lips exposing exquisitely white teeth, and continued down the aisle.

'You old dog,' Hens said, jabbing a stiff finger into Peter's right thigh. Peter hoped it meant accidents were rare, rather than there being a conspiracy of silence on such matters which he'd now have to uphold for the rest of the trip.

He and Hens bonded over their non-existent command of Chinese, and by the time they touched down they were united in wonder at the mystical sprawl of Shanghai. Old markets lurked in the corridors between rising glass spires. Bunting bridged the passages where neon fought the dark. The newness of Shanghai's cityscape had co-opted the old into its architecture, and to them it was otherworldly, a near-future metropolis. In a restaurant apparently catering exclusively to exhausted businessmen, Hens tucked into what could well have been a bat on a stick. To his credit, it had looked like a steak in the photograph accompanying its listing in the menu. Peter's soup was watery and tasteless, but he took great comfort in knowing it had never beaten wings.

Jet-lagged and unable to sleep, they walked the waterfront of the Yangtze River mouth late into the evening. The rain was a thin and pleasant wash, not the clatter that bombed the streets outside his apartment in the fall. When Hens's cheap umbrella buckled he dumped it into a bin and they let the drops dance upon their skin.

Boarding buses involved blind faith and guesswork. With the good fortune bestowed on them by an after-dinner cookie, they only went wrong twice. Once Peter was suitably convinced they were heading in the right direction, and Hens had stopped caring, they slept the rest of the way. The humidity in the air made Peter dream of being crushed beneath a boulder shaped like a man.

In the morning, a translator that Hens's botanist colleagues had helped arrange met them at the bus station as planned. She was young, eager to help and would drive them the rest of the way. Both men were relieved that she might open up the shell of a world they knew they'd never really penetrate, if only enough for them to peek in. Hens made lewd jokes about what else she could show him. Peter suspected she'd pretended not to understand.

Li Min, who lived in a modest home on the Lushan Mountain, Jiangxi Province, was astonished when the translator told her how far the two men had travelled, but she gave them her blessing to enter the house without hesitation and they took one last look at the view, where outside Mount Lu was beheaded by milky cloud. They removed their shoes and sat on the floor, struggling to fit their legs beneath the table, and drank tea. The flower had waited three thousand years to be seen. A few more minutes wouldn't kill anyone.

The translator listened intently to Li Min, and then recounted her story to the two men. She had filled a bucket with soapy water and decided to clean the kitchen. It was there, beneath the washing machine, that she saw what she thought was a cluster of worm eggs, each no more than one millimetre in diameter. Where most would have boiled water and flushed out the ground, or swept hard through the nest with a stiff, unforgiving broom, she paused for reflection. Her life had been lived by one virtue above all others – to never knowingly harm another living thing. So, she left the washing machine where it was, in the middle of the kitchen, finished wiping down the wall behind the sink and prayed, as she did every night, for the reincarnation of Buddha.

The next morning she glanced down at the cold ground and found that the barely there stems had grown eighteen tiny white flowers on top and smelled fragrant. As frail as frost. As tiny and white as the eggs of a lacewing. The plant had no root, no link to any living thing outside of it. It was as if it had just landed there. A Sage King had answered her call.

Peter and Hens followed Li Min into the kitchen. There it was, on the ground in a divot of dirt, where the washing machine once juddered above it. Rootless, it appeared to float, a tiny, delicate and impossible cloud. It was no more than two inches across in all, yet entire belief systems bent to its existence. This was the Udumbara, signifying the reincarnation of Buddha. It was the most beautiful thing Peter had ever seen. It didn't need a name. There wasn't one worthy. He retreated to the far corner of the room, as though his excited breath might blow the Udumbara out of the window. It was a clear day, and through the gap that winked between the oval-shaped mountains, he could see a glinting sliver of the Yangtze River far below to the north. Above them, the mighty rock fist of Dahanyang Peak, the grandeur it imposed over the Flower Path, noted home to awestruck poets and the occasional white deer.

He pictured the house after Li Min's death. How the grime would collect first in the corners. How the rain would soften the skirt of the wooden walls until they ballooned, then gave, with a rot you could taste in the air. How her bones would hold together, shaped in prayer.

Li Min and the translator went for a walk while Peter and Hens photographed the flower, sketched and measured it. A part of him would forever be amazed that they didn't try to take it home. But no, it belonged where they saw it, underneath a Chinese lady's washing machine, and where they left it, with her, searching inside herself for God.

Back home, Peter's mind was flushed of dirt and filled with rare bloom. Sitting in a sunken leather armchair, he stared at the love letter for so long that Angelica joked it had hypnotized him. And in a way it had. He knew he'd never learn what happened to the man who wrote it or the woman he wrote it for. He could only hope it resulted in a long and loving union. But still the letter pulled on him. Angelica smiled. There he was, lost in thought again. He threw a cushion, a lucky shot that hit her right in the mouth, and they both laughed so hard their ribs ached.

Peter began to fastidiously read books on the topic of flowers, plotting the countries he might find them in on a dog-eared world map that covered his desk.

Hens was busy finishing a paper on how humans shared memories with each other. Peter asked him about it once, as they sat together in the library, Hens researching while Peter pored over maps and charts and photographs of flowers. Hens leant over Peter's textbook and pointed to a picture of the Parrot's Beak, an extraordinary bloom of bright oranges and solar yellows. In shape and size it looked exactly as its name would suggest, with the top petal forming a claw over the bottom one to make a pincer.

'Take the *Lotus berthelotii*.' Peter rolled his eyes but Hens paid little attention. 'The *Lotus berthelotii*, native to the Canary Islands, has been classified as exceedingly rare since 1884 because it was originally pollinated by sunbirds, and sunbirds are extinct there. Some people, like me, believe it to be extinct in the wild . . .'

'Not me. I think it might still exist.'

'Precisely. We are approaching the flower with two very different attitudes. Now, say that you and I went to the Canary Islands and came across the *Lotus berthelotii* nestled behind some rock. My memory of discovering it might be one of shock, because I have been proven wrong. Your memory of discovering it might be one of relief and satisfaction because you have been proven right. But it is the same memory, that of discovering the flower, and we both lay claim to it as the definitive version of events, even though the feelings it arouses are significantly different. We might even alter the event, and both lay claim to have been the person to actually first discover the flower . . .'

'Why on earth would I do that?'

'Memory is not made of clay. You can't always do with it what you want. But I could convince you that my memory is the definitive one, or vice versa. It will not be pinned down.'

'Your point being?'

'Other people's memories are never your own, no

matter how much you might think they are. But you can still share them. That is what my research is concerned with. Can we truly share memories, or are we doomed to communicate in two entirely different languages?'

Peter was still looking at the photograph of the Parrot's Beak and didn't realize Hens had finished talking. He rolled back his sleeve to check his watch, the silent chamber of the library amplifying the ticking of the second hand enough that he quickly rolled it down again.

'I have to go,' he said. 'I have to meet Angelica.'

'Who the hell is Angelica?'

'My assistant.'

'You have an assistant?' It was a gut feeling of discomfort that had prevented Peter introducing Hens to Angelica, one he hadn't quite come to terms with. And anyway, he was running late. Punctuality was something he prided himself on. He pushed his chair beneath the table and buttoned his jacket up to the neck until it pinched his Adam's apple.

'This Angelica. Is she . . .'

'Hens, I have to go.'

He was almost at the revolving doors by the time Hens caught up with him.

'I forgot to tell you,' Hens said, holding a finger in the air. Peter shuffled impatiently.

'What? She's waiting for me.'

'They think they found a *Silene tomentosa*.'

'Jeez, Hens. Save the Latin for your university friends.

I was out of school by the time I was fifteen years old. I barely did basic math.'

'A Gibraltar campion, you ignoramus. They think they found a Gibraltar campion. Just like in your stupid love letter.'

Peter spent the next five nights after work reading everything he could find on the Gibraltar campion. On three different evenings he was the last person ushered out of the building by the librarian. When the library opened late on a Thursday he stayed until it shut and then took what books he was allowed to borrow home with him, where he read until four in the morning and fell asleep at the kitchen table, bruising his cheek. He was two hours late for work on the Friday, and found Angelica quietly seething. She'd cleaned much of a dead woman's kitchen on her own and remained unappeased when he told her what a good job he thought she'd done. He gave her a pay rise, and didn't care that she now felt duty-bound to listen to him tell her all about the Gibraltar campion.

The Gibraltar campion was a pretty flower with five petals that were each cleft in two at the tip. Its form was round and curious and when spun it beguiled as easily as any kaleidoscope. It was not like the common campion, which was undiscerning, white and dirty, growing on wasteland and clustering on graves. No other flowers grew where the Gibraltar campion did. It was unique, endemic to the island. It grew only in the furthest reaches of the rock face, in holes where it could have the sun to itself.

It was not plain, but the colour of pale violet found in the sunsets of Turner. It, too, was the work of a maestro.

Peter spoke of the flower so passionately, Hens agreed to accompany him to Gibraltar if only to shut him up.

A man had apparently spotted the Gibraltar campion from a passing boat, through binoculars, on a day when the water was too tempestuous to get any closer to the rocks. Today, the sea stilled to record the sun's vanity, but travelling this far to an unconfirmed sighting was a huge risk, one that none of the other botanists Hens knew had been willing to take.

Hens had a little climbing experience and friends who kindly lent their equipment. Eager that he be the one to test it out, Peter let Hens go first and he spent the entire morning on the cliff face, dipping his hands into the rock's nooks and scaring resting seabirds. Peter's job was to maintain the security of the rope and help hoist Hens back up to the top of the cliff when he tired. But Hens never tired. His muscles were a show of beauteous harmony, slinking beneath his skin like a puma's.

Lying on that clifftop, fine grass tickling his back, listening to the staccato song of Iberian gulls hovering in feathered crucifixes, part of Peter hoped that Hens would find the campion, take the glory, and that he would be told exactly where to look.

A solitary cloud strayed across an otherwise unblemished sky. Peter let a stiff brown beetle search his navel. A welcome breeze swilled his ears.

'It's not here,' Hens said from below. 'I think the old bastard's crazy.' Peter leaned over the edge, saw the wash on the rocks and instantly felt dizzy. Hens dangled, grumpily kicking his legs against the cliff face. 'I told you this was stupid. We might as well go home.'

'It's the first morning. We've barely covered any ground. Did you think we'd be presented with the flower in a gift set when we arrived?'

Hens rubbed his shoulder. All that time at the mercy of the sun and still he hadn't burned – some Scandinavian he'd turned out to be. 'Then you try.'

'Gladly,' Peter said. He hoisted Hens up to the top and unbuckled his harness, before slipping his own legs through the holes. An inch-wide gap hung around the circumference of his thighs. 'Wait a second. Is it meant to be this loose?'

'No,' Hens said, 'it's just that you have legs made of twine.' Presuming this was a Danish saying, Peter let it go.

Hens tightened the harness and lowered Peter over the edge, where the waves were louder than he'd ever heard. For ten minutes, fifteen perhaps, he hung as steadily as possible some twenty feet down, fighting the urge to summon the hotel continental breakfast he'd eaten that morning and make it answer to daylight. Eventually the movement of the water beneath him made a perverse sense. His inner compass settled and he was able to traverse the rock face, though nothing of his movement proved nimble and the sun scorched his skin.

Ninety minutes – less than half the time Hens had

spent searching – were all that Peter could manage before his buttocks numbed.

As a preliminary outing, it could be deemed successful. Neither of them had died, he had learned how to use the ropes, hadn't vomited, and Hens had an impressive tan he might be able to put to work on the women in the tango class their hotel was hosting that evening, which was all he'd talked about since the moment they'd checked in.

Peter tugged three times on the auxiliary cable.

'Hens!' Nothing. He waited for a small flock of noisy gulls overhead to move on, then shouted again. Still nothing. Peter began to panic, a fear he could only liken to that a child experiences after losing sight of a parent in a crowd – the feeling that all as it was would now be lost forever. 'Hens!'

He began to fiddle with the clips that fastened him to the rope, thinking he'd remembered how to manipulate the pulley system and slowly lift himself up the cliff face. But he knew as soon as he'd unfastened it what it was that he had done wrong.

The rope began to feed through the buckle, faster and faster, going up as he was moving downwards, dropping, not quite free fall, still attached to something. Thirty, forty feet, fast enough to smash his bones like china.

He thought of Angelica. He thought of his sister, Susan, how she'd always warned him to be careful. How he'd scoffed. How he loved her.

At fifty feet he was overtaken by an impulse to save himself. Suddenly, everything seemed obvious. As happens in proximity to death, Peter remembered why life was worth living. Still falling, ropes whipping at his thighs, he reattached the secondary clasp. Its metal teeth bit the rope and he came to a halt six feet above the rocks with a bounce and a snap that echoed off the cliff face. Gulls scattered. Speckles of sea foam dripped down his calves.

There was peace down there by the water, eighty feet from the top. He dangled for a minute, catching his breath, and spun in circles as the rope unwound. Then he saw it.

There, on a ledge no bigger than an upturned hand, was the Gibraltar campion. It was about forty centimetres high, with sun-kissed green leaves, no more interesting to the casual observer than any houseplant, quite ugly even. But nestled amongst the leaves, swaying, Peter found a small and beautifully detailed bilobed flower. White from a distance, up close an ethereal explosion of colour washed across the petals, from pink to purple. Elegant and soft, but surviving here, battered like a lighthouse by the wind and waves, a candle lit inside a tempest.

Peter was overcome by the sheer unlikeliness of its existence, and felt a kinship with the flower that seemed to distort him for a second. Above them, an infinite number of galaxies, planets and possibilities. Unknowns of a number that cannot be expressed. Yet here, on a protruding ledge and at the end of a rope, endless variables had colluded to bring him and the flower together. He was sure then that if anything could happen, then anything would.

And better yet, there was not one flower, but two, rocking gently on the breeze.

'Are you OK!?' Hens's head appeared five minutes later, leaning over the edge of the cliff.

'Pull me up!' Peter shouted, his rage disguised by the smash of the tide. Inch by inch he rose, until Hens was lying back on the grass exhausted, whilst Peter counted the lashes scored into his legs. 'Where were you?'

'I didn't think you would want to come up this early. I'd only just lowered you down. But I was here . . . I was here.' Had Peter not known Hens was lying, he'd have guessed from the way he couldn't make eye contact for more than a second. He chose not to argue the point now. He just wanted to get away from the clifftop.

'Let's go,' he said.

'Did you find the campion?' Hens asked. Peter's teeth clenched in anger. Hens didn't deserve to see it.

'I don't think it's here.'

'I knew it. Didn't I tell you? I knew it.'

In the car park, beside the rental vehicle, was a Volkswagen camper van that hadn't been there when they'd arrived. Inside it were two women. They waved at Hens and he pretended he hadn't seen them. Peter loaded the car with the gear and stood in silence eating the sandwiches the hotel kitchen had kindly prepared that morning. Nothing made a man homesick like stale bread and waxy cheese.

They searched the other cliff faces on the remaining

days and found nothing. Hens knew the campion was extinct. Peter knew it wasn't. They each had their own memory. They each had their own truth.

SIX

Just two days after finding the flight recorder of The Long Forgotten, Professor Cole looks out at the reporters convened for a press conference on the matter in the garish lobby of a Sydney hotel. His hair is combed neatly to one side to disguise the fact it's all but disappeared at the back, he is wearing a suit one size too small, and only a glinting gold tooth identifies him as the same man who stood on the deck of a boat covered in whale blood, the black box of PS570 held above his head.

That stupid whale. Cole is starting to wish he'd tossed it back into the sea like a rod-caught Atlantic salmon. Concerned that he looks like he isn't taking the press conference seriously enough, he sits up straight. A dozen or more photographers jostle for position. This is one of many times over the last couple of days he's noted a lack of respect for the lost passengers of The Long Forgotten. Relief that his wife isn't there to see it only just overrides the myriad ways in which he misses her.

He imagines himself in his kitchen, carefully dividing some of her delicious homemade Key lime pie so that they have exactly half each. Any more of that, though, and he definitely won't fit into this suit. These days suits are so unspeakably dull. As a student at university he had one made of a deep-purple velvet, with bell-bottoms wide enough to swallow an entire boot.

Beside him is Dr Nipa Dash. She is in her forties but younger looking – her skin babyishly smooth, eyes as round and brown as the knots in an imperfect plank of wood. She addresses the throng of reporters, flashbulbs and microphones thrust intrusively towards her.

'It is still early days. The black box recorder of flight PS570 had considerable damage done to it on its journey, even before it ended up inside the whale.' An animal rights campaigner who has sneaked into the press conference stands up at the back of the room and shouts something, too far away from the closest microphone to be decipherable. The camera catches a fleeting glimpse of her T-shirt, emblazoned with a photograph of the whale, belly sawn open, glistening on the deck of the ship. Next to that is a target transposed over the image of Professor Cole's head, shown on television for a split second before the protestor is quickly bundled from the room by men who move along the wall like shadows. Cole watches the drama unfold on a monitor, snapping the pen in his hand.

'As you already know,' Dash says, recovering well, 'we have assembled a team of specialists, experts in air disaster recovery, in an international effort to retrieve the data and conclusively establish what happened to flight PS570 from Jakarta to London, thirty years ago. It was immediately clear to the team that the challenge is a new one, a unique one, and they need to approach it in ways they haven't considered before. To that end we've had to use all of the considerable resources at our disposal to develop new methods, new systems, of data extraction. You're already aware that we have been able to feed power into the flight recorder. I can now announce that we have been able to plot the plane's final movements . . . information available to us for the very first time.'

A large digital display behind Dr Dash blinks into life – a map of the world. A yellow line links Indonesia to England with an angled course running below China, above India, over Turkey and through the heart of Western Europe.

'This,' she says, 'was the scheduled flight path of PS570.' A new line appears, in red, reaching Romania and then taking a southerly path over the north of Italy, where it stops. 'This is the course we know that the plane took, and here, close to the Swiss border, is where we inexplicably lost all contact with the flight.' A third line appears, this time in green, flying over the north of France, just shy of the south coast of England. 'This is the trajectory we have plotted from the new data.' A big blue dot flashes west of Cornwall, England, a few miles into the Atlantic Ocean. 'And this is where we now have reason to believe that flight PS570 came down.' Her face strobes in a sudden explosion of camera flashes. Professor Cole shields his eyes with a clipboard. The journalists caw, until a lone voice speaks.

'If it crashed that close to the coast of Great Britain, then why didn't we know about it?' Dash manoeuvres her microphone into position, but before she can speak, Cole leans forward into his.

'The sea is big. A plane is small.'

'Isn't that a little flippant, Professor Cole?' the journalist asks. He is a large man with unhealthy-looking skin, collar clinging to the sheen of sweat on his neck. 'Isn't this the question the loved ones of those who went missing on the flight will want answered?' There is a dull murmur of agreement from the journalist's peers, or rather, Cole thinks, the sound of their column inches being filled, and it is this, the tawdry state of most modern reporting, that draws his indignation. This man isn't interested in bringing to a close the grief of those who lost loved ones on The Long Forgotten. He's interested in perpetuating it to sell newspapers.

'It's a fact,' Cole says, 'and to think anything different is to completely misunderstand our insignificance in the face of nature. We're a speck of dust. And you, sir, are a speck of dust on the speck of dust.'

'I beg your pardon?'

Cole fixes the man with a grimace. All the joy of his unlikely reprieve when the whale saved his life has vanished for the time being, and won't return until he sees his wife again.

Dash scrapes her hair back behind her ears and starts speaking into her microphone too eagerly, creating a screeching feedback loop she has to shout over. 'What

Professor Cole means is, aeronautical tracking equipment has advanced at a fantastic pace since the loss of flight PS570. These days we can track flights on our mobile phones. But back then, as you'll know, things were very different, and until we ascertain exactly what went wrong on the aircraft, we'd simply be speculating. As Professor Cole was trying to say, we're not in the business of speculation. It'll be at least a few days before we get any more information from the flight recorder.'

Cole slides backwards in his chair and closes his eyes. Homemade Key lime pie. Damn, if he can't just taste it.

SEVEN

Dove sits in bed waiting for the last vestiges of his headache to fade. Keen to distract himself from the disconcerting memory of Hens Berg on the clifftop – the anger and betrayal Peter felt in his bones still resonating in Dove's – he checks Facebook. That's when he sees a photograph of Lara Caine and remembers an anger of his own.

The images have appeared on her page overnight, which has piped them directly into Dove's timeline, despite him making every effort to block them, so he couldn't be reminded of the relationship he'd destroyed ten whole years before, when he was kicked out of university. Whenever he saw her picture, whenever he read her name, that awful excerpt of history swirled in his stomach – a sneak attack on his senses in the form of a photograph. Lara Caine standing outside her brand-new apartment. On her thumb, thrust out at her side as though she'd hitch-hiked to get there, were hooked the keys to her new home.

Dove immediately recognized the building. One of the newly built blocks beside the canal before the water disappears into the tunnel that shepherds it in darkness from Islington to Camden. Expensive small flats like this were popping up all over London, capitalizing on a hunger to live in the expanding centre of the city by flushing out the old and the poor. No thought for the past, no thought for the future, these were ugly monuments to the now.

The photograph of Lara with her new keys was not the only one that appeared that morning. There were twenty-seven more. A virtual tour of a life. Inside, the rooms were small, with walls painted white. The floors were faux wooden, the worktops grey marble, lights hidden in a false ceiling, and the living space open-plan. Chrome taps bent to resemble swan's necks. She'd had a house-warming party at which a neighbour who knocked to complain about the noise was persuaded to stay for a drink. Dove now knew this just as he knew which gym she attended, where she was buying her wedding dress, even what she ate for brunch at weekends. All of these things, events, people, places: someone else's memories, suddenly, wrongfully his.

This is why he's walking to work along the canal again, where riverboats part the algae like curtains drawn to mark a death, and then standing outside Lara's apartment block. Because this is what Peter Manyweathers would do. Dove knows it from the memories. He'd move forward. He'd carve his own path of happiness into the future, just as he'd begun to hunt the flowers in the love letter. He wouldn't sit and wait for life to happen to him. If Dove could just make amends with Lara, then he could do the same.

He looks up at the building with its almost sheer glass facade, where once stood a pub servicing the men who built the waterways, and he imagines the view from the windows at the top. Until recently it would have afforded Lara a near-full panorama of south-east London, but the opposite bank had been developed in tandem, and so now, if she looked out to watch evening drape its tired body across the city, she'd be met by a row of tiny but expensive, identically furnished apartments – her own life mirrored back at her.

For a second he thinks he might ring the buzzer with her name beside it. Her voice will crackle through the intercom and this will be it, his chance to finally apologize for that night, years ago, when, consumed by an anger he couldn't control or even source, he was carried out of the student union bar by two campus security guards while she watched, the disdain on her face almost scything him in two. But then something about the proximity – it is still early, and in real terms she is only metres away from him, in bed with her fiancé no doubt – snaps his senses back into focus. She's better off without him in her life, a life he wishes for the mercy of knowing nothing about. Dove wonders if she's as happy as her online presence suggests. Whether it's possible to tell any more. Or, as is more likely, whether there are two versions of her, two versions of everyone.

Dove has always felt there are two versions of himself, and this had been precisely what interested Lara most about him in the first place. The discrepancy between the life an abandoned child lives, and the life it would otherwise have lived. His twin fates. After a while, at university, she'd been preoccupied by the idea of Dove as a foundling, and he'd grown to trust her so implicitly that he told her everything she wanted to know, things he'd not talked to anyone about, before or since.

He moves away from the door of her building as another resident exits, knowing with some sadness they'll never be as close as they were back then. He leaves, continues on down the canal, lungs filled with the phosphorous scent of algae. In some sense, he'll always be outside the door now. And that's OK with him. But still he remembers with fondness those days where he talked and she listened, and he'd told her exactly where he was when he first felt different to Len and Maud.

They were sitting in the garden. Dove was eight years old, watching Maud drag a trembling razor blade down the crest of Len's throat. The sound of it scraping on his stubble and the whisper of insects. She washed the blade in a red plastic bowl.

'I have another question,' Dove said, and Len and Maud both smiled. He'd been chatting incessantly for close to an hour, and so far they'd struggled to adequately explain how rainbows were formed, why penguins huddled together for warmth, and why he should always go to bed at 7.30 without them having to ask twice. But this next question was different. He could see it on their faces, how Maud let her hair fall across her eyes.

'Why did you keep me?'

'Why you?' Len asked, sparing his wife. Dove nodded. 'You weren't number eighty-three. Oh no. You were much, much more than that.'

'What was I?'

'You were our son. We fell in love with you, and that was how our bread was buttered.'

Dove just said it, or rather, it tumbled out, what had been stuffed down inside him for as long as he could remember.

'I'm not like you, am I?' In one sense or another he'd always known. He didn't have their ruddy skin, nor Len's big feet, nor Maud's coiled hair and hooked nose. He had brown eyes, tanned skin, dark hair and a button nose. They always seemed so peaceful to him, which made the tempest of his feelings all the more inexplicable.

'Not like us how?' Maud asked, pouring dirty water into a flower bed.

'We're not the same.'

'Of course we're the same. We're all human, aren't we? Doesn't matter what you look like.' She ran her fingers through his hair and he felt the stiffness that lingered in her knuckles.

'I don't mean that.'

'You mean because we're not your parents?' Len rose from his deckchair, holding his hip like he might flip a gun from its holster. 'No, we're not the parents you were born to. But we're family. Family is what we are.'

The dog forced itself through the flap in the back door,

waddled onto the lawn and turned a circle before collapsing on its stomach. Its health had been waning lately. Twice Dove caught it cowering behind the shed, and from what little he understood of overheard conversations between Maud and Len, a recent visit to the vet's had resulted in discouraging news. But he was fond of the musty cigar smell of its damp fur after a swim in the ponds. Of the way it nuzzled the soft flesh behind his knee when he climbed out of the bath, licked the suds crawling down his legs.

'What's wrong with Doggle?'

'He's just old, that's all,' Maud said, as her and Len's breathing reached slow synchronicity, both lost in the same thought, if only for a fraction of a second. 'He's just old.'

'Will he die?' Dove asked, voice faltering. Len pressed his thumb against the nape of Dove's neck, drawing perfect circles both conciliatory and ineffectual.

'We all get old,' he said.

As suddenly as a dry match sparks aflame, Dove felt a great surge of anger shoot up from his stomach, through his neck to fill his head. He exploded from his seat and ran as fast as he could to the bathroom, the only door in the house he could lock, his instinct when he felt this way to be cocooned, imprisoned, so that whatever it was trying to escape him could go no further than this. He took the showerhead and smashed it hard against the tiles. He only stopped when the tears on his cheeks cooled.

Maud was outside the bathroom door when he opened

it. She held him against her chest the same way she always did, rising, falling, rising, enough that afterwards, when he was calm again, there was a phantom motion to everything, and the universe was a boat adrift in a sea that knew nothing of the tempers in its past.

'It's OK,' she said, 'it's OK.' She smoothed his hair, and eventually he fell asleep knowing they too would leave him, one day.

That's what he told Lara. He didn't know then that one day she'd see his rage for herself.

Early evenings are always relatively quiet in the Pit. People are arriving home from work. They're making spaghetti bolognese, watching soap operas, sitting on the sofa; activities that don't tend to require the attendance of an ambulance. While in the real world outside, those more dangerous pursuits that do – drinking, fighting, falling, the three often connected – have only just begun. Dove considers a society working towards a future where there are no emergencies because nobody actually does anything. He'll be out of a job, but he doesn't care. All he cares about now is Peter Manyweathers, and what happened to him next. It's been on his mind all day, how Peter knew his and Hens Berg's destinies were somehow bound from the moment they met. Dove can feel it. He can feel how Peter feared and yet wanted this closeness, a link with another. Peter Manyweathers' life feels so much more seductive and romantic than Dove's own that he is beginning to lose himself in it completely, longing for the next memory, the next instalment of Peter's story to make itself known, because every time it does, his own world becomes that much more colourful and complete.

'Dove?' Cliff is standing behind him, hopping from one foot to the other like a horse in a dressage competition. 'Is now a good time for a chat?'

'With me?' Dove asks, suddenly wishing for a call. An emergency tracheotomy, anything.

'Yes, with you.'

Dove follows him across the floor and into his office, where Cliff draws the crooked plastic blinds on the internal window, then leans against the slats, smearing them open again.

'How are the headaches?'

'Fine.'

'Maybe you should see a doctor?'

'Really, I'm fine.'

Cliff straightens, uncomfortable enough with the conversation that he rubs his hands across his scalp.

'Do you know what I want to speak to you about?' Dove knows. But a part of him wants to make Cliff say it.

'I've no idea.'

'I hate to do this. I consider you a friend, you know that. But I'm your supervisor, so I must. A complaint has been made about your behaviour.'

'A complaint?' Dove lowers himself into a seat as indifferently as he can, instantly undermined by the squeaking of its wheels.

'Come on, Dove, let's not make this any more awkward

than it already is. Tania says you lost your temper with her in the middle of the office.' Dove can see a small group of colleagues have positioned themselves by the vending machine for a better view through the gap in the blinds.

'I didn't lose my temper.'

'I saw you with my own eyes.' Cliff stares up at the ceiling, as though he can project there things he's seen before, play them back and use them as evidence. 'You raised your voice.'

'Hardly.'

'You held her arm.'

Dove pinches the bridge of his nose hard enough two tiny pressure bruises appear and remain for the rest of the day. What would Peter do?

'I'll apologize,' he says. 'If you need me to apologize then I'll do it.'

'Good,' Cliff says, a smile on his face far smugger than he could ever mean it to appear. 'I appreciate it. Thank you.'

'Any time.'

'I hope next time we sit down and talk it's over a beer, huh?'

'Right,' Dove nods.

'And maybe you could be on time tomorrow? There are only so many blind eyes I can turn.'

When Dove exits the office his colleagues scatter in a hundred different directions, ants beneath an upturned rock.

Road traffic accidents are difficult to deal with at the

best of times. It's often too noisy to get a clear grasp on what the caller is saying. Usually they've witnessed something that has left them in a state of shock, making it hard to extract the key details needed to dispatch the correct response. Where. What. When. Sometimes there are multiple callers, each offering different perspectives on the nature of the incident. And this one is no different. But as the woman on the other end describes the way a white van shunted the rear of a blue Toyota at the junction of Holloway Road and Seven Sisters Road – three casualties, walking wounded, an ambulance is on its way – he can concentrate on only one thing. Jed's voice, four desks away, increasing in volume as he tries to get Tania's attention.

'Flowers?' he asks.

When his ambulance has arrived, Dove patches himself into Jed's line using the access code he's watched Cliff use a hundred times. The voice of the woman Jed is talking to is fragile, unsure. She is on the verge of hanging up, Dove can tell.

'I know I shouldn't be calling this number again, and I don't want to waste your time,' she says, 'but I think he might be in real pain. It's so difficult to tell with Zachariah.'

'Zachariah?'

'That's his name. Zachariah Temple. He's holding his head, really holding it. You have to understand, he doesn't move much, let alone speak. He's only really here in body, not mind, if you know what I mean. But he's looking at the flowers in the yard and holding his head and I don't know who else to call.'

'What's the address?' Dove's voice in Jed's headset makes him almost topple off his chair, exactly as he might in a cartoon, his arms flailing until he can finally reassert his balance.

'Dove?' Jed says. 'What are you doing?' But Dove repeats himself to the woman on the phone as though Jed was never there.

'The address?'

'What's going on?' the woman says, confused by the introduction of a second voice.

'Exactly,' Jed says, standing now, waving until he gets Cliff's attention. He hits mute. 'What the fuck do you think you're doing?'

'Your address? For the ambulance?'

'Blackatree Crescent Nursing Home,' she says. 'Zachariah doesn't have friends or family we can call. No wife. No kids we know of. No brothers or sisters.'

And the pain in Dove's head is growing, stronger this time, a fist of stone bunched in his skull, pushing his brain down into his neck. He remembers Peter's sister, Susan.

Cliff's voice comes from behind him.

'Dove, what the hell is going on here? Are you patched into Jed's call?'

Dove remembers. He remembers how Peter thought of Susan as he lay helpless, bloody, dying. How Peter wondered if it was Susan who'd sent the angel to save him.

'Dove! Are you OK?'

And the woman, still on the line.

'The flowers. It's Zachariah. He's doing it again. He's looking at the flowers.'

'Who's Zachariah Temple?' Dove asks.

He remembers Susan. He remembers the angel and the sheep-eating plant.

EIGHT

Peter met Susan in the diner on 10th Street, a gleefully shabby joint, halfway between two of the city's more notable churches, St Mark's-in-the-Bowery and Grace Church on the corner of Broadway. Both tussled for the title of Peter's favourite building in Manhattan, depending on his mood on any given day. The former struck him most on solemn mornings, when waking alone imbued the day ahead with a certain hopelessness, which he could usually shake with a brisk walk by noon. Perhaps it was the famous tomb, the solitude it brutally evoked. Come lunchtime, he was generally happier, and the awe-inspiring spire of the latter lifted him, as if it had risen proudly from his chest.

On this day, he was in a Grace Church mood, which is why he didn't mind too much when Susan ate half his eggs and links. Regulars sat at the dirty tables by windows cloaked with condensation, and the chef scraped burnt fat from the griddle. Peter made a mental list of the hygiene regulation contraventions on display. Perversely, without them, the diner might have lost both its charm and his custom.

They were so clearly siblings; the same stubby nose, the same tiny ears, like pasta shells. Susan's mousy hair was flat and unkempt, and yet she was somehow perfect. He could have watched her steal his food all day.

Susan said she worried about him every time they met. Usually, that he worked too much, or that he didn't get out enough, and apparently the worry was enough that it ruined her appetite. She took a bite from his final slice of toast, then slid the plate back across the table. Of more pressing concern was his new hobby, which she hoped he'd drop as quickly as he had all those when they were young. She swore often and loudly these flower expeditions would get him killed one day, that he'd be kidnapped by an unknown tribe in a jungle somewhere, impaled on a spit and roasted on a fire.

'I worry myself sick,' Susan said. 'And I worry that you'll pick up some deadly virus at work, in all that dirt. You don't know what bacteria is in there.'

'Actually, I know exactly what bacteria is in there. And anyway, don't be ridiculous,' he said. When she over-thought things her chin puckered, like their mother's, the dimpled peel of an overripe fruit.

'And now you're off around the world trying to kill yourself.'

'I'm not trying to kill myself.'

'What about the time you almost fell down that cliff?'

'What cliff?'

'Don't tease me. In that place . . . the place with the monkeys.'

'Gibraltar?'

'Yes, Gibraltar.'

'I was attached to a harness. It was perfectly safe. I wouldn't call it falling down a cliff.'

'You need to find yourself a woman, Petey.'

'Don't call me Petey.'

'There's a lady who uses the same dry cleaners I do. Pretty. Looks ten years younger than she is. Beautiful brown skin. Think her parents are from the Indian sub-continent somewhere. Divorced . . . but no children.' Through the window, he watched an enraged taxi driver climbing out of his car to throttle a cyclist and was able to empathize with them both.

It had been three weeks since they had returned from Gibraltar, but Peter had not heard from Hens, nor wanted to, though he'd thought of him daily. Hens' guilty conscience belatedly awoke. He called and invited Peter out for dinner. Peter accepted, expecting a more conventional apology than the one he would receive.

Hens chose the restaurant, somewhere on the Upper West Side. Peter was sure he wouldn't like it the moment he stepped out of the cab. Inside, it was gaudily decorated, expensive and badly lit.

'Here,' Hens said, sliding a brown envelope across the table.

'What's this? A bribe so I don't tell people what a thoughtless rock-climbing companion you are?'

'A gift, to say sorry for being a thoughtless rock-climbing companion.'

'Oh, Hens, I'm joking. This meal is enough.'

'Just open it.' Hens placed his hand over Peter's and Peter was struck by the difference in their sizes, like a crab concealing her young from a gull. In the envelope, a plane ticket. Destination: Chile.

'What's this?'

'You know what it is.'

'And you're giving it to me?' Hens nodded. 'How much did it cost?'

'Don't argue with me. It's being covered by the university as part of a research grant. There is a woman who lives there. It's unconfirmed but apparently she's 116 years old. And she looks it, too. Like a tortoise. But she's got this amazing history. This woman has seen Chile through revolutions, dictatorships, everything. But she's got all of her, how do you say, faculties?'

'Right.'

'She remembers all of it. Face of a tortoise, memory of an elephant. So I am going to interview her about what she remembers and, more importantly, why. And you're coming with me as my glamorous assistant. Except, not glamorous at all, you understand.'

'Where is your actual glamorous assistant?' Peter had seen Hens talking to a demure-looking woman in spectacles when he'd met him from work on a cloudy Friday evening. Overcome with shyness at her beauty, he hadn't dared approach.

'She's not my assistant. She's just some woman who works in the offices.'

'That's very kind, Hens,' Peter said, 'but I know nothing about your work, you know that.'

'No, you ass! You're not really coming to interview the old woman. That's my job. You, my friend, have other work to be concerned with.' He opened the envelope further and a passport-sized photograph of a plant fell out into a patch of Béarnaise sauce on the tablecloth. Peter already knew he wouldn't be able to resist the offer that was coming. A chance to put another tick on the list. And on someone else's dime? He might as well lie down in the palm of Hens's hand. 'While I work, you go find this. When you find it, we go see it together. I give you . . . the *Puya chilensis*.'

'The what?'

Hens made a clicking sound with his tongue against his bottom teeth.

'The sheep-eating plant.'

A fortnight later, Peter watched as the copper-rich deserts of northern Chile gave way to thick forests, then became vast volcanoes and lakes, fjords, inlets, islands and great twisting peninsulas.

They checked into a drab hotel in Santiago, sharing a noisy twin room off the old town's main drag. While Hens took a cold shower, Peter called Angelica, who reassured him that business would be fine, that he should enjoy himself and his stupid hobby, that this was no time to be calling her on the other side of the world. He gave her the number for the hotel, just in case.

Hens wanted to go drinking but Peter was too exhausted from the journey. Rest, for Hens, was a chore and he could survive perfectly happily on four hours' sleep a night. This might have been useful, were he a head of state. But his primary interests were drinking and meeting women, and the women that were awake at four in the morning in Chilean bars were not the calming influence Peter thought Hens needed. Hens came back seventeen hours later, blind drunk, without his wallet and with his nose now a botched, swollen prism, bleeding in the middle of his face. He talked incoherently about the woman in the university office who had spurned his advances – how dare she!? – while Peter half listened, then vaulted into unconsciousness. It was already morning, so Peter showered, then waited for the hotel manager – who'd told him she could locate a knowledgeable tour guide – to ascend the rickety stairs outside the door.

The landlady introduced Peter to a driver who knew the plant well. Max Sosa drove him out of the city, into the arid hillsides of the Chilean Matorral. The journey was longer than Peter had predicted by examining the map, and though the heat was stultifying, they had no choice but to keep the windows up to fend off the red dust that coated their hair.

Max was a young man whose eyelids hung at half mast, so he appeared to be just shy of sleep at all times. For the first hour they didn't trade a word. Peter's command of the dialect was non-existent, and Max apparently found it funny to watch the inappropriately dressed passenger in the back, sweat collecting in the grooves of the seat, like it would be a story he'd tell his sons when he returned home.

The back wheels bucked as the car hit a pothole, and the two men seemed momentarily weightless. Though Max was a clear half a foot shorter than Peter, both banged their heads on the roof with a thump when it found the ground again. Struggling to bring the car under control, Max yanked the steering wheel left, then right, almost tipping the entire vehicle onto its side before it came to a stop in the middle of the road, an undulating S-shaped track stretched through the dirt behind it. Peter looked into the rear-view mirror, where he caught Max's eye, and they crumpled into laughter, bonded by the universal language of a close escape.

'The roads,' Max said, the words clipped. 'They are shit.'

'You can say that again,' Peter said, mopping his brow with his sleeve. Max straightened the car in the road, took a deep breath, and they carried on, slower than before.

'It's no trip to Chile if you don't cheat death.'

'That so?'

'That's what they say.'

'And where are they now?'

'Dead.' The men laughed again, louder this time, and Peter clambered over the seat into the front.

After another hour's driving in which the conversation

never faltered, Max dropped Peter off with some water, a map and a compass, and told him to meet back at the same spot in six hours' time.

'Good luck,' he said, grinning, his accent a twanged string. 'Remember, Mr Manyweathers, you are not the little sheep. You don't get snagged in the Puya or I bring knife to cut you out!'

Sharp leaves on the roadside lashed Peter's legs beneath the hem of his shorts, raised red scratches flecking the skin. He pictured his trousers, neatly folded on a shelf beside the bed, and wanted them with the same tired lust these tropical shrubs had for the contents of his water bottle. He laughed, if only to mask the profound sense of regret he was experiencing, then seriously considered sitting down on the spot for six hours and pretending that he had fruitlessly searched for his quarry. But no, he had come too far to stop now.

'You're sure it's here?' he said.

'If it is anywhere in the world growing wild, it is here in this square kilometre. The question is not *if*, Mr Many-weathers, it is *when*!'

After Max had driven away, Peter took a reference book from the rucksack Susan had given to him as a gift. Already well thumbed, it fell open at the page he was looking for – a picture of the plant that he now saw all around him. The sheep-eater. Max was right. It wasn't a matter of if, but when. The sheep-eater was an evergreen perennial bromeliad, native to these unforgiving climes. It stood up to two metres high and at the top formed a large dense rosette of grey-green, swathe-like leaves covered in hooked spikes, so that it resembled a mace. They were everywhere.

Peter approached one, dabbing a finger against the weaponized tips. Though the plant is not uncommon, the sheep-eater flowers just once every twenty years, and only for a week at most, a flash of green and yellow as pretty as a picnic in a meadow. But the beauty of the flower betrayed the grisly means it had adopted to live. The outer two-thirds of the leaves' blade bore spines and were so tough that Chilean fishermen used their fibres to weave robust nets. This prevented herbivores from reaching the thick fleshy stalk at the centre. The plant had evolved to defend itself, just as a child grows to learn that fire burns, and pins prick, and not everything in the world – other humans included – will be its friend.

But more than that, the plant had learned to attack. It used these sharp spines to snare and trap animals – sheep – that slowly starved to death, bleating their last under the hot sun that rose behind the Andes to the east. They then decayed at the base of the plant, acting as a fertilizer in the otherwise parched ground. The plant feasted on the nutrients, drawing the good from all the bad around it. They stood as proud monuments to nature's merciless dependence on death for as far as the eye could see. But to find one in bloom would take tremendous good fortune. And a decent pair of walking boots.

Peter headed north-west in as straight a line as possible, through the rocks and leaf-daggers. When half the time had elapsed he'd scaled eight hundred metres. The air was thin, his lungs dented ping-pong balls, battered and reluctant to reassert their shape. He'd found nothing but a new lexicon of profanity to describe the pain of the blister that had appeared on his right heel from nowhere, and a new-found respect for the Sherpa. Anxious not to miss the lift back into town, he rested for a few minutes and then began a slow and steady descent.

He was perhaps an hour back down the slope, a little confused and looking at his compass when he heard it, the noise: one note, distorted but sustained for four, five seconds or more.

Brrrrrrrrrrrr. He'd no idea where it had come from, and though he looked all he could see were rocks, shrubs and monolithic stalks.

Brrrrrrrrrrrr. Not so loud this time. He took a few short steps back.

Brrrrrrrrrrrr. To his left was a bank of spiky, hard-skinned bush leaves, so thick and sturdy they looked as though they could survive a nuclear blast. The sound was coming from beyond them, but there was no getting through it. He would have to climb around them, up the steep incline that penned them in to the north, and shimmy across the sheer face for a good fifteen minutes. It would blow his timing. He'd be late, with no guarantee that Max would wait. He had already been paid, and it wouldn't be the first time Peter had mistakenly placed his trust in someone else. But he'd seen in Max's eyes, when they'd almost flipped the car, a kindness: a shared belief in what is precious far stronger than his word.

It came again, shorter, more urgent. *Brrrrr.* He began to climb.

The rock face was solid and simple, if laborious, to navigate. He managed it faster than predicted and dropped onto a thin patch of flat ground on the other side of the scrub, no more than a metre in width. This formed the lip of an almighty crevice, unseen before, now splitting the landscape in two. The rocky valley bent the buzzing sound, so that it became sourceless and infinite. But it was in there somewhere. He took a torch from his rucksack and shone it into the void. Two eyes lit up, staring back at him from the blackness. 'Hello! I can see you!' he shouted.

Brrrrrrr.

With utmost care he lowered himself over the precipice and eased down, slowly, carefully, thinking of the close call in Gibraltar, while the torch in his mouth picked face-shaped pools of shade from the rocks.

'I'm coming,' he mumbled, reaching the bottom, jaw aching, sweat stinging his eyes. He let his sight adjust. There was light at the bottom from a thin split in the rock. Plants, unseen before, thrived in the gloom. Emerging. Surviving. Finding a way on their own. Central among them was the *Puya chilensis*, in glorious bloom. Its flowers glistened like coral jostled by a Caribbean tide. Frail yellow petals, bursting forth from delicate lime buds, intricate little buttons on the face of a peculiar monster.

And at its base, snared in the vicious spikes, a sheep. Wizened by weeks of hunger, wool damp and bloody from where, driven crazy by starvation, it had begun to eat its own flesh.

Peter clutched his stomach, more through shock than sickness. He poured water from the bottle into his left hand and put it to the sheep's mouth. Weakly lolling over the crumbling brown slabs of its teeth, its tongue felt like a dying animal in its own right. The stench of shit and infected flesh didn't bother Peter – his work had prepared him for worse. No, it was the dawning of an awful truth that turned his stomach. The sheep was beyond saving. Mercy, or something similar, meant killing it. He had never knowingly killed anything, let alone something so big as a sheep, which in that moment, shivering, scared, tired and in pain, seemed human. It was just as he'd always said to Angelica: we're all nothing more than organic matter. We're all just the same, in the end. There was, he supposed, a little comfort in that, so he clung to it.

He lay with the sheep a while, until its bleats collapsed under the weight of silence, stroking its knotted wool and hoping it might find peace. Its breath faded, then returned, then faded again. When he thought it might perish, and its eyes blanked and watered, from somewhere it found life in the grey. It could have survived another hour, another day, but he could sense its frustration in the to and fro of its weight shifting on his lap. It wanted an ending. It wanted him to kill it.

Peter lifted the torch above his head with both arms,

as if he were fishing in a low river with a spear. The sheep turned its head into the leaves. They had conspired, together, in what was coming. Or so he thought.

He quickly brought the torch handle down towards the sheep's skull. Filled with a sudden energy, the sheep flinched, its last survival instinct jerking from its body, leaping the gap between life and death. With one final almighty kick it shifted, still stuck in the leaves but a foot or more lower, and Peter's momentum, now unstoppable, toppled him over onto the plant. The spines of the *Puya chilensis* tore open the skin on his legs, arms and chest, exposing the squirming pink of muscle. He was impaled on a leaf, sharp as a boning knife, stabbed through the soft flesh just above his hip. His rucksack, out of reach, taunted him from the ledge where he'd rested it, though his water bottle was still clipped to his belt. Pain rose slowly through his body, as if he was lowering himself into a bath of it. When it reached his head he took a final look at the sheep, recognized what he took to be sympathy in a gentle nod, then felt his own consciousness flit wildly away.

When he woke, a cold sweat was soaking through his clothes. At night the valley sky was a velvet curtain, peppered with the moth holes of stars. A stalactite of coagulated blood clung to his back. The pain had plateaued, but he couldn't move, couldn't twist the key of the spike through the muscle. Looking down to the lower of the two bunks he had accidentally made, he saw the sheep was dead. He cried for it, or that's what he told himself.

Were it not for the freakishly warm summer nights the area had been subjected to, he'd have frozen to death at the foot of the *Puya chilensis*. Over the next eight days Peter watched its flower bloom, wither, then die, from below. It was beautiful, to be witness to this brief and wondrous lifetime of colour. Just as the sheep had enriched it, so it had enriched him. He prepared to die with the flower and had just one regret. That he couldn't share this glorious sight with someone just as ecstatic to see it.

On the ninth morning, water long gone, he knew his body only as an endless piano of ribs.

A woman's head appeared at the top of the crevice, scattering a nest of lizards across the cool face of the rock. He wondered how long it had taken her to get there from heaven. She repeated, in a mesmeric broken English he heard in his veins, that he would be OK, that he would be all right, that he should not give in to sleep. An angel? Sent by Susan? And her face, as it came closer to his, was a work of fragile intricacy, like the centre of a flower, simple and perfect. He loved her then, as quickly as that. He knew because his heart unfurled, the way he'd heard they do.

That's all he could remember of his rescue. Powerful drugs flooded his system, but weakness kept him under. Most of his vital organs had malfunctioned. Dehydration had come for him, but he had not been taken. The angel had seen to that.

The medical care was good and thorough, though the hospital was basic. Mould grew in the corners by the floor, and the bedrails were sticky with a nameless gunk, the residue of another's suffering. For those first two weeks, whenever Peter drifted into the open water of consciousness, all he wanted to do was clean. Other patients paced the ward during the night, screaming or scraping bedpans along the bars in the windows. Short of any real, sustained feeling, he still managed to be grateful that they mostly left him alone.

As soon as he was well enough to be moved, Hens, who'd apparently left Chile after visiting the hospital a few times, had the university pay to fly him home, where he woke with a sudden and stunning clarity he had not experienced in over seven weeks, in a hospital ward in Manhattan with Susan holding his hand.

'Where is she?' he said, the words stuck in his dry mouth.

'The nurse?' Susan reached for the emergency call button.

'No, not the nurse. The woman.'

'What woman?'

He grabbed her hand and squeezed it white. 'The woman that rescued me.'

'How the hell should I know?'

He wanted to yank the drip from his arm and run to the exit, but pulling back the sheets to see the pale ropes of legs he didn't recognize, he knew he'd never make it.

Susan tipped a glass of ice water to his lips. 'I've been worried sick, Petey, worried completely sick. I can't sleep. I can't eat. I can barely sit down.'

'Susan . . .'

'And to think you told me none of this was dangerous. I should have handcuffed you to your goddamn radiator.'

'Susan!' She stopped, swallowed, looked up and down the ward as though expecting security to come and escort her from the building. 'I need to know what happened to me.'

'All I know is they searched for you for over a week. Thought you'd fallen or something, maybe broken a leg. But they were pretty sure you'd be dead when they got there. They said that even the guys who lived there thought no one could survive. Normally, anyway. Then some lady found you.'

'Some lady?'

'Yeah. And get this. She's a flower hunter too! What are the chances, huh? That a woman, an *actual* woman, has got the same stupid pastime you do. When they told me that I didn't stop laughing for the rest of the day. She was looking for the same thing you were, apparently. I don't think she thought she'd find a man trapped in it, though. My God, you're an idiot.' She chewed the tips of her hair, her attention waning fast.

'How do you know all this?'

'Your friend Hens told me. He said the lady stayed with you at the hospital until they could track him down and he could get there. Something a little odd about him, isn't there?'

'So he met her?'

'Yeah, I guess. And you're aware you've left your business in the hands of a moody teenager, right? I've been passing by the lockup to check on her, and either I'm getting on her nerves or everything gets on her nerves.'

'Probably the former. Look, Susan,' he said, 'I need you to get Hens for me.'

'I can't do that,' she said. He turned to face her but was beaten back by a sharp pain in his lower abdomen.

'Why not?'

'He's not here.'

'Not in the hospital?'

'In America.'

'Not in America!? Then where is he?'

'Who cares?'

'*Where is he?*'

'Calm down, Petey, you'll do yourself even more lasting damage. Do you know how much candy I've brought you over the last few weeks? How much of it I had to eat?' He took a deep breath, then repeated himself as sternly as he could.

'Mexico, or some place like that. Said there were reports of some rare flower. Apparently they found a whole load of them. Like a fieldful. They reckon they're all gonna go at the same time. At least I think that's what he was talking about. I'll be honest, I wasn't listening. That guy gives me the creeps.'

'A flower.'

'Uh-huh.'

'Do you know what it was called?'

'Something stupid. Something like the Queen of the Night. How come you lot wouldn't know romance if it took you out for dinner but you can name a flower like you're Shakespeare?' Peter clung to the bed frame. He thought of the Kadupul, and was suddenly full of foreboding.

Almost anything desired can be owned. But no one, no emperor, president or king, could ever own the Kadupul flower. No one could lay claim to the Queen of the Night.

Not only was it rare, the Kadupul couldn't be picked without causing devastating damage to its form. Plucked, it perished within hours. To hold it was to kill it, a conundrum of heartbreak, a newborn baby that burns at its mother's touch. So it belonged to no one.

Better still, it only bloomed at night, for one night only, emanating a unique fragrance, a heavenly death rattle of the senses, before it died at dawn. The Kadupul – technically a delicate white cactus – could be seen by anyone patient enough to wait. It flowered once a year. So it wasn't rarity that earned it its place on the love letter he found in the library. It was pricelessness. What else was truly priceless? Only love.

He knew that Hens did not feel the same. Hens Berg lacked many things, but chief among them was the patience that the Kadupul demands. He'd sooner pull it from the earth, reasoning that to hold it as it died was better than not to hold it at all. And to make the trip alone seemed completely out of character. Hens was too fond of an audience. The only reason he'd invited Peter to Chile with him was because he needed a drinking partner long enough for the whisky to kick in, so that he might find someone with whom to share his bed. No, he had another motive.

Against the doctor's advice, Peter checked himself out of hospital an hour later. Susan reluctantly helped him dress, then pushed him towards the exit in a wheelchair.

'I can't believe you are forcing me to do this.'

'I'm not forcing you to do anything,' he said, 'you're doing it because you're my sister and you know it's important.'

They took a cab to Peter's apartment and Peter was relieved to find Angelica was out at work; he didn't want to have to explain the teenager living there rent-free to his sister, and luckily there was little sign she'd ever been there other than the fact the whole place was spotlessly clean, unless you knew where to look. The kitchen countertops beamed back a gaunt reflection he didn't dare examine. The windows were so spotless he had to touch the glass to believe it hadn't been blown out onto the street.

'Well, this is depressing,' Susan said.

'You don't have to stay,' he said, ambling to the fridge, which was empty because Angelica seemed to subsist on air alone.

'Of course I'm staying.' He kissed her, just once, on the forehead.

Peter slept for three hours. When he woke he ate a few mouthfuls of the lunch she'd been to the supermarket and bought for him. Honey-glazed ham draped lazily over thick white bread, mayonnaise oozing from the ends.

In the shower he ran a razor over his face, shearing off the growth that seemed to concentrate on the right cheek, lopsiding him. He brushed his teeth and it felt like discovering them anew. For a while he sat on the rim of the bathtub, letting the steam swirl around his wet skin. He listened through the door to Susan singing as she moved through the lounge, her voice joyfully lilting from one note to the next.

She found him standing by the wardrobe, its contents spread at his feet. On the bed he'd put a moth-eaten pea-green tent, a head torch with a cracked plastic case and a limply stuffed pillow.

'What are you doing with all that?'

'Nothing,' he said.

'Come on, Petey . . .'

'Peter.'

'Stop changing the subject and tell me what you're doing.' She removed a small brain of gum from her mouth and flattened it between her fingers.

'I'm going to Mexico.'

'You're not serious.'

'Yes,' he said, 'I am.'

'You're not going to Mexico. It's the stupidest thing I

ever heard.' She took the mirror from the wall and held it up in front of him, a sight he'd been desperate to avoid.

'Look at you,' she said. 'You wouldn't even make it to the airport.' It was abhorrently true. He'd been confronted with the reflection of a man cut down from a noose. He sat on the corner of the bed, caressing his narrow wrists. Outside, a break in the traffic gave the rare illusion of absolute peace.

'You're not well enough. Who do you think you are? Superman?'

'I'm fine, Susan.'

'You look like an actor playing a ghost.'

'I promise you, I'm fine.'

'You know it's because I love you, right?'

'I know,' he said, 'I know.'

'Then don't put me through this shit any more.'

He placated her by ordering takeaway pizza, but again only managed a few mouthfuls before his appetite faded. They watched movies while he summoned up the courage to tell his sister she wasn't going to be able to change his mind. She winced, squeezing her eyes together as though trying to magic him into a cell he wouldn't be able to escape.

'For a flower?' she said.

'No.'

'To catch up with your stupid friend?'

'No.'

'Then why? Give me one good reason why I should ever let you out of my sight again.'

'For a woman,' he said, and where he expected her to shout, a smile slowly edged across her mouth, her entire face rising with joy.

'You can't go there alone,' Susan said, 'you're not well enough.'

'I'm fine,' he said, 'honestly. Wait. What do you mean, "alone"?' She stood, bracing herself as though she had no idea what effect her next words might have on her body – that she might explode, or collapse, or even take off.

'I'll go with you.'

'Susan,' he said, waggling his finger in a way he knew would annoy her if she looked at him, 'that's very kind of you, but . . .'

'This isn't an offer,' she said, 'it's a promise.'

'What?'

'I'll go with you.'

'Come on, Susan.'

'You need me,' she said, and it brought him to his knees once more.

NINE

Dove wakes at home before sunrise with little recollection of how he got there. Not of Cliff helping him out of the office, travelling with him in a taxi, coming into his house, taking off his shoes. This is the series of events he pieces together when he sees the note beside the glass of water on his bedside table.

You've taken two paracetamol. Stay in bed. I wish you'd let me take you to hospital. Call me when you wake up, no matter how early or late it is. I am really worried about you, regardless of whether or not you want me to be. Your friend, Cliff.

He checks his phone. Two missed calls already. He switches it off and flings it to the other side of the room, where it lands behind the rusted metal rear of his refrigerator with a clang that brings to an end the quiet hum of next door's baby snoring.

The headache is beginning to dissipate. He can feel it, moving slowly downwards through his body, a warm fuzz, melting. Only when it's passed over his collarbone can he drag himself out of bed. He inches across the floor on all fours like a dog expecting punishment, finds the open pack of painkillers in the drawer beside the oven and washes two more down with a sweet, sticky orange juice that chills a column from his throat to his gut. Only then can he leave the house, weak, but closing his eyes and remembering Susan's hand in Peter's, imagining it in his. Guiding him forward. Isn't this exactly what he wants? Feeling what Peter once felt is in some way sharpening his own experience. Where before the world has seemed dull, it is clearer now. He doesn't want to shy away from it, but to seize it in both hands.

He takes two buses busy with the early commuters. Cleaners. Security guards. Carers. People only seen by those who are looking. Living beneath the surface of the city they keep running. His train heads overland from Highbury, south through East London, to cross the Thames near Canary Wharf. Standing at the front, eyes against the glass, Dove is giddy with a childish excitement. Below, the wonky seams of old London twist into buzzing carriageways, down towards the centre of the city. The houses become towers rising on either side, each with a hundred glass eyes brightening in the sunrise. Ramps dip to carry cars through the underpass, rising again in tight brick canyons. Behind him now, a view from the south, the city's overgrown steel canopy. Commuters scurrying around in the mulch. When he alights, it's into the wide, serene expanse of a leafy Blackheath readied for the day ahead. Only there, where the air fills him completely, can he breathe properly once more.

Blackatree Crescent Nursing Home is a sprawling one-storey building emerging from florid grounds where neat beds patchwork the lawns. A brook trickles gently around the periphery, the water clean and the damp rocks blinking as the clouds block the light above. Beyond the walls on the other side is a magnificent garden, where bees bump into one another like corks strung from a hat. It feels removed from the city, which is perhaps its aim. To let people forget it or its inhabitants exist. It's easier that way.

He unlatches the gate. Approaching the door and ringing the bell, he clenches his fist tight until his hand stops trembling, pressed against the wood.

A woman appears with a sponge of tightly curled hair, held in position by a net and strip of worn elastic.

'Yes?' she says through the glass. Dove recognizes her voice from Jed's call, a musical timbre barely wrestled under control. The woman he spoke with. 'Can I help you?' His lips fall open with the weight of sudden realization – he doesn't know what he's going to say.

'I'm here to visit somebody.'

'What, anybody?' She chuckles to herself, hands on hips.

'Not just anybody, no.'

'Then who?' He looks at the flashing red light on the numerical keypad, the security cameras positioned just above her head. Had he assumed he might walk straight in?

'Well, it's a funny question.'

'A funny question?' She frowns. He can smell the sulphuric tang of overdone scrambled eggs escaping a kitchen somewhere behind her.

'I'm here to see Zachariah Temple.'

She twists to look over her shoulder, down a long empty corridor with doors on either side, and he reads the name badge pinned to her chest. Rita. She has long, almost bovine lashes and large brown eyes, which narrow as doubt sets in.

'Can I ask you again why you're here?'

'I just told you. To visit Zachariah Temple.'

'And who are you to him?' Dove sighs, suddenly feeling like a con man.

'Nobody.'

'Nobody? Zachariah doesn't get visitors, ever, and you just turn up saying you're nobody?'

'I work in ambulance dispatch. You called us.'

'I beg your pardon?'

'About his headache.'

'You're offering follow-up house calls now?'

'Not really, it's just that, well, I . . .' He adjusts his posture – straighter back, aligned shoulders – something, anything, that will give him the air of someone she should take seriously, prevent her slamming the door in his face at any second.

'Please, Rita. I have ID.' Dove squeezes his wallet to a yawn and shows her an out-of-date driving licence he's never actually used. She reads it aloud, the higher register of her voice finally unshackled.

'Dove,' she says. 'Dove.' Repeating his name. Rolling it around her tongue. Checking it for leaks. 'Dove. Dove. Dove. Strange name, isn't it?' The golden plait of her necklace jiggles, weighty and mayoral.

'About the headaches . . .'

'Forget about any headaches for a second. There is nothing here to steal, you know, unless your thing is shortbread.'

'I'm not a thief.'

'Then what should I tell the police?' She smoothes down the pockets of her pinafore, searching for a phone that isn't there. 'Because that's who I am going to have to call unless you leave the premises immediately.'

'Please,' he says, still holding his driving licence against the pane, knuckles paling.

'You expect me to believe you're just a good Samaritan concerned about the migraines of an old man he's never met?'

'No,' Dove says, withdrawing into the shade of the porch. 'I'm just a visitor to an old man I heard about who doesn't normally have any.'

He is nearing the gate when the door's electric lock clunks behind him. Turning, he finds it open, with Rita impatiently tapping her foot.

'You catch me on a charitable day. It's not always this way. So hurry up. And don't leave my sight.'

Rita ushers Dove into a large hallway, the air damp with steam. Somewhere, a television is turned up too loudly, its levels distorted, voices indecipherable. The walls

are lined with photographs of faraway beaches and mead-
ows, calming seascapes and clearings in forests filled with
warm golden light, little different to the ones in the Pit,
except here, potentially, of use.

A bedroom door opens as they pass to reveal a morose-
looking priest, no older than Dove, who shakes Rita's
hand. Young priests make Dove uneasy; not a symptom
of any aversion to organized religion, more a distrust
rooted in something deeper: the surety with which they've
committed to their calling. Isn't it the malaise of his gen-
eration, to have no clue what they're meant to be doing?
Infantilized by the digital age, freed from the preset
destinies of their parents and grandparents and every gen-
eration before them, yet unable to choose in a world of
infinite choice; a swathe of young adults drifting, flotsam
and jetsam from which the priest has escaped with an un-
erring display of devotion. It must be good to put on a
collar every day that tells you exactly who you are.

'Don't be upset when he doesn't speak to you,' Rita
says, guiding Dove down the thin corridor. 'Zachariah has
been here many years. Longer even than me. He doesn't
speak at all. Never has.'

She stops outside a set of double doors, behind them
the deafening television, and shrugs. She plugs her ears
with cotton wool, jewellery wobbling on the lobes. Dove
declines two plugs of his own and enters the room.

There are armchairs, thirty or more, but none of them
match. Half are full, but empty ones hold the shape of

whoever sat there last, the prints of their hands tightly gripping the arms. They hold on.

'You didn't come here to watch TV,' she says from behind him. 'Did you?'

He looks from one person to the next, each face lined with the puzzles of age. Not one of them acknowledges his presence. He feels no more than air.

Rita taps her foot against the skirting board to a skittish, impatient rhythm. He turns to see her pointing towards an old man in the corner of the room with his chair facing the window.

'Mr Zachariah Temple,' she says.

And the first thing Dove thinks about is Len.

He was twelve by then, and the years he'd been with Len and Maud had ironed out many of the issues he'd arrived with. He was less shy around strangers. More trusting of others. There were still problems with his mood – he became jealous and angry easily – though he could largely control sudden fits of temper, and his sullen episodes were fewer and further between. He still feared abandonment, but no longer feared Len and Maud leaving the room and never coming back. It had become a background radiation, always there, only sometimes building to an all-consuming nausea, like the one he was experiencing sitting in the hospital room, Maud beside him, their hands pressed together.

The room opposite had a light box screwed to the wall,

and if Dove craned his neck he could see the image pinned to it: a cauliflower print of brain, blackness surrounded by the dense white of bone – a tiny galaxy.

'See,' he said, squeezing the sodden fabric round her wrist, 'looks like outer space, doesn't it?'

'I suppose it does if you look at it a certain way,' Maud said, huffing on her inhaler, a rattle in her lungs. She stared at the door like she did at the dog flap in the kitchen. As though it might open at any minute, the corners of her mouth curled upwards in hope.

Len lay perfectly still on the hospital bed, a likeness of a man carved atop his own tomb. His eyes were caves in his skull. A fury of tubes ran from his arms and nose. A doctor explained: the tumour that felled him had been there for some time, lurking in the black space of his brain.

'It's pressing on the temporal lobe,' he said. He was young and handsome, a cleft in his chin. 'It could explain any loss of cognitive ability he was suffering. It would certainly explain any pain he was in.'

'He wasn't in any pain,' Maud said.

'That he mentioned.'

'I'm his wife. He'd have told me if he was.' The doctor didn't lift his eyes from a form he'd been filling in since he entered the room.

'What about memory loss?'

'No more than anyone else our age.' Dove knew that to be true. They'd spend many evenings, especially on nights when he didn't have school the next day, with Len telling him all about the wild things he got up to as a young man. His stories were rich and colourful, recounted in a level of detail so fantastic that, as Dove had grown into the first flushes of adolescence, he sometimes wondered if they were inventions. Like the time Len was a fireman during the war and he and two friends had to wrap themselves in a mattress and jump from the third-floor window of a burning building. Or the time he hitchhiked all the way home from the Mull of Kintyre with a man he convinced himself was an escaped prisoner, only for a newspaper article three days later to confirm his suspicions were correct. Maybe it was the way he told them, or how he pinched the back of Dove's neck as they drew towards their climax, but the stories excited him. He couldn't wait to grow up. For the first time in his life, he wanted to reach the future. To see what happened next.

'That's good,' the doctor said. 'The mind is a fragile instrument. Almost anything else there are pills for.' Dove scowled at the doctor from his seat in the corner of the room, unappreciative of his manner. Too flippant. Too functional. Did he think they were discussing the engine of a broken-down car? Only years later did he see that what he'd assumed to be nonchalance was in fact a coping mechanism, deployed to help not only Maud, but the doctor himself. How else could a man hold the lives of others in his hands?

'And you,' he said to Dove. 'Don't you be worrying about your grandad.'

'He's my dad,' Dove said. But his voice was quiet and tired and the doctor spoke over him, more from efficiency than ignorance, as he tapped his pen against various machines and recorded what it said on their displays.

'He's in the best possible care here. If he does what I tell him to, everything will be just fine.'

That was when Dove knew the very opposite was true.

It was early evening – the thin curtains couldn't keep out the milky glare of the moon – when Maud fell asleep in the armchair at the foot of the bed and Dove was the only one awake. Yearning for closeness, he stood on the tips of his toes to kiss Len's forehead, then his chest. He took Len's fingers and caressed them with his lips. They were brittle. Len opened his mouth, so slightly his tongue stayed trapped inside, a dying animal, peering through the bars.

'Dove,' he said, a low grumble.

'I'm sorry,' Dove said.

'What for?'

'She'll kill me if she knows I woke you up. The doctor says you need to rest.'

'Pffft. Rest? And who will put the bread on the table if I do that?' Len often used analogies involving bread and butter. Dove was astonished at the range of things he could apply them to: moving furniture, rebuilding a car's engine, even worming the dog.

Fighting an urge to scoop Len into his arms, Dove shoved his hands into his pockets. At twelve he was big for his age, but his muscles were still slight and sinewy.

And yet, with Len before him, the tumour having shorn the weight from his bones, carrying him home seemed not just possible, but something he should definitely attempt.

The nurse came with a plastic cup and, in it, the jumping bean of a fluorescent sedative. Maud woke and forced Len to eat the solid round lump of mashed potato they served him. The gravy was thin, with suspended crystals of salt, giving everything on the plate the same anaemic hue.

'I'm thinking of going to a nightclub tonight,' Len said to her as she wiped a thin band of dribble from his chin.

'Is that so?' Maud asked, and they laughed together. 'Then I'd better get you cleaned up.'

'I can get you some help,' the nurse said, straightening the blue paper curtains. Maud smiled.

'Thank you, but it's fine. I've been looking after Len in one way or another since the day I met him. I could do it with my eyes closed.' There was truth to this too. Dove had seen her rub his skin with moisturizer until he smelled of cloves. She had a way of lifting him, turning him, almost one-handed, so that they were one body, each an extension of the other.

Len waited until the nurse left.

'Maud, go home and get some rest, will you? I'm meant to be the one in hospital. Not you.'

'Fat chance,' she said, pinning another photograph to the wall beside his bed; the two of them with a little girl named Annabel, who was an adult now and had promised a visit yet to materialize.

'Then go get yourself something to eat in the canteen. Something. Anything. Put up those bloody feet of yours.'

'My feet don't need putting up.'

'Don't give me that,' he said, 'get out of here. Go. Dove can keep me company for a while.' Eventually Maud left – a wiggle in her walk concession that yes, maybe a sit-down and a hot meal was a good idea after all – but not before kissing Len on the lips with a teenage enthusiasm that made Dove want to hide beneath the bed.

'Don't go anywhere,' she said, gently closing the door behind her.

After a while of Dove holding Len's hand in a sad but pleasant silence, Len pressed the back of Dove's to his cheek and he felt wetness on it.

'Are you being good?' he asked.

'Being good?'

'For Maud. Helping around the house. Doing what she tells you to do.'

'Uh-huh.' It was true, he had been. In Len's absence he'd quickly realized she needed him every bit as much as he needed her.

'You're a good boy. I always said keeping you with us was the best decision we ever made.'

Dove stood then, looked Len in the eye through a glaze of tears.

'You're coming home, aren't you? Maud said you were coming home.' He laughed, but it quickly petered into nothing.

'You think I'm staying here eating biscuits all day,

staring out of the window like in some old folks' home? Come on, Dove. Of course I am. Of course I'm coming home.'

Dove approaches Zachariah from the side so as not to startle him, but the old man doesn't move, even when Dove's shadow falls across his face.

'Hello,' he says, lowering himself to head height. 'Zachariah?' No answer. 'Mr Temple?'

The man stares straight ahead and Dove is nothing in his vision. 'Mr Temple?' His hand, pallid and limp. Nothing. Though right in front of him, he could leave now and believe this man had never seen his face.

'Mr Temple. I'm here to talk to you about flowers.' Still nothing.

Rita appears at Dove's side and hands him a biscuit. They walk together, to what feels like a polite enough distance.

'Not who you thought it was?' she asks.

'I don't know who I thought it was.'

'God bless you for trying.'

'He has Alzheimer's?'

'You can call it whatever you want. But like most of our residents here, what he doesn't have is himself. That's the only important thing.'

'Who was he, though? I mean, before he was here.'

'I'll tell you what I know. I know that he likes to be clean, and he likes his surroundings to be clean. So I do that for him. He likes to be positioned by the window so that he can see the garden outside, and that's the only time I ever see a smile in those old eyes. But maybe I'm imagining it. Maybe thinking someone is in there helps me get through the day.' Rita wanders slowly away, her trolley wheels squealing. 'I'll give you a minute to say goodbye.'

Dove draws back towards the chair and quietly crouches down beside the old man's legs.

It is not his features Dove recognizes. His face, layers upon layers, folded like the head of a dying rose. No, he does not look like Peter Manyweathers, not the Peter Manyweathers in the memories. But, in the tilt of his head, the vague clue of an outline – the same otherly sense by which a lover can be spotted across a crowded room – he also does.

'Mr Manyweathers?'

The old man's pupils hang in the centre of his eyes like targets on the back wall of an abandoned shooting range. 'My name's Dove.' Taking his hand, running a fingertip over the electric-blue map of his veins.

The old man snatches back his arm and presses his knuckles hard into the front of his skull, while at his feet, Dove does the same. The pain is more intense than before, sharper, faster, a blade carving open the space inside him, splaying it out, and filling it with something new.

A memory of his mother.

TEN

They were on a flight to Mexico. The plane was full. Cigarette smoke snaked across the ceiling and slithered into the vents. Susan's fingernails were mottled by the imprint of her bite. The magnitude of her snap decision was taking hold. She stared out of the window at the cloud tops, whipped to form ranges in the sky, convincing herself that at any moment they might crash.

'Do you know how rare plane crashes are?' Peter asked. His teeth punctured the apple she shoved into his mouth.

The way she gripped her seat when the plane banked reminded him of how she'd clutch his arm as a child, whenever they crossed a busy road. When she did it, he felt like the only other person alive.

They landed in Guadalajara, and a relentless Mexican heat blasted the cool film of plane sweat from their skin. Susan carried the bags while he limped along on crutches borrowed from a neighbour. They let the arrivals lounge clear, then approached a tour guide with a map he'd had annotated by the more knowledgeable members of the etching group.

'I'm looking for the Kadupul flower,' he said. 'It'll be in one of these areas, somewhere.'

'You are serious?' the tour guide said, a laugh drowning out the flight announcements. The circled areas of the map covered over two thousand miles. Jalisco lay in the transition area between the temperate north and the tropical south, on the northern edge of the Sierra Madre del Sur at the Trans-Mexican Belt, home to all five of Mexico's natural ecosystems. Arid and semi-arid scrublands, tropical evergreen, deciduous and thorn forests, mesquite grasslands and temperate forests with oaks, pines and firs. Finding a specific flower, or even a field of them, was as futile as hunting a solitary, bashful flea on the body of a dog.

'Yes,' Peter said, 'I'm serious.'

Keen to understand what his colleague had found so funny, an older man approached the counter, where this apparently impossible quest was translated. The conspiratorial sound of their conversation, combined with the curt way a stamp had been punched into her passport, had convinced Susan they were going to be arrested and imprisoned forever in a cell with thirty strange, sweaty, sporadically violent men. Peter told her to calm down, but in reality he was almost as anxious as his sister. To relax, he found an opportunity to remove the love letter from his pocket. Still it inspired him, and again he lost himself in its romance. The thought of finding the flowers, but more than that, the slightest chance of seeing the woman again who'd rescued him from the sheep-eater, left him bristling with determination.

The older man whispered something in his native tongue, then picked up the telephone.

'You might have a lucky day,' the first man said, guilt for having mocked the Americans drawing his face into a frown. 'Irving might know someone who knows.'

Irving was tall, with owlish grey eyebrows that looked almost metallic against his brown skin. He was a slow conversationalist, and spent almost fifteen minutes on the telephone as the heat closed in. By the time he'd finished, Susan was hyperventilating into a sick bag she'd picked up on the plane. But Irving came good. A friend of a friend of his, a keen botanist, had heard about the field of Kadupul, somewhere at the foot of the Volcán de Tequila, the flower perhaps lulled into delusions of safety by the 200,000 years that had passed since the volcano's last eruption. Irving helped them board a bus in the right direction, Peter tipped him five dollars, and Susan complained about how uncomfortable the seats were for the next two and a half hours.

They dumped their excess luggage at a hostel, where Peter quickly cleaned the room while Susan showered. The volcano's shadow grew as the moon rose over the town. Tequila train tourists pigeon-stepped through the tight adobe corridor of the main strip, with stucco, ochre lime-washed walls, arches, quoins and odd-shaped window frames. Three bells marked 9 p.m., when the parish priest emerged from the honeycomb brickwork of his church to bless the town. Everyone stopped what they were doing, even turning off their radios to mark the moment, as if it was the first or the last night of their existence. For the Kadupul, it could have been both.

Late the next afternoon, the hostel owner's wife kindly drove them out of town, dropping them where the volcano's gargantuan silhouette loomed like an incarnation of the devil. Susan stopped to look up, and her breath was robbed by its majesty. He realized she was wearing heels – the first time he'd seen her in them since she graduated – and that they were sinking into the mud.

'I don't care if they're inappropriate,' she said.

'Susan,' he said, staring down at his crutches, 'it's going to be a long old walk.'

If they were in the right place there would be many other flower hunters ahead of them. As with any clique, they perpetuated their own existence with the promotion of a strict and exclusive code, assuming others didn't understand the grace of an orchid, or the siren song of a sweet lily. Peter found them to be dullards, unable to comprehend that the recognition of a flower's beauty was, in all ways, enough. To his ear, calling the Kadupul an *Epiphyllum oxypetalum* was grossly unedifying. He wished his arms were stronger, so that when they inevitably noticed his sister's inappropriate shoes and rolled their eyes at the amateur in their midst, he could spark them straight out.

They walked the path for two hours, guided by the

wonky torch of the moon. Susan was quiet, moving her hands through the warm night air, letting it wash over her skin. Fields of blue agave swayed on the breeze, giving way to the shivering leaves of a forest canopy. And then, without warning, a clearing, and a swathe of resting Kadupul, stretching as far as the eye could see. There was no sign of one in bloom. Yet. They had made it in time, for this at least. Setting up their tent beneath a wide night sky, Peter used binoculars to scan the undulating hats of the flowers. Dotted around the field, two here, three there, were other tents, flagged by balls of dim lamplight. Outside some sat lone searchers, and outside others small groups, huddled together over reference books, keeping watch on the field for the first showing of a petal. But there was no sign of Hens or the woman who had rescued him.

Susan surveyed the stems of the Kadupul – some erect, some sprawling, all profusely branched – as if it were a fragile lake of ice.

'This is it, huh?'

'Yes,' he said, 'this is it. The shyest flower of them all.'

'Then tell me about it.'

'In Sri Lanka they believe that when the Kadupul blooms, a semi-mythical tribe known as the Nagas descend from heaven to present the flower as a gift to Buddha. The Chinese use it to describe someone who has an impressive but brief moment of glory . . . an instance of great luck. You know, like a lucky strike.'

'I could sure do with a few of those.'

'Wherever you go, people will interpret it differently. That's what we do with things we can't begin to understand. We give them magic, and so they become magic.'

Susan lay back on the long grass, alive with the lullabies of insects, becalmed by the brilliance of stars. Even the mosquitoes seemed to sense her blood was too still to drink. 'How do you interpret it?' she asked.

'I prefer its Japanese nickname. Beauty under the Moon.'

'We're not all as brave as you, y'know, Peter?' The more she spoke, the more she spread out across the ground.

'What do you mean?'

'Other people settle. But you. No. A list of six flowers on a letter and you decide you're gonna see them all.'

This made him smile so broadly he couldn't sleep for the ache in his cheeks. She was right, of course. But he didn't use to be brave. It was the letter that emboldened him. It felt as if the list of flowers was a path he had to follow. As if it had been mapped out by whoever wrote the letter to guide him to something greater, something the writer himself had been seeking when he put pen to paper. Love.

But that feeling was fading. They waited for three days. Peter used all the cash he had to buy food from opportunistic vendors who'd come from miles around to capitalize on the flower hunters' hunger. He struggled with his own unwillingness to confront a growing number of possibilities. That the woman wouldn't come. That Hens had found her first and spirited her away. Or, simply, that he'd been a fool. To yearn this way, for something that had never been his in the first place, hurt enough that he wouldn't have minded if the volcano had erupted and lava had engulfed him while he slept.

By the fourth day, they were both tired. Susan didn't once complain, but Peter knew they'd need to return to the hostel soon. The Queen of the Night rewarded patience, but even his was thinning. Susan rubbed his shoulders with the balls of her thumbs and whispered, gently, that they should stay another night, just in case. He thought of the campion, how it waited. But he was spent.

'This is stupid,' he said, disconsolately squeezing his head between his knees. 'If she was coming to see the Kadupul, she'd have been here by now. Or she came and left already, which is even worse.'

'You don't know what's going to happen.'

'That's the problem.'

'Come on, Peter, you're just too tired.'

'No,' he said, 'I'm just too late.'

They shook dirt from their belongings and packed them tightly into bags, until all that remained was the tent and the binoculars spilling out of their case. He wearily put them to his eyes for one last look at the flower. Strafing over the horizon, he saw, beyond the Kadupul, a sight that instantly soothed every ache in his limbs.

She appeared, on the far side of the field, out of the trees that seemed to open for her like velvet stage curtains. Though she was miniature in the sight of the binoculars, he recognized her instantly. Not from her face or her hair, the way she moved or how her brown skin bathed in the celestial glow – a beauty under the moon indeed – but from the way his heartbeat pummelled his ribs. Without another word, or his crutches for support, he limped around the perimeter of the vast field, not once taking his eyes from her white shawl, until he arrived behind her, and placed a shaking hand on the soft apex of her shoulder.

'My name is Peter Manyweathers,' he said.

'You're alive!' she said, and he was. Susan's excited yelp cut through the night.

A column of smoke pirouetted from the campfire, wood crackling. She sat barefoot on the ground and said her name was Harum. Susan, who'd barely spoken in an hour, apologetically gave her a peach that had browned on the journey.

'Harum is a nice name,' he said, everything that emerged from his mouth a mortifying cliché. He'd afforded hours of silent rehearsal to this moment, yet here he was, fluffing his lines.

'Thank you,' she said.

'What does it mean?'

'It's Indonesian for "smells good".' She laughed.

'In truth,' Susan said, inhaling, 'you do smell good.'

'I don't think that's me,' Harum said, smiling. 'It has been growing all night. The scent of vanilla. It means the Kadupul are coming.'

Peter showed her his reference book of flowers and she

nodded as if it were a yearbook of old friends. She pointed to a bright-pink bloom, with so many petals it looked like a hundred camellias in one flower.

'The Middlemist's Red. They say there is just one in the world now, in an English country garden. There is not a single one left in China, even though it is Chinese. I think it is proof that we do not belong to a certain place, but that we belong to the world. It is a flower I cannot die until I've seen.'

'It's beautiful.'

'You're a man after my own heart,' she said, her face lifting whenever she used a phrase she'd heard from another culture, unsure whether she'd deployed it quite right. He nodded. What she'd said was perfect.

She was thirty years old, with a pretty nose. Her silver necklace – two dainty birds – caught the firelight. When the wind filled her dress, billowing like the cloak of a jellyfish, she straightened it again with a single neat stroke. She described the buttery stamen of the Franklin tree she'd found in the Altamaha River valley, Georgia, the first recorded wild growth since the early nineteenth century, and the urgent red of the Koki'o flower in Hawaii, where only twenty-three are thought to exist.

'Peter?' Susan said. How long had he not been listening? Harum's voice had entranced him. He swore the flames moved to it.

'Huh?'

'Harum's asking you a question. I'm gonna go to sleep now, let you answer it.' Susan climbed into the tent, clucking, the way she had as a girl when she found something cute.

Harum sat beside Peter, and even the hairs on his legs seemed to reach out to her.

'I was wondering how you survived,' she said. 'When I found you, I thought you were already dead.'

'You were just in time.'

'Then it was better than seeing the sheep-eater bloom.' She held a hand across her heart.

'I don't remember any of it.'

'I came to hospital with you until they found your friend.'

'Hens.'

'Yes, the Dane. He was very kind. He wanted to take me to lunch, to say thank you for finding you. I told him, he did not have to thank me. Perhaps he had to thank a higher power, but not me. But he insisted, and so, of course, I had to accept his offer. We got quite drunk.' Peter prodded a stone through the dirt with the rubber tip of his crutch and imagined Hens's hand on her back, guiding her through the swinging wooden doors of a Chilean restaurant. How big his fingers looked curled round her dainty waist. How they dwarfed the shot glass he forced into her hands. He could smell the stale musk of tobacco on Hens's breath, stronger now than the vanilla in the air.

'Did you have a good time?' he asked, picturing Hens's expression, the way it went blank when he talked to a woman without listening to what was being said.

'He was very interested in the flowers I have studied.

141

Very charming. A real gentleman. In fact, we talked for most of the afternoon, swapping stories and sightings.'

'You did?'

'Oh yes. He told me about the Youtan Poluo, in China. I must admit, I was very jealous.' Peter didn't suppose she could ever experience a jealousy akin to his own at that moment. He tried to concentrate on his legs, but his time in hospital had left them so puny, an afterthought compared to the generous trunks Hens walked around on, that they embarrassed him, and he wrapped his arms around his aching knees.

'Yeah,' he said, 'that was a good find all right.'

'And the campion of Gibraltar. He told me how he searched the cliffs for a whole week until he found one, just one, in the furthest possible place.' Peter swallowed the bile climbing his throat. He was trapped. If he outed Hens as a liar now, it would seem bizarre. In her mind, they were friends, flower hunters bound by the brotherhood that supposedly united everybody else gathered here. Harum would doubtless run as fast as her feet could carry her over such hostile ground.

'It was a difficult expedition.'

'But I can see why he is driven to do it. I mean, finding the love letter in the library like that. It is so—' she seemed to search her hands for the right words '— it is so romantic.' Peter tossed his crutch aside. It bounced, then slid into a ditch. She jumped, and to save face he made it seem like the result of a spasm by affecting another.

'It's the painkillers they put me on.'

'I can imagine. I just wanted to know you were surviving. And now I do.' She pinched the bird necklace between her lips.

'I like the birds,' he said.

'Doves,' she said. 'Dove is my father's name. Tradition means that one day it shall also be my son's.'

Just then, the moon emerged from behind a purple swirl of cloud, lighting the field to its furthest corners. And it appeared, a blanket of delicate white flowers, as if it had been there all along, like snow that falls as you sleep. The Kadupul. The Queen of the Night. The beauty under the stars in blissful symphony. They had come to die together. Harum squealed, and they embraced, then waited, melded by this spectacle, for the dawn to come. When it did, the flowers wilted. No price could be put on them, or on the experience they'd just shared.

Hens Berg arrived with the sun.

His face was bloated and red. When the breeze picked up they could smell the alcohol that welled in his pores. But Hens had an ability to project a certain strength, and as he approached – chest puffed, shoulders straight – it was as though he'd come to save the day. Peter could barely watch but found his eyes disobeyed him as Hens kissed Harum's tiny hand, then scooped her into a pelvis-crushing bear hug. Susan seemed to sense her brother's unease as she watched the giant man drenched in rust-coloured sweat pluck the cap off a beer bottle begged from the natives.

'Peter!' Hens said. 'How amazing that you're here! Last time I saw you it looked like you wouldn't make it. To Mexico, I mean.'

'Who'd have thought I'd get here before you,' Peter said.

Hens smiled and whispered, his mouth close to Peter's ear.

'The way you speak reminds me of a cat I had back in Denmark. It hissed when frightened. Had to put it down.'

Peter spun away, keen for Hens not to see the goose-bumps rising up his neck.

'My goodness,' Hens said, turning back to Harum, 'my journey here was not what I expected. But didn't I tell you I'd come!'

Nobody had reason to believe the story Hens told was anything other than plausible. That he'd been robbed not long after arriving in Mexico, losing all his money and the paperwork and maps he had telling him where to find the Kadupul. That he'd hitch-hiked the whole way, a procession of truckers having taken pity, and detours, across the Mexican wilderness. It certainly seemed true, the way he said it, standing there with only the clothes on his back. Peter stopped listening. He felt too sick to listen. Hens hadn't once looked at the Kadupul, its dead petals fluttering to the dry ground. Harum would see through his pretence, Peter was sure of it. Ignoring all the times he'd poorly judged character in the past was the only way he avoided throwing up all over his feet.

'Too late though, eh, Hens?' he said.

'Yes, I'm devastated.' Hens inhaled a breath that for a time seemed never-ending. 'Story of my life.' Harum gave him a conciliatory stroke of the arm, which Peter could hardly bear.

'I have a car,' she said, 'we could go to the airport together.' Both men agreed in unison. Peter packed the remainder of his belongings. Hens loaded himself up like a packhorse, carrying almost everything down the long dirt track to the road, while Peter sidestepped to avoid his shadow.

Claiming that he had the longest legs, Hens sat up front. Peter and Susan squeezed together in the back. In the rear-view mirror, Hens's eyes flitted between Harum and Peter for the whole of the drive.

'Where will you go next, Harum?' Hens asked.

'Namibia,' she said. 'To see the Welwitschia.'

'The Welwitschia!'

Peter kicked the back of Hens's seat, an involuntary response, not hard enough for Hens to feel.

'You should come!' Harum said.

'I should!'

'And you, Peter? Don't you think it would be a wonderful adventure?' He leaned forward between the two front seats. Her hair smelled of smoke and wood. As bitter as the words tasted on his tongue, he said them anyway.

'It certainly does.'

'So you'll come with us?' she asked. Peter pretended to think about it a while, if only to keep Hens guessing.

'I wouldn't miss it for the world.'

Hens rapped the club of his knuckles on the dash-board. 'What about your cleaning job?' he said.

They locked eyes in the reflection. Peter couldn't have felt more confident that Angelica was taking care of business back home.

'There is nothing for you to worry about there.'

'You know me, I do worry.'

'I know,' Peter said. 'I know.'

If Susan thought the exchange odd, she was apparently distracted. It was clear to Peter that the power and passion of the field of Kadupul had left her mind on other matters. She no longer seemed scared of the flight home, even though she'd be doing it alone.

'Peter,' she whispered as they unloaded their bags from the car, 'do it. It's a long way to go otherwise.' Peter nodded, and when she kissed him goodbye he held her tightly, as though he'd never see her again, not knowing he wouldn't.

ELEVEN

A loud, infuriatingly catchy jingle blares out around the studio, and that's what first makes Professor Cole uneasy. If it hadn't been for the unfailingly pleasant Dr Dash accompanying him on this ludicrous press tour these past few days he'd have given up and gone home a long time ago, as is his urge now – to get the hell out of this green room, where the sandwiches laid on by the production team are laughably small and unreasonably bland. He watches the monitor mounted on a metal arm in the top corner of the room, wondering if he can refrain from tearing it off the wall. An immaculately groomed female host, with popcorn-coloured hair and eyelashes as tidily splayed as the fan of a geisha, whips the studio audience into a manufactured frenzy. This, apparently, is his cue.

Professor Cole and Dr Dash emerge from a recess built into the wall of the set, designed to look like a door. A famous television actor, James somebody or other, who Professor Cole swears on his wife's precious life he's never seen or heard of before, but whom he already feels inclined to punch, shuffles aside to make room at the fake breakfast bar where they sit in wait for the perfectly timed dissipation of applause. Cole already looks uncomfortable, as though he'd rather be anywhere else. An undeniable truth. I'd include in that, he thinks, being back at the bottom of the ocean. With oxygen, and probably without it.

'Now. The Long Forgotten. We welcome two people who have found themselves at the centre of a story that has had everybody hankering for news 24/7, hasn't it, James?' The actor recounts how his fellow cast members discuss nothing but the black box of flight PS570 during breaks in filming, much to Cole's annoyance. Why the hell does it matter what a bunch of failed movie stars get up to in the queue for the catering truck?

'It's been a remarkable few weeks,' Dash says. Cole fingers his collar, regretting wearing a woollen suit under the scrutiny of such hot studio lights. He retells the now well-rehearsed story of the whale and how the staff aboard his research vessel had posthumously named it Gobbler. The audience laugh. Buoyed by this, Cole adds a short anecdote about the pungent smell that is released when a whale's carcass is sliced open.

'Rotting flesh and burning sulphur,' he says, 'of a strength so powerful that one might question their own will to live, as if to have it enter the nose is to let death inside you.' James scrunches his nose and wafts his hand in front of his face, but his ham-fisted attempt at silent comedy is met with Cole's total indignation. 'Oh, I'm serious,' he says. 'The senses are extraordinarily powerful things. To smell death and be disgusted is what makes us, *us*.' Ever mindful of the lunchtime viewership, the host returns to Dr Dash.

'And unlocking the secrets of The Long Forgotten's flight recorder has been a difficult task?'

'Yes,' she says, jiggling the tension out of her shoulders, 'more difficult than we could possibly have imagined.'

'But there have been successes?'

'Oh yes. We can say for sure that we know where the flight entered the sea, off the coast of Cornwall. And using that information, with what we know about the movements of tides and weather conditions, we've been able to finally locate what remains of flight PS570 on the seabed, as you may have heard.' Another round of applause. Professor Cole brings his chin to his chest, his mouth closer to the microphone clipped to his shirt.

'What you're actually clapping right now,' he says, addressing the audience, 'isn't the discovery of a plane at all. You're clapping the idea of a mass underwater grave.' The host fixes on her autocue and swallows, her earpiece alive with the commotion of a panicked director's gallery. Dr Dash swivels in her seat, resignedly coming to the flustered woman's rescue.

'What he means is, it's proving perilously difficult for us to access the crash site. Weather conditions have been tricky, to say the least.'

'But you have managed to record some remarkable pictures,' the host says, an ill-timed camera cue catching her reading from her notes.

'That's right.' The picture cuts to subdued blues and fuzzy browns, murk suspended in the water. 'This is footage from an unmanned craft we were able to send down to the ocean floor. Obviously it's quite hard to see what's what. That there, the large strip of fuselage' – it looks like a rusted upturned pigsty, almost entirely obscured by barnacles – 'is a part of the plane's cockpit, still intact, it seems.' The camera moves to what is indisputably the corroded structure of two wheels, separated by a stanchion of metal pipe, like a crucifix, with a flag of seaweed floating ethereally on the drift. 'That appears to be the landing gear,' she says, 'and from what we can tell the actual body of the plane is scattered across some considerable distance, maybe half a mile or more.' Cole thinks of skeletons strapped to their seats.

'But the black box isn't able to tell you what happened?' the host asks. The camera cuts back to Professor Cole in the studio, a frost of sweat descending his forehead, as he defers the topic once more to Dash with a nod, so that beads land on her dress.

'No,' she says, 'for the moment it looks like we might not be able to get any more information from the flight recorder. It's damaged in the extreme. You might say it has forgotten.' There is more laughter, the audience apparently glad that things have set at least one foot back on the safe terrain of light entertainment. The host returns her practised glare to the camera lens.

'It appears Flight PS570 might just have fallen from the

sky. And why? We may never know. For with the finding of the fuselage it is finally confirmed, as if it ever needed confirming, that there were no survivors. Regardless, this story continues to captivate, and after the break we'll be talking to someone you may have read about in the newspapers, who claims to have witnessed something strange on the day flight PS570 disappeared.' Hairs rise on Cole's forearm. He strokes his fingertips across them. Could be Braille, he thinks, or Morse code; writing on his skin. A cutaneous signal, a warning, a memo to put a stop to this whole shambolic circus once and for all. As the music blares once more, they are joined by a woman whose soft blonde tresses hang at waist length, splitting at the ends. In her hand is a glass, the surface of the water trembling.

'This is Anna Gray. Now, Anna is a little nervous . . .'

'Yes,' Anna says. James leans over, his thinning hairline intruding on the shot.

'Don't be. I have that effect on people.' He pats her lap, sending a snicker through the audience in a way Cole finds quite objectionable. Anna pretends to giggle, then fiddles with the microphone attached to the lapel of her pristine mauve cardigan, clearly bought for the occasion. The floor manager's shadow can be seen on the monitor, frantically trying to discourage her from behind camera, but to no avail. The host shows a perfect set of white teeth to the actor, who sits back, happy with his input, as Professor Cole rolls his eyes as if he is about to squeeze drops into his pupils.

151

'But Anna, you have a very interesting tale to add to the mystery of flight PS570?'

'I do.'

'Go on.'

'When I was six, my father lived on the Cornish coast. You couldn't get a good television reception then, and there was very little to do. No video games, like there are now.' More laughter. 'And my mother was allergic to most animals, they made her face itch and swell, so we couldn't have pets. Plus I was an only child . . .' The host dabs a fingertip to her ear, eager to hurry Anna along.

'And what did you see?'

'Well, early most mornings I would sit in the window. One morning, I remember that I saw what looked like a star, except it was light, and it was moving, and it was on fire. I called my father to come and see, but he was too busy. It went along sideways, then it seemed to spin and slow and come down to where the ocean was, which I could hear but couldn't see, and then it disappeared.'

'So you think you might have seen flight PS570 crashing?'

'Yes. I didn't know that's what it was at the time, of course. I was too young. But it all comes back to me now, since I saw the professor with the black box, and found out the route the plane took.' She warms to her role. 'I even made a wish on a shooting star, like they do in Disney movies.'

'They?' Professor Cole asks.

'Princesses,' Anna stammers.

The host faces the audience.

'But that's not all that makes your story remarkable, is it?'

'No, I suppose . . .'

'Tell the folks at home what happened to you later that day.'

'I was out on the beach collecting shells in a bucket. There was nothing unusual about that, I often did it, and I hadn't wandered very far from home. That's when I saw a man. He was dripping wet, like he'd just been swimming in his clothes.'

'What did you do?'

'I didn't dare go close. I was scared, I think. He had blood on him. I remember where it had mixed with salt water, so it was like a deep-red goo in the cuts on his arms. And he was carrying some kind of box, or something. I was maybe twenty metres away, when I shouted hello to him.'

'And what did he say?' the host says, loading that final word with emphasis to skilfully pump the anecdote for drama.

'Nothing. Nothing at all. He just walked away. But I have never forgotten his face.'

'It would make an excellent movie, and I know an actor who is made for the role,' James says. The audience titter, expanding his grin until he sees, from the corner of his eye, Cole frantically shaking his head.

'Bullshit.' Cole's stool scrapes backwards across the faux kitchen floor. 'If you were six years old, you'd barely remember your own mother's face if it was the last time you saw her, let alone a fleeting glance of a stranger on the beach.'

'Mr Cole,' the host says.

'Professor Cole. I'm a professor. Not a talking head on a panel show, or whatever this is.' The audience gasp, as though sharing one big mouth. Dr Dash hides her face in the folds of her turquoise neckerchief. 'What you're telling everybody is a fiction invented in reaction to the saturation of the story in the news, and the producers of this show know it. They know that people will watch it and believe it. This is not how memory works. It's how the media works.' He unclips his microphone and throws the battery across the pinewood counter. Feedback squeaks through the studio, shrill enough that members of the audience in the front two rows shield their ears. He turns to the host. 'Now, if it's all the same, I'll leave you to it. I won't be talking about flight PS570 again.' He faces Anna, who appears close to hyperventilation. 'I'm sorry, Mrs Gray, for my outburst,' he says, and exits the studio through the pretend door. Dr Dash mouths the word 'sorry' into camera, and the house band stumbles through the opening bars of the show's theme tune, woefully out of time.

TWELVE

Despite it being early in the morning the television in the communal room of the nursing home is so loud it vibrates. Rita's voice is louder still. There's a thickness to its middle frequencies when she shouts that make it seem somehow solid. More than a noise. An object. A baton, beating Dove about the head. Beating him back into the present. At first the words don't make any sense, but as she repeats them they right themselves until he understands.

'Come!' she's saying. 'Come quick!' Not to Dove. To someone else. But close to Dove's ear, close enough that it forces him out of Peter's memory, and suddenly he is back in his own body, at the feet of an old man in a care home, cheek pressed against the gnarled wool of his slippers. Except the old man is standing now. He is standing for the first time in decades. And when Dove looks up at the old man's face, he sees it not as it is, but as it used to be, because he knows who the old man is. This is Peter Manyweathers. This is the man whose life he is remembering. The man who had once loved his mother, Harum.

Rita wraps her arms around Dove's midriff and yanks upwards, like she's trying to expel a bone from his throat.

'Oh my Lord, are you OK?'

'I don't know, I . . .' The pain in his head still hangs there, the lingering din of a cymbal crash. She pulls harder.

'I'm not talking to you.'

And now Dove is behind her, looking up at Peter Manyweathers, whose arm is raised, finger pointed towards the window, at the flowers beyond the glass. Stranger still, Dove realizes he can name them. Each and every one of them. Not just the blush crowd of a rose bush, and two imperious sunflowers, but fists of billowing lilac hydrangea, parades of globe thistles and cherry-red fuchsia hanging like the unworn hats of fairies. All this knowledge he never learnt. The things Peter remembers.

'Quickly!' Rita shouts. Two nurses rush into the room, the second of them with a half-cocked fire extinguisher held above his head, which hits the ground and rolls into the centre of the rug when he sees Peter, and suddenly everyone is standing completely still: Dove, Peter, the nurses, until Rita cajoles her two colleagues into circling Peter, ready to catch him if he falls.

'What did you do?' she says, with a panicked glance over her shoulder in Dove's direction. He tries to answer. But his tongue is thick and heavy. He can do nothing but look at the blank expressions of the other residents and wonder what it is they see.

'Just relax,' the first nurse says, 'just relax and everything is going to be OK, Zachariah.'

'That's not his name,' Dove says, clinging tight to the arm of a cracked leather sofa.

'What?' the second nurse asks.

'His name is Peter Manyweathers.'

'And who the hell are you?'

'My name is Dove Gale. I'm his son.'

So it is with this that Dove meets his second father; the only one he has left.

Maud's reaction to Len's death was one of astonishing pragmatism. All those things he used to do. Tending the garden. Feeding the animals. Painting the sills. These were her pastimes now. 'He is working through me,' is what she always said. 'It's not me that has to get out of bed in the morning. It's always me and him.'

Whereas, despite her grief, her response was wholly constructive, Dove's was entirely the opposite. The anger he'd begun to tame before Len fell ill was renewed and potent.

He was expelled from secondary school when his head-mistress called the police saying he'd threatened another kid in art class with a pair of scissors. Even immediately after the incident he had no recollection of what took place. Maybe he threatened him. Maybe the kid deserved it. Maybe he did what many had before: mocked Dove's name, or the colour of his skin, or the fact that he was adopted, or even Len's death. All these things were of value in the cruel currency of the playground. What surprised him least was his own violence. It had always lurked. Len's death just gave it an outlet.

They lived far enough away from any other school that if he was to remain in public education they'd have to move house. Maud didn't consider that an option. These walls were Len's arms around her. So after Dove's expulsion, she homeschooled him instead, and he found a certain relief in knowing he wouldn't have to try to make friends any more.

As a young woman Maud had worked as an accountant for a local newspaper, and she retained a deft understanding of basic mathematics. Her efforts to instil the same in Dove were largely wasted. When he looked at numbers on a page the ink moved, jiggled and webbed together into a frustrating, indecipherable mess. Most lessons ended badly and at a time dictated by his temper. But Maud persevered, developing methods Dove could use to stifle his frustrations before they became outbursts of rage. Closing his eyes. Breathing deeply. Reminding himself that he wouldn't be abandoned again. Saying it, over and over. Eventually it yielded fine and unlikely results. He achieved good enough grades to attend a college a fifteen-mile bus journey across the moors that to him felt like long-haul travel.

Once there he largely kept himself to himself. That's not to say he was lonely – he had a few casual acquaintances that he purposely kept at arm's length. But the time spent alone was put to good use revising in the library.

Acing his exams left him with a shortlist of university offers he could afford to take only because of the small sum of money that remained when selling the house became an unfortunate necessity. He protested, but Maud said moving into an assisted living facility had come to make sense. Besides, it wasn't like an old folks' home. She'd have her own kitchen, a small garden and, more importantly, her independence. And, crucially, it would be worth it for Dove's sake. She said she identified his great potential as a journalist, or writer of some kind. She'd known talented writers herself from working on the newspaper, some of whom had subsequently written novels or collections of essays. Many had been her friends for long periods. What she identified in all of them was a quality she believed she also saw in Dove – an innate instinct for empathy married with the need to remain in some way apart from their subject (which was always people) in order to survive. To lock themselves out while plugging themselves in.

Maud stood at the rim of the vegetable garden. There were still two weeks before Dove was due to leave for university in London. A pleasant spring had given way to a warm summer and now autumn was approaching, but the carrots, cabbages and turnips she planted had all failed to grow. Her only plausible explanation was some strange disease she couldn't name causing the taproots to decay before they'd properly developed. The few vegetables she'd found were small and misshapen, abandoned attempts at living things, never fully formed from the outset.

Dove held a basket that so far contained little beyond soil and leaves. Maud edged her walking frame up the path towards the back door and they went inside. He sat her down in her favourite armchair and arranged on the trestle table beside her the familiar array of objects that had come to define her widowhood. A delicate silver cross on a chain (they never talked about it, but Dove caught her praying once or twice), a dog-eared deck of cards for solitaire, and Len's pipe, which hadn't been cleaned and to this day retained the faint aroma of tobacco that used to announce his entry to a room. Then Dove returned from the kitchen with a plate of cheese sandwiches on springy white bread, and a pickle so tart it stung their nostrils.

He looked down at the half-eaten crusts in his hands.

'I can see you fretting,' Maud said, setting a crumb-covered plate down beside her. 'You only don't eat when you're fretting.' This was a marked point of difference between Dove and Len that he'd always struggled to comprehend. Len had not indulged in more than a second of introspection in his entire life.

'I'm not fretting,' Dove said. This was a lie. The prospect of leaving her alone had been chewing him up for months. Wouldn't he be consigning her to the fate he feared most?

'Go, for goodness' sake. I want you to. Len wanted you to. Go to university. You think I'm going to fall over and die the minute you walk out of the door?'

'Of course not.'

'Then go. Otherwise all that teaching I gave you is a waste.'

'What about you?' he asked. Maud shivered, coiled a blanket tight around her thighs.

'What about me?'

'What will you do?'

'I've got my new room to decorate and all those other widows to chat to. And when you come back to visit, which had better be all the time, I'll have a whole lot of sandwiches to prepare.' She smiled, toothily, theatrically. It was a running joke they shared, to answer the other's question without really giving an answer at all. But Dove wasn't in the mood for joking, and she sensed as much, sipping loudly on her tea. 'Come on, Dove,' she said. 'You know I'll be fine. You know you have to go.'

He sighed. She was right, of course. He had to go. But without Maud he'd have no one. He'd be where he was at the start. And this is what made the fear unfold in his gut. The fear that would inevitably turn to anger, if he didn't stay in control, as she'd taught him.

The fortnight they had together after that passed quickly. Soon they were standing in the doorway of the house, the hot pall of smoke in the air from a bonfire somewhere on the hill behind which he'd soon disappear. It was almost time to go. Maud threw her arms around him. Her flesh pressed against his neck. The looseness of her aged skin, slack muscles, creaking joints. The tightness with which she held him, the ache it must have struck through her bones. All these things in fragments; memories much easier to carry as shattered pieces of a whole.

'You have your smart shoes, for lectures?' she asked.

'Of course. I shined them.' He didn't have the heart to tell her he wouldn't need smart shoes for lectures, but the longer they stood there with her asking him questions, the longer they would be together.

'And your winter coat?'

'I packed it.'

'The big one? With the fleece-lined hood? I know they say it's warmer down south but that's nonsense if you ask me. Len and I took a young boy we fostered down to London once because he was obsessed with the soldiers that stand outside Buckingham Palace. You know, the ones with the big black hats and red tunics. Anyway, it was cold enough to freeze the you-know-whats off a brass monkey. I swear the Thames iced over. So . . .' She suddenly wilted, on the verge of tears, and made the sign of the cross; her crooked, swollen knuckles.

'I promise I packed the big coat. With the fleece-lined hood.'

A chill was blowing under the door, the occasional leaf skittering beneath it.

'I can fix that draught for you,' Dove said.

'Nonsense. There is nothing here I can't do myself.'

The car was packed and they had held one another. It was time to leave. Maud moved back into the shadows but her eyes were still dewy and shone. Dove would be the last of her children to leave her, and the hardest one to lose.

'Thank you,' she said.

'For what?'

She looked down at the floor and he saw a brief glimpse of a different woman altogether. A version of her she'd never let him see before. This new Maud was solemn and tired. This was the version of Maud that worried herself sick Dove would be OK every night after she went to bed. The version of Maud who harboured a secret guilt for having adopted a young boy when she herself was old. The version of Maud who hadn't coped so well after Len's death, but who knew she must hold it together for his sake. All these things to protect him, behind the mask worn by a mother.

'Thank you for being our son.'

The old man is standing by the window looking at the flowers outside, his palm pressed flat against the glass. It's been almost an hour.

'I'm surprised his legs still work,' Rita says. They sit at the back of the room and Dove tells her all about the memories. Of meeting Harum, of the man he is sure is his father, of the woman he is sure is his mother. Rita's face freezes, equal parts compelled and incredulous.

'Why else would I be getting them?' Dove says. 'The headaches. Why else would they be coming to me?'

The nurse who dropped the fire extinguisher comes

back into the room with a dusty plastic tub of disorganized paperwork, which he places at Rita's feet as he scowls in Dove's direction.

'Out of the loft,' he says, 'and not easy to get to either.' He hovers for a while, his hand extended like a tip-fishing bellboy. Rita waits for him to leave, then spreads the tattered files across the carpet.

'Here,' she says, opening a folder worn at the binding. Dove peers over her shoulder at the two crumpled sheets of paper inside it, the ink so faint it's barely legible.

'That's it?'

'That's it. Nineteen eighty-four. Zachariah Temple. Says here police found him wandering the streets, confused. Couldn't speak. Didn't know who he was. Identified by the passport in his pocket: the only thing he had on him.' Rita lifts the first piece of paper to reveal a photocopy of the passport, so faded it's almost impossible to make out the features of the man in the photograph, except for one stark detail. He is wearing an eyepatch.

'But he has both eyes?'

'Yep.'

'And no one came to find him?'

'Apparently not.' She flicks back to the first page, traces a scrawled bottom paragraph with the tip of her index finger. 'Says they turned up no next of kin, no friends, no missing persons. Nothing. Zachariah Temple became the responsibility of the state.'

'But his name is Peter,' Dove says, still looking at the document in her hand.

'Not according to his passport. He's been called Zachariah the entire time he's been here, so that's the name
we'll use, thank you very much. He doesn't need to be any
more confused than he already is.'

Dove slouches in his seat. He's sure the old man is Peter
Manyweathers, but has no idea how to convince Rita she
is wrong, especially not with a copy of his passport in her
hand.

'And no one ever came for Zachariah?' he asks.

'That's what I said. Not a soul's been interested in him
since the day he arrived. Until you turned up this morning,
that is.'

As if in response to the sad truth of his time here,
Zachariah slowly retreats back to his chair. His eyes glaze
over again. Everything is as it was, except Dove has a
father.

This is when it strikes him: he's devoted his entire life
to the dismemberment of this man's character. It has only
been possible to comprehend the duality of his existence
and absence by imagining his real parents as, at best,
negligent oafs, and at worst, latent evils. He'd only ever
known his father as a man who looked into the eyes of
his newborn son and gave up on him; gifted his future to
the wind.

Equally, it's only been possible for Dove to counten-
ance his own flaws by allowing himself to believe they're
a reflection of his father's. *This is his anger. This is his fear.
I am who I am because of him.* A shadow, doomed to
imitation. Wasn't that why he'd so rarely allowed himself

to get close to anyone? Not because they might one day abandon him, but because he might one day abandon them – just as his parents did. Is that what he'd done to Maud?

But this is not the man falling asleep in the armchair before Dove now. He knows because he remembers. Because he felt it too and still does. This man is honest. This man is kind. This man loved Dove's mother with an instant and utter totality. Yet this is a man whose life is ending in loneliness, sadness and silence, and so who maybe, just maybe, knows even more about abandonment than Dove.

'I need to get him out of here,' Dove says to Rita, who is straightening the folders and loading them back into the tub, quietly thanking God for the advent of computers.

'What did you say?'

'I need to get him out of here.' She searches his eyes for an indication this is a joke – a sign that doesn't appear. 'He's my father.'

'Not according to the paperwork. You'd have more luck talking me out of my life savings.'

'So I have to leave him here?' Rita drapes an arm over Dove's shoulder as she ushers him towards the door.

'What do you think?'

An old woman, who until now hasn't opened her eyes, stands from her seat. She says something about her daughter not having visited, crosses the room and exits in entirely the wrong direction, chased by a day nurse just arriving for her shift.

'Where is her daughter?' Dove asks.

Rita sighs. 'She doesn't have a daughter.' And he sees how, in her line of work, it's easier to sidestep reality in a way in which her patients have no choice but to do.

They're almost at the door before she speaks again, quietly and with her head at an angle that tells him she could get into serious trouble for this.

'Tomorrow's my day off. Can you make it your day off too?' Dove thinks of Cliff, of the Pit, of the emergencies that will happen whether he is there or not.

'I think so.'

'Well, I'm sure it wouldn't do Zachariah any harm to have a little while out of here, and in some company, given how he seems to react to you.'

'Really?' Dove feels like falling to his knees in gratitude, but the other nurse watches from the far end of the corridor.

'Chaperoned, of course.' He nods and she closes the door behind him.

'Thank you,' he says through the glass, knowing that if he recovers another of the memories it'll be of how his mother and father fell in love. Of how he came to exist. He can't wait.

That night, head squeezed in his hands, he remembers how his father and mother ran away from Hens Berg. And their fear is his own: it is coming and vast.

THIRTEEN

As their plane flew towards a pinkish Namibian dawn, Peter watched the sunlight strobe on Hens Berg's skin. They'd barely spoken since leaving Mexico. The silence was souring fast. Though Hens hogged the armrest and leg space, Peter was glad when Hens finally fell asleep.

He reread his notes on the Welwitschia. The living fossil. All of his research concluded it existed in mastery of adaptation and resilience, the two essential components of survival. Survival, for the Welwitschia, was an art form, and that – he had no doubt – was how it had earned its place in the love letter. But that word, *adaptation*, jarred. Grievously bending a laminated crash safety instruction card, he couldn't quite figure out why.

The flight landed with a short screech as the wheels kissed the runway. They disembarked together – Harum had enjoyed a whole row of empty seats behind them – and waited for a snaking conveyor belt to bring their bags, Hens bursting into action as Harum's trundled into view.

'Let me get that for you.'

'It's OK,' she said, but it was too late to stop him snatching it from the belt, and they could only watch as he made a great, apparently effortless, show of hoisting it over his shoulder.

'I'll carry it for you – it's not a problem.'

'I can carry it, Hens.'

'Please. It would be my pleasure.' Remnants borrowed from a gentleman's lexicon tripped clumsily off his Nordic tongue. That's when Peter was struck by why that word, *adaptation*, bothered him so. It applied to Hens every bit as much as it did the Welwitschia. Hens was adapting too. As ignorant as he seemed, he wasn't ignorant enough not to realize that Harum's heart couldn't be won with the bullishness he'd applied to previous conquests. So he was being kinder, more thoughtful. His old braggadocio was still detectable, but had been shorn of its brashness, applied with a lightness of touch. It was almost (though it pained Peter to think it as he dragged his rickety case towards the escalator) charming, enough even to smother the phoniness at its heart.

He toyed with giving it to him straight.

'Hens. Would you mind leaving us alone? I think Harum might be "the one".' But standing before Hens now he just couldn't say the words. It would be wrong. This wasn't some dumb lust. He had no right to Harum just because he cherished her company, because he liked the way she looked. Ultimately this choice would be hers, if indeed she chose either of them, and he knew it.

In a bathroom at Hosea Kutako International Airport's

arrivals lounge, Peter splashed his face with cold water and searched the glitter of drips in the sink for perspective. All he could do was adopt the Welwitschia's other great quality: resilience. Because he was sure in the depths of his being that Harum would pay no mind to the impression of the man Hens was trying to build. Someone strong. Someone dependable. Someone heroic. All things Peter knew Hens wasn't, in his soul. She was too pure for his lies to stick. She moved in the pursuit of truth. That's why he could feel himself falling for her so tumultuously. Surely she would hold that filter over Hens, see him for what lay beneath, pick away the petals and survey the rotted stem.

He quickly dried his face on the sleeve of his jacket and ran to catch them up in the arrivals lounge. Leaving them together for longer than a few minutes bolstered his paranoia. Hens could have said anything in the time he'd been away. Truth was not such a preoccupation of his as it was of Harum's.

As he rejoined them, Peter could hear Harum's laughter waning.

'What's so funny?' he asked.

'Nothing,' Hens said, clenching his jaws until the muscles pulsed, and the battle lines were drawn in their unspoken, shaky truce.

Windhoek's sprawl lapped at the feet of steep rocky mountains on each side of the city, hints of the inhospitable terrain they'd traverse in the days ahead. The Ceiling

170

of Africa Hotel in the east of the capital was shabby but charming, taller than the buildings around it, as if presiding in judgement over a street teeming with people and traffic. Whatever concoction they'd washed the walls in mostly worked to ward off flying insects the size of cotton reels. Bats hung from the trees above the courtyard, biding their time before an unknown duty.

They took a room each. Peter responded first when the hotelier tossed the keys onto the counter, artfully choosing the middle room for himself, a physical barrier between Hens and Harum. Spinning the key around his finger, he could rest a little more easily in the knowledge this space existed, whether or not it was of any use.

The cauldron of the hotelier's paunch had torn the buttons from his shirt; material flapped at his hips. Glimpses of a coffee-blackened tongue could be caught between his lips, and his fulsome laugh seemed to echo inside itself.

'What brings you to Windhoek?'

'The Welwitschia,' Harum said. 'This is the place to be for the real big ones, we hear.'

'You hear correct.'

'We're going searching tomorrow,' Peter said, and the hotelier smiled at the sound of his accent like a man for whom a dollar went a long way.

'Tomorrow? You Americans. You are always rush rush rush. First you must acclimatize. In Namibia, we don't rush for train. We only rush to get out of train's way.'

'We'll decide what we do,' Hens snapped, stepping

forward to rest a giant fist on the counter. 'And for future reference, I am not an American.'

The hotelier was unmoved. Peter noticed a shotgun by his feet. Black holes peppering the door arch were testament to that, if not to his aim. There was little likely to intimidate him about a brusque Scandinavian, even if he was the width of a buffalo.

'Actually, Hens,' Harum said, her hand on his back, 'acclimatizing might not be such a bad idea.'

'She's right,' Peter said, and smiled so that only Hens could see it. Hens removed his hand from the counter, picked up his bag from the floor and tossed it over his shoulder, narrowly missing Peter's head with a force that would have shattered his cheekbone had it hit.

'My name is Lazrus,' the hotelier said. 'Like the saint. I'm here twenty-four hours a day, seven days a week. And sometimes more. If you need anything you know where to find me.' He slapped a scuffed gold bell on the desk, a chime hanging in the air around it. 'Ding ding, I come running.' Peter couldn't imagine Lazrus running, not after seeing the star chart of stretch marks round his navel.

They drank chilled cucumber water while Harum unfolded a large map across the table in a small dining room, and plotted the point in the Namib Desert where she'd heard on good authority the largest recorded specimen of the Welwitschia was found.

'Apparently there is nothing like it. They say it's a living fossil. Can you imagine?'

'No,' Peter and Hens said together. A small electric fan

moved the hot, dry air between them. Harum hadn't even broken a sweat.

'I'm Sumatran,' she offered by way of explanation. 'This is nothing.' Hens sat in the corner and removed his shirt. Peter's feet tapped with delight when Harum didn't seem to notice.

'Know what I want?' he said. 'An ice-cold towel draped across my face.'

'You've picked the wrong pastime,' she said.

Hens stood, arching his back.

'You guys put your feet up and kick back,' he said. 'I'll go find us all something to eat.'

He returned with an impressive tray of food. Only then did Peter realize how long it had been since he'd consumed anything more substantial than a biscuit. They shared veldt bread freshly baked on the premises, the choicest cinnamon any of them had ever tasted, sweetened with honey that lingered in the throat. Afterwards they rested, their stomachs gurgling in delight.

'Hens and I,' Peter said to Harum, 'we know each other inside out. But you. What's your story? Why are you hunting flowers?'

Harum blushed. 'It's boring, really.'

'And I've already heard it,' Hens said, after which the room fell quiet for a few seconds. It fell to Peter to lift the mood.

'Well, I haven't. And I'm willing to bet it's not boring, too.' When she started to speak he leaned towards her like he'd take an exam when she was done.

Harum told them she had fled Indonesia after the anti-communist purge of 1965–6, which her progressively politicized parents died protesting. Though she had been heartbroken to go, and vilified for questioning the acts of her own people against the ethnic Chinese who lived among them, she had used her exemplary command of the English language to get private teaching work in China, tutoring for the children of rich Western families that had moved their factories there, taking advantage of the cheap labour and negligible workplace law.

Peter felt suddenly embarrassed by his relative privilege – even though he was just a cleaner – but Harum selflessly moved to put him at ease, joking about how she ended up teaching the daughter of a celebrated botanist whose husband mass-produced the grotesque tie-dye T-shirts worn by only the most annoying travellers. It was the botanist who turned Harum on to the magnificence of the plants she had grown up beside, but never appreciated. A passion for flora was born.

'They show me peace,' she said, 'when I come from war. One day I would like to go home and teach others what this peace is. My people should know of the beauty that surrounds them in Sumatra, the land they destroy.'

'Uh-huh,' Hens said, nodding, and Peter wondered if he'd already stopped listening.

After stints in Japan and Vietnam, Harum returned to China in search of the Udumbara. But it was a catastrophically unlucky hunt. Rumours, misunderstandings and lies led her down many fruitless paths. After a year of looking, which included two months in a Chinese hospital fending off a nasty infection, and an incident in which she'd either given all of her money to a monk, or been robbed by a man pretending to be one (she still wasn't sure which), she had conceded it was time to give up, heeding the words of the Lotus Sutra:

> *Such people too, are rare,*
> *Like the Udumbara flower,*
> *In which all take delight,*
> *Which the gods and humans prize,*
> *For it blooms but once in a long, long time.*

Peter remembered what pleasure he'd taken when he'd read these words for himself back in Brooklyn Library. He wanted to tell Harum, but couldn't, preferring to believe that deep down she'd know he had read these same words too as she continued her story.

She travelled to Europe, settling in Venice where she studied botany with some pioneers of the science. One of her tutors took a liking to her and offered cheap lodgings in his enormous, draughty house overlooking the city's higgledy sprawl. 'We became lovers,' she said, blushing. Peter, disguising his own jealousy by looking anywhere but at her, noticed Hens was suddenly paying full attention again. 'Then we were engaged to be married. But he liked to fight. We argued all the time. Eventually we split up after an argument about a rose.'

'A rose?' Peter couldn't help but laugh, and she joined him.

'A humble rose. He dismissed it as a cheap prop for the troubadours who sold them to tourists in the piazza. I told him he had a tin heart.'

Via the dense black forests of Germany and the velvety countryside of southern France, Harum hunted the hardy gems of shrubs withstanding the Greenlandic tundra, then criss-crossed the Americas, collecting sightings of everything from Minnesota snow flowers to the punishing spines of Nevadan desert cacti. South to Chile, where she'd rescued Peter from a sheep's fate and spent a long evening in the company of Hens – which she quickly skirted over while Hens smirked to himself – to Paraguay, a wasted trip, and Mexico for a rumoured field of Kadupul, the reality of which far exceeded her dreams.

'That's how I got here,' she said. 'The short version, anyway.'

Once they retired, Peter showered, swept the floor of his small beige-walled room with a brush he always carried in his hand luggage, and repaired a rip in the insect net flimsily hung across the window. When they'd arrived the street outside buzzed with commotion. Now it was silent. This allowed his fears to take form. Twice he closed his eyes and heard the heavy footsteps of the Dane padding past his door. Twice he checked the corridor and saw nothing. He drained a glass bottle of water with the full intention of resting it in the darkness on the floor in the middle of the landing where Hens would surely kick it over if he passed to reach Harum's room, but as he opened the bedroom door it seemed somehow pathetic, certainly unbecoming to a grown man, to lay a booby trap this way, as though Harum was a possession and could be stolen.

When he wasn't being charming, Hens was a lot of things. Brash. Selfish. Self-indulgent. Underhand, maybe. But was he truly worse than that? Am I suggesting he's evil, Peter wondered. He hadn't acted this irrationally since he was a teenager, when he'd had such a crush on the tomboyishly beautiful Alice, whose father ran the local gas station, that he'd waited for the days she worked and spent his last dollars on fuel, which he carried home in buckets, even though he didn't have a car.

He finally got to sleep three hours later, and only once he'd locked the door, it having occurred to him that if Hens was awake and in the mood for walking, it wasn't necessarily Harum he'd try to visit.

A thud. Peter woke with a start, as if he'd suddenly been born of particles colliding in the air. His watch said 4.16 a.m. The thud again, fainter than before, but nearer. Sitting bolt upright, he took the bottle from the side table, his fingers curled tight around its neck, and held it down by his side as though trying to convince himself it wasn't a weapon, even as he rehearsed in his mind how he might bring it down on a human skull. He'd never fought in his life. In fact it was now a matter of some regret that no one had made his blood hot with the anticipation of violence quite like this.

He slid across the floorboards to the door. The handle had creaked when he opened it before. If he pressed it slowly he'd be heard. But if he pressed it quickly the door would swing open and he'd be cast out on the landing clutching this glass club, and what of Hens's temper then? What if he was wrong? All he could be sure of was that he had to act fast, so he turned the key in the lock – click – and put an ear to the wall. But the movement had ceased. That's when, with his head pressed flat to the edge, he realized he could see through a narrow split in the old wooden beam in the corner. He brought his eye to it. On the landing he saw the shape of a man, detail erased by the dark, moving slowly towards Harum's end of the corridor. Peter's sweating hand slipped against the glass of the bottle. The shape dithered outside her door. Peter knew he must make a decision, that he couldn't falter. He slammed down the handle, pulled the door towards him and burst onto the landing, the bottle brandished close and high, like a knife he was pulling from his chest.

'Hey!'

The shadow of the shape twisted to face him, and moved forward into the thin patch of starlight bounced off a mirror, only stopping when its gut came to rest against the thick glass of the bottle bottom.

'Can I help you, my friend?' Lazrus asked.

'Thought I heard something.'

'Just me, doing my rounds. Same every night. We have many problems with intruders in the past.'

'I see.'

'Please accept my apologies if I woke you.'

'Not at all. Sorry to have startled you.' Peter heard

Hens's door click shut behind him, but when he turned to see, there was no one there.

The next day neither man mentioned what had happened, and Peter began to believe he'd imagined hearing Hens's door after all. When Hens slept he slept deeply. There was little chance of him hearing Peter's quiet conversation with Lazrus, and even less of him bothering to climb out of bed and check. Hens was too lazy for that. Peter put it down to paranoia clouding his judgement. Tiredness had set him on edge.

The three of them spent the afternoon adjusting to the heat and altitude, visiting the springs of Windhoek and drinking cheap wine. They wandered the Zoo Park in as few clothes as was reasonable, Harum in a white linen dress that danced with the breeze blown through a lion's cage. The evening brought a coolness to the air. Harum retired to bed early. Peter and Hens sat in the courtyard drinking cold beers in near silence.

'You will go back to New York after we see the Welwitschia,' Hens said eventually.

'Huh?' Peter said. It hadn't sounded like a question.

'New York. When we've seen what we came for.'

'Maybe. What about you?' Hens slugged his drink and watched the bubbles in the backwash pop.

'Peter,' he said, slinging his bottle into the tall grass on the roadside, 'please. Don't you be concerning yourself with me. You're not even back to full health yet. You're weak.'

Early next morning, Lazrus helped them hire a truck, scarlet rust chewing through the sky-blue paintwork. So began the hunt for the living fossil.

The bowl of the Messum Crater, arid, vast and red, could have been Mars. Namib chameleons congregated on the high rocks, stabbing tongues at the air. Lonesome springboks skirted the rim, and a pair of oryx sauntered with a grace out of time. The volcano once arisen there, that provided basalts for the surrounding Goboboseb Mountains, had long collapsed in on itself like an overbaked pie.

Hens insisted on driving, too recklessly for Peter's liking, though he didn't dare complain. They left the car to the mercy of the dust by the dry bed of the Swakop River, then shouldered their rucksacks, laden with water. According to the map, it would be some hike into the mountains. Depending on pace it might take two days, though with Peter still weary from his stay in hospital, and having chosen to leave his crutches behind, he privately suspected three. They walked ten minutes and already his shirt needed to be wrung of sweat. He flirted with the idea of squeezing it straight into his mouth.

'Do you think this is a stupid thing to be doing?' he asked. Harum was already ahead of him, charging into a steep first ascent.

'If we find it, I'll make sure you don't get stuck in it,' she said. Ahead of her, Hens was setting a brisk pace Peter already knew he couldn't match.

'Hens,' he said, 'can you slow down a little?'

'Why?'

'We don't want to exhaust ourselves too early.'

'I won't get exhausted.'

The words echoed behind them, gave chase.

By late afternoon, with little more than Harum's compass to thank, they'd reached the band of fog where the cold, north-flowing Benguela Current met the constant rub of the Namib Desert's hot air. By night it turned the sky a mysterious, rich purple. These were ideal conditions for the growth of enormous Welwitschia. Its lumbering, downward-pointing leaves collected the fog as condensation, allowing it to drip feed its roots in the scorching summer months, when the rain refused to come.

Dust united them in ochre skin, the matt colour of mannequin plastic. As the shroud of darkness fell they set up camp in a cave of billion-year-old rock. The air inside felt reverent, the cave a church to an earlier form of man. Peter arranged a circle of black stones to hold a fire. Hoping the matches in his pocket weren't too soaked with sweat to spark, he rolled a kindling ball from paper and dried tumbleweed. Outside he could hear a jet of Hens's piss oafishly hammering the hard ground. He turned to Harum, who was massaging her shoulders with a smooth, hypnotic twizzle of her thumbs.

'Jeez,' he said, 'couldn't he have done that further away?'

'It's a man thing.'

'A man thing?'

'Passed down from the monkeys.'

'What, taking a piss?'

'Marking your territory.' Shamed though he was to admit it, there was an overtly animalistic quality to their behaviour. Even this, the building of a fire, was part of a choreographed mating dance, and thinking of it now made him rigid with self-awareness. He could see the beam of Hens's torchlight outside, bouncing off the yellow river coursing round his boots.

'He could at least mark it round the corner, though, huh?'

'It would be preferable.' She laughed. He closed his eyes and hoped she would never stop.

'What's so funny?' Hens asked as he came back.

'Nothing,' Peter said, crouching by the fire.

'Nothing? Why would nothing be funny?'

'It's just a figure of speech, Hens. Don't sweat it.' From below, Peter saw Hens's sharp knuckles, protruding like sawn-off tusks. Only when the plump blister on his heel burst – a sharp sting – did he realize he'd edged backwards out of Hens's reach and was almost flat on his buttocks.

'Don't sweat it?'

'Another figure of speech. It means don't . . .'

'I know what it means.' Hens nudged the kindling with his foot. 'We won't be sweating anything if you don't build a fire properly. We'll be freezing to death in our sleep.' It wasn't that Peter didn't have time to respond, more that he couldn't. Hens ground his sole onto the lit red ends of straw. The fire was extinguished before it had begun. A thin wisp of smoke drifted out of the cave mouth.

'Hens!' Harum said. For a second it seemed as if they'd forgotten she was there. 'What did you do that for?'

'To start again,' Hens said, slugging another shot of whisky from a worn silver hip flask engraved with the name of a woman he'd never mentioned.

Perched on a barrel-sized boulder at the rear of the cave, Peter watched Hens build a fire that he admitted, though only to himself, was better than his own effort by any conceivable measure. Flames filled the space with heat and light, animating the textured rock roof above.

'Better?' Hens asked. Harum shrugged.

'The first one would have been fine before if you'd gently blown on it a little.'

'And wait in the cold and dark?'

'I'm going to the toilet now. Far enough away that I can't be heard.'

Peter watched her go through the short lifetime of sparks leaping from the flames. The soreness in his limbs vanished with them.

'Wanna make a bet?' Hens asked, turning his hands above the fire as if they were lambs on a spit.

'A bet?'

'Yeah.'

'I don't have much money left, Hens. All these flights are draining my account. Not sure I should go frittering the rest of it away on a stupid bet.'

'You don't know what it is yet.'

'OK,' Peter said. It had seemed silly when he'd put it there back at the hotel, histrionic even, but right then he was gladdened by the cool of a flick knife's blade against his ankle. Maybe he'd learned his lesson from the incident with the sheep-eater. 'What's the bet?'

'The winner is the first person to spot the Welwitschia tomorrow.'

'And the stake?'

'You know what the stake is.'

'I do?'

'The loser leaves Windhoek. Goes home.'

'I don't know what you're talking about, Hens,' Peter said. He couldn't lift his eyes from the stones in the gut of the fire, glowing red.

'I think you do.' He had the hotness of his hand against Peter's cheek now, caressing it almost, pushing heat into him, feeling the chatter of his teeth through the skin.

Just then, Harum returned. When Peter lifted his head, Hens was back in the firelight, twisting the tip of a cigarette against the flames.

'Keep this lit,' he said. 'I'm gonna go smoke.' And he went.

'You OK, Peter?' Harum asked. He nodded a little too exuberantly. The trembling wouldn't stop.

'Uh-huh.'

'You are cold. Come closer to the fire.' He did as he was told and she sat down beside him, casting a blanket over their shoulders.

He didn't feel it happen. Perhaps the shock numbed his senses. But when he looked down, they were holding hands. He had to concentrate to make sure that one of them was his. And as soon as the synapses aligned to send a signal to his brain that, yes, it was, Harum was across the other side of the fire, lowering herself into a sleeping bag that swallowed her up like a hungry python, and it was as if their hands hadn't been pressed together at all.

Hens was drunk when he returned. Peter could tell by the way his pupils rolled back, and the whites of his eyes smiled beneath them.

'What happens now?' he said.

'Now?' Peter said, unsure exactly what 'now' meant in this context. After something? Something he had seen?

'Yeah, now.'

'I don't know.'

'We sit around the fire singing camp songs or some-thing?'

'Actually, Hens, we have an early start,' Harum said. 'We could just go to sleep.' Hens swung his arms over the fire. Flames licked his cuffs. Peter heard a drumbeat of hooves in the distance, running away.

They set off before dawn sprayed the sky gold. These were the few weeks of the year when prolonged missions around the crater were possible. Rain came in occasional bursts, meaning grass and tsamma melon plants could grow down by the Messum River. The rest of the time, the crater was an unforgiving host, where only specialists in extremely arid ecotopes dared venture.

Occasionally Harum stopped to caress the X scrawled onto the map. It was now clear that the pen had been too thick relative to scale, and the ink, where the two lines met on the page, obscured an area in reality three or four miles square. Peter did his best to help navigate, but could think only of Hens, which dizzied him like a sugar craving. Hens was pale, plainly mired in a swampy hangover, the likes of which he wasn't used to, and had barely said a word all morning. Peter preferred him vocal – he could feel Hens's mood darken in the silence – and encouraged conversation wherever he could.

'Hot, huh, Hens? You know, you don't have to walk at the back all the way if you don't like?' Hens grunted, and the offer was rebuffed. Soon, he was fifty metres or more behind Harum and Peter.

'I thought it would be you holding us up,' she said. 'But look at you, strong as an ox.' Peter took it as a compliment, though it was clear she could outrun him over any distance whether he was injured or not.

'I think *ox* might be overstating it a little.'

Hens was a third of a mile behind them now. Peter observed him through the binoculars. He'd been wrong when they met. Yes, they were both lonely, but in their own very different ways. Peter's was where he'd found himself, looking for an exit. Hens's was a construct of his own. A house without a door.

He swung the binoculars to Hens's left. Cracked red

terrain flooded the view. Somewhere out there he'd find dirty black vultures, fighting over the starved corpse of an antelope. Then to the right, past a full sun crowning a midday sky, and the direction they were headed. That's where he saw it, in the distance. The exact centre of the X.

'Harum?' he said. 'You might want to see this.' She put the binoculars to her eyes, almost garrotting him with the strap, and shrieked. There it was. The living fossil.

They skipped across the next mile, and along a precarious ridge to a short flat in the cleft between two mighty boulders. Harum helped lower Peter from a thin pass to the plant's level. He caught her bag and she joined him at what he realized was the most breathtakingly bizarre thing, living or otherwise, he had ever come across. An adult Welwitschia. Harum fell to the ground in amazement.

At 1.8 metres high and 8.7 wide, the Welwitschia hadn't shed its leaves in two thousand years of continued existence. Now they were huge and leathery, carpeting the ground around it and tattered with age. Thick, corky bark encased a rigid, hollow stem. This was it all right. The biggest specimen ever discovered. This plant, looking more like a B-movie alien, had adapted to survive the most extreme weather and the harshest terrains. It had survived eras, empires and billions of men. It was one of the oldest trees on earth, every one of its grooves a trophy from its ongoing fight against adversity. A second spent in its company was a reminder of the fleeting nature of existence. Overcome with exhaustion, Peter sank to his knees behind

Harum while she photographed the shallow roots. It had granted them an audience, and was in the ground beneath them, holding them, like a hand rising from the earth, offering them to the heavens.

After what seemed like a Welwitschia's glorious lifetime, Hens appeared at the top of the pass. He climbed down the ridge, glugged a mouthful of whisky, then held the flask upside down above the leaves. Three drips and it was gone.

'Ugly old brute,' he said. Harum moved around it, taking photographs from every reachable angle.

'It's not meant to be pretty,' she said.

'A monotypic gymnosperm genus. The *Welwitschia mirabilis*. Division: Gnetophyta. Class: Gnetopsida.'

The dial clicked beneath her thumb as she wound the camera on and continued taking pictures.

'Know what I think?' Hens said, tossing the hip flask into the middle of the growth, where it couldn't be retrieved without injuring the stem. 'I think what's the point?'

'The point?'

'Of existing in complete isolation.'

'It breeds. It's dioecious. There are male and female plants. This one is male.'

'It waits hundreds of years' – Hens was staring at Peter now, spitting to get his attention – 'for a bug to come along, to carry pollen to a mate it will never even see.'

'Not all living things share your notion of romance.'

'Shame,' he said, 'shame.'

Harum was on the far side of the Welwitschia where she'd found sticky traces of nectar. The heat was affecting Peter now, and he sought shelter in the shade of a boulder, where Hens came to join him.

'Don't suppose you brought any whisky, did you?'

'No.'

'Even after getting yourself stuck in the sheep plant. Need to learn your lesson, man. A good drink might have kept you going another few nights.'

'You're talking like I died out there.'

'But you didn't.'

'No, I didn't.'

Peter closed his eyes and tilted his head back against the rock. When he opened them, it was because Hens had two fingers in his sock and was removing the flick knife. Seeing it now, in the plate of Hens's palm, it was obvious how it would hardly have nicked him. It could barely have fought off a fox.

'Thinking of catching your own dinner?' Hens asked. Peter licked his lips, nice and slow. Even here, thirty kilometres or so from the coast, he could taste the sharp salt of Atlantic Ocean air.

'Like you said. Gotta learn my lesson. If I'd had that knife in my sock in Mexico, maybe I could have cut myself free and I wouldn't be feeling as shitty as I do right now.'

Sprinkles of stone drizzled over Peter's hair. Shielding his eyes from the sun, he peered up to see Hens carving initials into the face of the boulder.

'This'll be here long after the Welwitschia.'

'Probably so.'

'My name. Hens Berg. Forever and ever, amen.' He slipped the sheathed blade into his pocket. Peter pretended he hadn't noticed, smoothing the stretched material where the knife had sat in his sock.

'Oh, by the way . . .'

'What?'

'Bad luck.'

'With what?'

'With the bet.'

'The bet?'

'Yes, the bet,' Hens said. He walked back to the bed of browned leaves, the letters HB now behind him for eternity. 'Fact is, Peter, I saw her first.'

Though the hike back was slow it was direct, and done with confidence they'd make it to their transport by nightfall. Harum talked incessantly about the Welwitschia. Peter could see how gleeful it had made her to behold it, and did his best not to prick the bubble of her high with a smile he had to force.

'Are you not thrilled?' she asked.

'Of course I'm thrilled.'

'And you, Hens?' Hens was far ahead of them, windmilling car keys on the tip of his thumb.

A cola-coloured sandstorm rumbled across the plain. They gathered pace. Peter walked as fast as he could, but his calves burned. The wind kicked up the smell of copper from the land, the scent of drought and death, and he could feel the dust in his lungs. He fantasized about coconut milk, a mirage of the senses; he could taste its sweetness, a chill on his lips. It only stopped when they reached the truck, which was coated in thick sand and hidden against the landscape like a frightened chameleon. Peter climbed in and lay across the back seat, glugging from the spare water they'd left warming in the trunk, kneading his thigh muscles, while Hens and Harum brushed the windscreen clean with old rags. A nausea he mistook for exhaustion came over him, before he conceded it was a sense of defeat. He slept all the way back to Windhoek, where he was woken by the nearside blast of horns. Hens weaved the truck through heavy traffic. There was something reassuring to Peter about the busyness of the roads. As unpredictable as Hens was becoming, there was a limit to what he could do around so many other people.

Lazrus was pleased enough to see them that he rose from his seat.

'You're back!' he said. 'And alive! I was wondering when to send a search party.'

'It's only been a couple of days,' Peter said.

'Sometimes people leave my hotel to visit the market for souvenirs and get lost for a month.'

'You're joking.'

'Oh no. You Americans. Not understanding of the size of the desert. How it can eat you up.' Peter knew the jibe was aimed squarely at him. His lips had shrivelled and cracked. Windburn pinked him from his chin to his ears. He looked every inch the tourist he was, whereas Harum and Hens could have walked straight out of a spa, but for a little dust in their hair.

'I appreciate your concern,' he said drily, and Lazrus gave him a firm, not unpleasant embrace.

'Did you find your flower?'

'Yes,' Harum said, peeling off her boots and socks to leave dainty footprints of sand on the wooden floor. 'It was enormous. The best that I have ever seen.'

'And you, big man?' Either Hens hadn't heard Lazrus, or he was more pig-headed than Peter had given him credit for. Lazrus poked a stiff finger into his shoulder blade. 'Big man? You are too high to hear me up there, uh? Like I am shouting to the top of a mountain.'

'I heard you,' Hens said. 'Do you have a bar?' Lazrus lifted his arms aloft, the ripped flap of his breast pocket revealing a chewed-up brown nipple hung in a state of permanent disconsolation.

'I have a kitchen full of food and drink, big man. You must want to celebrate after your success with the Welwitschia. If you like, for a few dollars only, I can give for you a table of meat and champagne. It will be a, how do you say . . . a banquet!' Buoyed by Lazrus's wobbly gelastics, Harum broke into spontaneous applause, then headed to her room to shower. Peter whispered to Hens.

'Listen, man, I don't have much money left.'

'I will pay for this.'

'You will?'

'A parting gift.'

Peter picked his bag up from the floor and held it to his chest. When he turned back, Hens was gone.

'You should shower too, Mr Manyweathers,' Lazrus said as he disappeared through the swinging kitchen doors. 'To eat like a king, a man must be clean like a king.'

Peter undressed in his room, flinging his filthy clothes across the dented metal bedstead. The wound above his hip had healed nicely into a scar the shape of Jamaica. He prodded the shiny new skin, let the shower jet beat hard on it, and paddled in the brown water that cascaded down his dirty body to pool by his feet. He turned the tap off. The pipes shrieked and soon the water stopped. No more than four or five inches away from where he stood, he could hear Harum – also stepping out of the shower – gently humming the melody of a song he half recognized. He could imagine her, just as clearly as if the wall had disappeared. How the water made her skin glitter. Nudity only compounded his longing. With a surge of defiance he decided to apply to himself what he'd applied to so many forgotten homes, and the possessions left behind by those that had passed. A gift for restoration.

Lazrus had worked through his laundry while they'd been gone, and it felt luxurious to pull clean jeans onto his legs; to feel the kiss of a fresh cotton shirt against his chest for the first time in over a week. He combed his hair into a smart side-parting, flossed, shaved, then dabbed a little of his most summery cologne on his neck. He buffed his nails, cleaned his ears. Finally, he shone his shoes with a vigour that reminded him how good he'd been at his job. The feeling of defeat had vanished. He held his chest high and stretched it wide: a king indeed. Angelica would have been proud.

'Harum?' He drummed three fingers against the door of her bedroom, loud enough that she might hear, quiet enough that it would not alert Hens down the corridor, but competed unsuccessfully with the drone of her hair-dryer. 'Harum?'

It was a full five minutes before she eventually answered.

'Peter. I apologize. How long have you been standing here?'

'A few seconds.'

'Come in.' She opened the door and he saw her fully. An exquisite emerald-green dress that clung to her body like oil. What gumption he'd been building escaped with his breath.

'I can meet you downstairs?'

'You are being silly. Come in and wait. As long as you do not mind me putting on my make-up.'

He closed the door behind him as quietly as possible and sat on the bed while she highlighted her cheekbones with small streaks of opal-coloured powder. The rooms had seemed reasonably sized before, but with two people in them he was suddenly aware of their closeness, as if his arm might spontaneously reach out to touch the slender curve of her shoulder and sate the smallest percentile of his desire, if he didn't concentrate hard on it remaining by his side.

'Harum,' he said, 'I hope you don't mind, but I wanted to tell you something.' A waver in his voice must have alerted her to his seriousness, because she set down her brush, twisted to face him and took his hand in hers, as was customary in Indonesia when entering into deep conversation. Rather than swelling his confidence, this made him feel like a teenager again, fuel leaping from the bucket filled at Alice's gas station to make flammable the baseball jersey his father forced him to wear. An inner monologue hit overdrive, the words 'Pull yourself together, man,' again and again, every repetition coaxing a new bead of sweat to form on his brow. Though outside it was nighttime, it was hot, too hot.

'I've been thinking about the death flower.'

'The Rafflesia?'

'Yes. I've been thinking how they grow in Sumatra, and that if you went home I could come with you to find one. With it being the last flower on the list in the love letter and all.' He mistook her silence for distaste at what suddenly seemed a grand imposition on his part, and was instantly prepared to carpet the room with apologies. Instead he found relief in her arms, a garland around him.

'You would come?'

'If you'd take me.'

'I know so few people there now. It would be a dream to take a companion.'

'Then it's a deal,' he said. 'I'll come.' He put his hand

out, reflexively, as if he'd just done a business deal on a condo-cleaning contract, and she awkwardly shook it, before they both toppled back on the mattress in a laughter intertwined, divine in his ears. There, pressed lightly together, he'd happily have remained for two thousand years, a living fossil of their own.

'And Hens shall come too?' she said. He blinked twice, three times, as if closing his eyes would rewind time to a few precious seconds before.

'Hens?'

'He found the love letter. I am sure that he would want to come also.' Peter shook his head, but it did nothing to right the wobbly tandem of the conversation.

'Hens didn't find the love letter,' he said, closing his eyes. 'I found the love letter. I found it in a book in Brooklyn Library. It is mine.'

'But Hens said . . .'

'It doesn't matter what he said.' Peter reached into the back pocket of his trousers and produced the love letter, worn in transit, but unmistakeable. She rose and walked to the door of the bathroom, switching on a small fan that oscillated creakily around the room. Peter was grateful when its cool blast roamed across his lap. It was in disappointment, the way she twisted the balls of her thumbs against her temples, he was sure of that. But disappointment at what? That Hens had lied? Or that Peter seemed so keen to split their convenient triumvirate? And to what end?

'Why would he make it up?'

'Oh, you know Hens.' Peter's inner monologue had reverted to its default position, chastising himself, over and over, for showing compassion to the Dane when it was so patently undue. Truth was, he still felt sorry for Hens. Whether he deserved to be alone was irrelevant. He was lonely. Does any human being deserve that? Of course not. But thinking this way seemed foolish. There was another thing Hens didn't deserve, even more than loneliness, and that was sympathy. He should have been running Hens's name into the centre of the earth. 'When he has a drink he just talks and talks. It was probably a slip of the tongue.'

'So you think he wouldn't come?'

Peter floundered in the quiet.

'Do you *want* him to come?' In that moment, with the simplest shift in inflection of a four-letter word, he had opened his chest and shown her his tiny beating heart. He didn't know how she felt about Hens, and was too scared to guess.

'Peter,' she said, 'I have something to tell you . . .'

She stepped towards him, just as a powerful thud rattled the door.

'Harum!' It was Hens, mouth pressed against the wood, as though he might bore through it with his teeth. Peter sucked his breath deep down inside him, locked it up.

'Yes?' She moved from one side of the room to the other so quickly it was as if she'd jumped over the bed. She rested her full weight against the door, and the sound of his voice muffled as it passed through her body.

'Can I come in?'

'Not at the moment, I am naked!' Outside, the floor-boards groaned as he shifted from his right foot to his left.

'I can wait?'

'Thank you, Hens, but there is no need. You should go downstairs and join the others.' Peter might have admired her restraint, were it not for the great fear swirling through his insides, one she had apparently overcome effortlessly, or at least that was how it looked to him. They hadn't taken their eyes off one another.

'Peter is downstairs?' Another silence, the room getting smaller still.

'He is not in his room?'

'I don't think so.'

'Then yes, he must be downstairs.'

'And I will see you there?'

'You will see me there.'

'We must celebrate.'

'Absolutely.'

'To the Welwitschia!'

'To the Welwitschia!'

Only when she was completely convinced Hens had gone did Harum open the door for Peter to leave, softly placing her lips on his cheek as he passed.

'I'll tell you later,' she said.

Peter heard Hens coughing in the garden.

Lazrus hadn't developed that paunch without knowing how to feast. It was a banquet big enough for nine, spread over a table in the courtyard that divided the bedrooms from the small apartment he called home. Peter limped towards it.

'Sorry,' he said, 'must have fallen asleep.'

'Understandable,' Hens said, gargling then swallowing a mouthful of fizzy amber beer. 'Must be tiring, being you.'

Peter let it pass and took a seat at the opposite end of the table. Lazrus appeared with Harum close behind. He took a glistening roast chicken in a tango hold, then tore its legs off and let its body land back on the platter with a plop.

'Eat,' he said. And they did, until all were low in their seats, their hands shining with sticky meat glaze. Harum sucked sweetness from her moist fingertips, doing her best not to make eye contact with anyone but Lazrus, who threw the chicken carcass to a skinny brown cat that had adopted a sentry position on the wall. The bats above it clicked in unison. Hens removed a bottle of champagne from an ice bucket, opened it and poured. His helping, the lion's share, was gone in two big gulps.

'More?' Lazrus said, rising, belching and shuffling towards the kitchen.

'Actually, Lazrus, I think we're OK for drink,' Peter said. Lazrus looked back at him as if he'd heard the world's funniest joke but forgotten how to laugh.

'Come on,' Hens said, emptying the flute Lazrus had left behind. 'I think tonight it is OK to celebrate.' He flicked the butt of a cigarette into the grass, its impact exploding in orange rain. 'Lazrus, bring all the bottles you have. I'm paying!'

Lazrus clapped a hand against his stomach and the bats fled. 'Not a problem,' he said.

On his return, Hens proposed a toast.

'To what?' Harum asked.

'To friendship.'

'To friendship!' they all said. Hens held his glass in the air until she clinked hers against it. Before Peter was even a quarter of the way down his own, Hens was wresting the cork from another bottle, rocking back in his chair as if gravity had ceased to apply.

'You know how to tell if a champagne is a quality one, Lazrus?'

'When you drink it?'

'No. When you remove the cork from a decent bottle of champagne it is supposed to sound like the fart of a princess.' Hens smiled at his own wit. Lazrus slapped the table in agreement, compelling the cat to drag the chicken bones into the bushes.

'I thought you Scandinavians were like the Russians, but I was wrong. You are funny.'

'Ever marry, Lazrus?'

'Me? Oh no.'

'Why not?' Hens was twisting the cork, but still it wouldn't give.

'It just didn't happen. You know how these things are.'

'Oh, I know how they are.'

'Almost though, a few times.' Lazrus lolled in a warm reminiscence.

'Why didn't it happen?' The cork burst to sudden freedom, pumping a small fountain of foam to the ground, before Hens took the neck of the bottle in his mouth.

'I'm sure Lazrus doesn't want to talk about marriages that didn't happen,' Harum said. Peter found that if he concentrated solely on the splendid alignment of her features, everything about this awful situation seemed somehow manageable, though it was one that had, in that very moment, turned as black as the night sky above them, and without the bright punctuation of stars.

'Come on, Lazrus, what was it?' Hens said. 'The Namibian women not doing it for you?'

'No, not that.'

'The opposite, huh? Too many for you to want to settle down.'

'Not that either.' Lazrus's demeanour had changed now, and he gripped the table's edge.

'What, then? Can't be another man in the world suffering from the same bad luck as me.'

'Hens,' Peter said, with as much firmness as he could summon up, 'seriously, man, Lazrus doesn't want to talk about it.' Hens looked at Lazrus, who was studying a baby cockroach crossing the paving slabs beneath his feet.

'Then he should buy better-quality champagne.' He tossed the grenade of an already-empty bottle onto the lawn, where it bounced and rolled to the wall. 'This one made a dumb sound when I opened it.'

'Lazrus, how about you put some music on?' Harum said, and Peter was pleased she'd successfully changed the subject. Lazrus agreed it might be a good idea, and had been gone only a few moments when they heard a gramophone hiss trickle into the fidgety opening bars of Steely Dan's 'Kid Charlemagne'. Hens sprang to his feet.

'That's more like it! Dancing music!' He spun around the courtyard, taking off his shirt and flinging it into the awning's rafters. Now he was wearing just a white cotton vest embracing the curvature of his muscles, a taut, unrelated footnote to the puffiness of his face, his handsomeness lost in this new, boozy composition.

'You really remember some moves,' Peter said, the best attempt he could muster at lightening the mood. Hens ignored him.

'Come, Harum, dance. Dance!' he said, shuffling past the ice bucket, taking and opening a beer in one swift motion, the cap dispensed behind him like a bullet casing. He approached her, his chest expanding, the eagle tattooed across it stretching its wings to full span. In that simple exchange, Peter had become no more powerful a presence than the lizards congregating at the cloud of flies around the bulb. But, he had to admit, Hens could dance, and was doing so now, pulling Harum from her seat into an uneasy rhythmic alliance she took on without any hint of a smile. She reluctantly jerked her hips in time to the music.

A low gurgle came from inside Peter's chest, chambers of acid angrily bubbling. Lazrus watched proceedings from the safety of the doorway to the porch. A new song began.

'I can't dance any more, Hens,' Harum said. Hens plucked a blue garden lily, sucked down its sweet scent, and thrust it into her hand.

'Can't or won't?'

'Can't, Hens, my legs will barely move from all the walking.' He hadn't let go of her fingers.

'Then perhaps you'll dance with Lazrus?' Lazrus dismissed the idea with a waft of his hand. It was clear his enthusiasm for Hens's drunken little show was waning fast. Peter wouldn't have been surprised if he'd closed the doors and left them out there with an audience of hungry bats for company. He was suddenly overcome with tiredness.

'Lazrus doesn't want to, and neither do I.'

'Maybe if Lazrus danced some more, he'd have less difficulty with women.'

Peter turned to observe Lazrus's reaction and found he'd already gone.

'Hens!' Harum tugged her arm sharply, but still it was in his grip.

'If you won't dance with me, maybe it's because you'd like to dance with Peter instead?'

'Hens!' Another sharp pull and she was free, leaving Hens swaying as he leant against a waist-high stone statue of a German corporal on horseback, an exact recreation of the controversial Reiterdenkmal which stood in the centre of post-colonial Windhoek a few kilometres away.

'Dance with her, Peter!' he said, rocking the statue so it crashed to the ground. 'If she wants to dance with you, then you should oblige!' Peter moved to put himself between them, thinking: the bottle. He would use the bottle. Smash it on the far wall where the geckos nest, ward Hens off with the fractured glass, like a ringmaster taming a lion with a chair.

'Please, Hens. Maybe we should all go to bed.' Hens planted both hands against Peter's chest, and with one strong push repelled him across the lawn as though they had opposing magnetic fields. Peter skidded across the grass on his rear, coming to a halt at Harum's feet.

'Sorry,' Hens said, ejecting an arrow of sputum into the stagnant pond water where cats had helped themselves to the carp long ago.

'Fuck you,' Peter said, staring wistfully at the narrow bumps of his biceps.

'I think that we must sober up and see each other again in the morning,' Harum said. Peter could hear her fury. She helped Peter stand, then left, slamming the door behind her in disgust.

Hens muttered under his breath, pausing only to squint at the moon as he lifted another cold beer to his lips.

'What did you say?' Peter asked.

'You heard me,' Hens said, swaying from side to side like a tree almost felled. But Peter hadn't heard him, and wasn't sure he wanted to. It was time for him to go to bed too. 'I fucked her. That's what I said. *I fucked her.* Your little girlfriend. When you were in hospital. Bet she didn't tell you that, huh? We went for dinner, we got drunk and we did everything you dream about doing.'

Peter couldn't turn around. He didn't know if he wanted to, but he couldn't. He concentrated on climbing the steps to his room, unable to feel any emptier than he did.

'A toast!' he heard Hens say. 'To friendship!'

At 4.30 in the morning, the blackness in Peter's room had a velvetiness to it, full and rich. The bulb in the hallway had flickered and died some hours before. But despite the still and the quiet, and the fatigue in his limbs, Peter couldn't sleep and didn't intend to. Instead he sat at the foot of the door, wondering what best to do next.

What Hens had said didn't make Peter like Harum any less. He couldn't pretend it didn't hurt, of course. But it was up to her who she chose to go to bed with. Besides, he was more upset for Harum than for himself. He could barely imagine how awful it must feel to sleep with someone only for them later to reveal themselves as Hens had, when faced with the prospect of her rejecting him. True, Peter couldn't stop visualizing it – the two of them together, their clothes in a heap on the floor – he could almost hear the lies Hens must have told her while Peter himself lay comatose in a Chilean hospital bed. But he couldn't let it dampen his elation either. That was the past. He'd been offered a glimpse of Harum's affection. Friend or lover, he wasn't sure he much cared. He just wanted to be near her, to burst through the thin wall that divided them now. For that, he'd have scratched through it until his fingers bled.

He looked out of the hallway window into the court-yard – a mess of smashed empties. It seemed Hens had finally gone to sleep. Maybe the smother of a bad hang-over might compound what guilt he'd feel for his behaviour come the morning. They could never be friends again, that much was clear. But they might at least part cordially. Peter considered leaving right this moment, and taking Harum with him, but Windhoek was not an easy city to cross by day, let alone at night, and particularly without speaking the language. Besides, it seemed exces-sive. No. He would wait until the booze was slept off. Hens wouldn't be easy to deal with when the sun was up, but he would be *easier*. And anyway, maybe Peter would derive a little joy from telling Hens to his face that he and Harum were leaving together. Didn't he at least deserve that?

It sounded like air being blown between teeth. It wasn't unusual to come across puff adders in Namibia, even in built-up areas like Windhoek. With their stout, strong bodies, they had little difficulty entering warm buildings through their foundations, pumping mice and rats with a yellowish haemotoxic venom. Evolution had gifted them brazenness too. Unlike most other serpents, they didn't take flight at the slightest tremor in the ground or recede at intrusion, which is why they were often found under-neath beds and in lavatories, and while they weren't particularly aggressive, they did bite, and would hurt.

Peter's instinct was to stand on a chair like the woman in the Tom and Jerry cartoons, and remain there as he tried to light a candle with the matches that had finally been rendered defunct by sweat on the trek back from the desert.

But then he heard it again. Closer. Clearer. Not a hiss, but the sound made by the dragging of a weight across the floorboards in the hallway. He struck a match, then another. A brief spark, but nothing. The drag moved slowly past his door. Another match, this one snapping, falling in two pieces and lost in the dark. Peter could feel the surge of his blood. Pinching the last match between thumb and forefinger, close to the head, he brushed it hard against the strike strip. It took, and the room was brought to life by a bopping yellow flame. Again, the drag, but shorter, further away, and stopping outside Harum's room. Peter assured himself that Lazrus was simply doing his rounds. But he knew better than that, even before he heard the jiggle of the handle on Harum's door.

Peter stepped onto the landing with the match held up. Weak though the light from the flame was, the silhouette of Hens Berg outside Harum's door was unmistakeable. He was opening it and about to step inside her room.

'Where are you going, Hens?' Peter said.

'What?' Hens slurred. Peter could smell the alcohol on his breath, even from this distance.

'I think you have the wrong room.' There was still the chance it could be an innocent mistake, and while there was, Peter had to believe it. The flame was nearing his skin. Soon it would burn. Hens turned towards him, but fell drunkenly against the wall. Harum's door clicked shut behind him.

'Shut up,' Hens said. 'Go back to bed.'

'Not until you tell me where you're going,' Peter said, more firmly this time. Hens began to fumble through the pocket of his trousers.

'I've got something that belongs to you,' he said. They both looked down – Hens was holding Peter's flick knife, the blade already exposed.

'Jesus, Hens, put that away, you'll hurt yourself.' Hens smiled, sighed and managed to stand up straight, but he didn't respond. 'Hens?'

The flame licked Peter's fingertips. He shook the match dead and all he had then was the sense of a giant shadow moving towards him. It was only now, as the blade came to rest against the side of his ribcage, that he allowed himself to believe Hens might actually hurt him. When it was happening. When it was too late.

'Hens!'

Peter didn't notice Lazrus appear, only heard him, or rather heard the thump the butt of his shotgun made as he brought it down on Hens's skull with a force that seemed to turn him off by a hidden switch. Hens first fell to his knees, then his face hit the floor, two front teeth skittering across the wood.

Harum had switched on the lamp in her room, and when she opened her door wide it filled the landing with light. Hens's hair was matted with blood, a trickle dripping around his left ear.

'You should go,' Lazrus said, breathing so rapidly that air seemed to enter and leave his lungs at the same time.

'Go?' Peter took the knife from Hens's limp clutch, tucking it behind the elastic of his waistband.

'Go.'

'What will happen?' Harum said. It was plain that a clock had been set in motion. They might as well have been standing over a bomb while a spark chewed its way up the fuse. He would wake. Lazrus shrugged.

'I shall take care of your drunken friend here.'

'He's going to be angry,' Peter said.

'He was already angry. That is his problem.'

'But . . .'

'Please, no buts. He will sleep this off, and when he eventually wakes up I am sure he will be more amenable.' Lazrus patted the shotgun, supported in his arms like a baby. The first sight of the sun through the window shimmered down the length of both barrels. Peter tongued the cracks in his lips. Was leaving right or wrong? Could he really ditch Hens in the middle of Namibia with an offended, gun-toting hotelier, albeit one that had potentially saved his life? Then he saw Harum, expectant, and he knew. Yes, he could. He had to. It was time to go. To adapt. To survive.

'We shall pack our things,' she said. Lazrus nodded sorrowfully.

'Your bill is taken care of. Your friend here gave me his credit card. I am sorry your time at the Ceiling of Africa has been cut short, but we hope you have enjoyed your stay here as guests and that you shall again return soon.'

'We will, I'm sure of it.'

'The big man would have no way of knowing where you are going, would he?'

'No,' Peter said, as sure as he could possibly be. 'Not at all.'

FOURTEEN

Professor Cole pushes a slice of his wife's delicious home-made Key lime pie around a plate with a spoon and imagines himself guiding a hockey puck towards the goal. Hobbies men in retirement are supposed to enjoy sounded frightfully boring. Steam trains? Philately? Lapidary? To hell with all that.

He sits by the window and looks out over the garden. His wife has done a fantastic job of tending it while he's been away, not that he can take any credit for its majesty. It was she that designed it. It was she that dug the earth. She that planted the seeds, watered them, coaxed them to grow. His wife hunkers over a bed of soil. Twin dimples duel like thumbprints at the base of her spine. He watches her turn the mud with a silver trowel, scattering pink and yellow begonia seeds. All these years later and still he wants her fingers all over him. When he feels her touch, his skin is tight and young again. She remakes him, every time. He is as contented as he can possibly be watching the shade slink across the grass, his sundial for the rest of the day.

His granddaughter will be visiting later that evening, no doubt pestering him to watch another awful television talent show. But he'll be true to his word: the promise he made in the submersible as his oxygen supply diminished would stand. She can watch whatever she likes. He's already seen in her glimmers of the verve, the acumen, the intelligence that means one day in the future, when she is the beautiful young woman she's already becoming, she too will be a scientist. She is his greatest achievement. She is his finest discovery. She is his biggest joy. Nothing Simon Cowell can say that will change that.

He pulls on the new slippers his son bought for him as a 'staying alive present', and walks slowly around the house. Its orderliness pleases him, and he allows himself a moment, eyes closed, to enjoy the peace and quiet found in each room. It forms a stark contrast to the weeks before, which now seem like a hellish psychotropic nightmare he'd been forced to endure. Is it possible his hair has turned even greyer since? His wife is too kind to say, but he is confident something about his appearance has been changed by the stresses of having such a grotesque duty of public perform-ance foisted upon him. And in such unlikely circumstances. He'd even been recognized by a gap-toothed gentleman old enough to know better while out to buy milk.

'Excuse me . . . are you the whale guy?' It had taken every fibre of composure not to unscrew the lid and splash the whole carton in the man's face. The indignity of celeb-rity. What a wretched aspiration. Makes him shudder to think of it.

He runs his finger along the mantelpiece and whistles the second movement of Brahms' Double Concerto in A minor. Most think it a rather mournful piece, with its lilting strings brattishly refusing to peak, but Cole considers it a perfect expression of true happiness. Perhaps it is because Brahms, unlike most composers, was a sceptic. He understood, as Cole does, that happiness in human beings is never complete, because we are just that: humans, by nature flawed, by nature wanting. If anyone ever dares ask Cole about belief – it happens rarely, but sometimes – he always takes time to explain how it is those who don't accept this notion that turn to God, blame Him for their shortcomings, just because they don't exist in a state of constant and unbridled bliss. It's far more likely their own fathers are to blame than the heavenly father. *Ha*, he thinks. *Chumps.* Cole knows this is as close as he'll get to happiness. It doesn't matter that he'll never discover new species of hydrozoans. He is pleased to leave them behind, along with all that talk of the flight recorder from The Long Forgotten. When he heard that they couldn't retrieve any more information from it specific to the plane's engineering, and therefore the reason for the crash, he allowed himself a wry smile. Some things are best left unknown.

The phone rings. Half hoping it will stop before he gets there, he ambles back through to the kitchen. No such luck.

'Yes?'

'Professor Cole?'

'This is he.'

'This is Nipa Dash.'

He's already identified her voice, and it's good to hear it. He does, however, fear whatever it is she has to say enough that he takes up the slack from the phone lead as though he might yank it from the wall. Whatever it is, a newspaper interview, another damn chat show, he'll just tell her, firmly but fairly. *Absolutely not. Never in a million years.*

'I'm sorry your efforts came to nothing more. That was some marvellous work you were doing with the flight recorder,' he says.

'Thank you. The chances of us ever actually finding out what caused the crash were slim.'

He clears his throat. Is it mawkish to ask? Or as a friend of Dash's, which he now considers himself to be, is it simply inquisitive? 'Do you have your own suspicions about why it might have happened? Privately, I mean.'

'It's difficult to say. There's a theory the pilot was a spurned lover. Took everyone up to 40,000 feet, knocked them out, drove the whole lot into the sea.'

'Unbelievable,' he said, and yet he believed it. More than that, though he'd never say it aloud, he could identify in it a certain romance. 'And what do you think?'

'I suspect standard engine failure. Seems more likely than a hijacking. There was no intelligence on that kind of activity at the time, not even from Libya. Chances are it was a catastrophic power outage, much like the one you suffered when you found the black box.'

'Funny how the universe works.'

'You're not saying it was the work of a higher power, are you, Professor Cole?' She laughs nervously, and he can hear the relief through the phone when he allows himself to join in.

'Hardly. And please. Call me Jeremiah.' He peers out of the window just in time to see his wife blow a kiss, which he imagines fluttering towards him on the back of a butterfly. 'So how can I help you today, Dr Dash? Do you have something you'd like me to get grumpy about and storm off again?'

She laughs once more, loud enough that he moves the receiver an inch from his ear. 'I don't think this occasion will afford you any of the opportunities for grumpiness you seem to relish so much.'

'Then I'm all yours. What is it?'

'There's a memorial service for flight PS570. I guess with all the press attention, and finding the plane . . . and then the disappointment of not knowing why it came down, it might be a way of laying all this to rest.'

He'd guessed this might be coming. As selfish as it is to admit, he'd hoped his non-attendance might be overlooked.

'Seems a little strange for me to be there, doesn't it? I mean, a memorial service should be for the families. Maybe having "the whale man" there might attract the wrong kind of attention to what should be quite a solemn affair.'

There is a pause, which he takes to signal dejection.

'I think you'd be very welcome. In a way, you've helped to keep the memories of those people alive.'

'Well, I'm sorry,' he says, 'but I'll have to decline. I think it's time to call it a day with regards to me and PS570, The Long Forgotten, whatever you want to call it. Let those people rest in peace.'

'That's a shame,' she says. 'You take care, Professor Co— Jeremiah. It's been quite an enlightening experience for me, this whole thing. I hope to see you again sometime.'

Cole bids Dr Dash goodbye and hangs up. He sits at the table and aggressively pulls apart a peach. A puddle of juice forms between his elbows. He flicks his fingers through it. When did he become this cantankerous? Wasn't he once effervescent? He was the man who'd whisk his young fiancée away to Rome at a moment's notice. He was the man who'd made love on the coarse black sand of an Italian beach. He was the man who'd stopped their honeymoon car on a hillside, opened the door, and let the confetti with which they'd been showered chase itself into the wind like a murmuration of tiny colourful birds. But it was gone now, wasn't it? Replaced with the crotchety temperament of his father. The one he swore he'd never develop. How disappointingly obvious it seems now. How dull, to become that man, how sad, how inevitable.

He dials, making a silent wish it will go to voicemail. 'Hello?'

'Dr Dash? It's me. Listen, I've thought about it, and it

would be my pleasure to accompany you to the memorial service.'

He gives her little time to respond and hangs up. There is every reason to believe she might still be holding the phone to her ear in disbelief as he walks towards his wife in the garden, arms outstretched.

FIFTEEN

Dove pushes Zachariah's squeaking wheelchair through the glasshouses of Kew Gardens.

'I hope this works,' Rita says, gently massaging the old man's shoulder – care for her more than a vocation; an impulse, even on her day off.

'It will work,' Dove says, because he knows them. He knows the beautiful flowers lining the walkways: giant, tiny, many and rare. He knows them because Peter knows them, remembers them because Peter does. Over thirty years ago, in a dusty corner of Brooklyn Library, Peter read about them all.

The goblet-shaped Chilean crocus, its unusually deep gentian-blue petals as thunderous as the sky over the Andes its forebears reached towards. The double coconut palm, thirty-four metres tall, its fruit the largest found in the wild, fed into island gigantism by the electric-blue waters of the Seychelles. The *Victoria amazonica*, three metres wide, its flowers morphing from white to pink on opening – the largest water lily in the world.

'What happened to you?' Dove asks, face so close to the

old man's ear he can smell the sandalwood in his shaving cream. 'What happened to my mother?' Zachariah's head lolls forward, his cheek resting on Dove's palm, a rough film of stubble unevenly shorn that morning by an over-worked nurse. Rita is standing over them both, protective of her charge, but also torn; should she be indulging Dove at all, when Dove's presence could be causing Zachariah stress, even though his headaches have eased? This is in stark contrast to Dove's own headaches, which are now so bad that the moment he snapped out of remembering the sickening wet thud of Hens Berg's skull cracking under the weight of Lazrus's rifle he'd run to the bathroom and spent the next hour vomiting into the toilet.

'You've got another half an hour,' Rita says. 'Then I have to take him home.'

'I can't force him to remember,' Dove says. 'It just has to happen.'

'And it has to happen soon.' She checks her watch, taps it three times and huffs out her growing impatience. 'I've a life, you know, outside of caring for old people. Not much of a life, but a life all the same. There are box sets I need to catch up on. I need my fix. I wanna know what happens next.'

Dove wheels Zachariah outside, through the airborne pollen of a million blooms scenting the air: pickling spices, cinnamon and nutmeg, wool wash and lanolin. They sit on the grass by the Palm House, a vast Victorian structure of glass and iron that from a distance looks like the upturned hull of a stricken cruise liner. Rita removes

Zachariah's shoes and socks, to reveal his feet turned sepia by time. Dove feeds him ice cream, swirls of chocolate and vanilla dripping into his lap, while a light breeze dismantles Rita's hairdo, still shaped like the hairnet she wore yesterday.

Dove closes his eyes, holds Zachariah's hand, wills the memory to appear. *What happened to my mother?* But it doesn't come. He's as still as the pagoda tree beside them: toughened, twisted and hollow.

'Dove,' Rita says, unpacking a picnic for three that strikes him as unusually prepared for someone so reluctant to be here. 'Did it ever occur to you that he doesn't want to remember?'

Why would he not want to remember? He'd been falling in love with Harum, and after the encounter in her hotel bedroom in Windhoek, Dove felt as sure as Peter that it was reciprocated. It must have been. Dove himself was the proof.

'Why wouldn't he want to remember?'

Rita takes a bite of her sandwich, butter smeared on her chin that she wipes clean with a hooked finger.

'I remember what my ex-husband's hands felt like when he put them on me. I remember what his voice sounded like. I remember what aftershave he wore. But it doesn't mean I want to.'

In the corner of his eye, Dove spots Zachariah's hand quivering, his right index finger slowly rising from it, trembling.

'That's the thing about what you remember,' Rita says.

'You don't get to choose. If you only remembered what you wanted to remember, there'd be no such thing as heartbreak.'

The finger, straightening, pointing towards the Rose Garden.

'But ain't it always the way – the bad memories burn in deeper.' And Dove is pushing Zachariah towards the Rose Garden, thinking of the things he can't forget. He knows she's right.

The first weeks and months at university were the hardest, and Dove struggled with the thought of having left Maud all alone. He called her as often as he could, and as time passed he grew used to his new life. Things slowly began to get easier. Still, there were moments. He regularly dreamed of Len standing over him, as tall and broad as he'd been when they met, a reminder of Dove's broken vow. Hadn't he promised to look after Maud? Dove knew Len would have wanted him to go to university – and Maud herself had implored him to – but at any given moment there was a voice in his head asking him why he wasn't with her. Instead he was studying for the bare minimum of time he could get away with, relaxing, enjoying himself even, successfully controlling the fits of rage that had blighted him for as long as he could remember and – he barely dared say it aloud – falling in love.

Lara Caine was the most beautiful woman he'd ever met in the flesh, and the first time she spoke he almost cowered in his seat in the lecture theatre. What was it she'd asked? Something about the chair next to him being free. An everyday question she'd rendered exquisite to his ear.

'So is it free?'

'It's free.'

She smiled and sat down as the lights in the auditorium dimmed. For forty-five minutes Dove thought about what to say at the interval. The best he could come up with was: 'You're American?'

She turned towards him, her hand already outstretched for him to shake.

'Chicago. Ever been?'

'I'm scared of flying.' He winced so hard he heard the sinew in his forehead crunch.

'You can get a boat to America.'

'I don't like the ocean much either.' At least there was some self-respect to be found in not having lied, even if he did now seem a little pathetic. But the truth as Dove saw it was that hurtling through the sky in a jet-propelled tin can was to any rational being a fool's errand. Fearing the ocean was harder to explain. The mere sight of the sea, a vast wall of blue diamond; foam on the waves like spittle in the corners of a madman's mouth, struck him with a fright that punched through his body. If Lara thought him as pitiful as he now felt, she didn't let it show. In fact, she seemed to delight in the absurdity of the exchange. Later, she'd tell him how most men tried only to impress her, and of the tailspins of arrogance she'd previously endured

222

for want of decent conversation with strangers. Dove's unfailing honesty proved unexpectedly endearing.

'My name's Lara,' she said.

'Dove,' he said, acutely aware they were still shaking hands.

'Nice to meet you.'

'Likewise.'

'Let's catch up later.' She tossed a glance over her shoulder at the lecturer, impatiently fingering his waxy grey moustache. 'I've a feeling this guy is gonna bore us some more first.' She was perhaps the only person Dove had ever met who hadn't immediately dissected his name: why he had it, where it was from. It was as though it didn't matter, as though nothing mattered but the moment and how they colluded to fill it.

By the end of the first term they saw each other almost every day. They met for coffee to talk through their seminars, read each other's essays, lent each other books. Soon they were no longer just studying together. Every Tuesday night they'd go to the cinema, taking it in turns to select which film they'd see. Dove found himself choosing films he thought she'd like and exaggerating how much he enjoyed them afterwards. On more than one occasion he was sure she'd done the same thing.

They'd eat out together on Sunday afternoons and Dove was even invited for dinner when her parents were in town, though for the most part he couldn't think of anything much to say, and he was shocked at the prices listed on the menu. It was perhaps the greatest relief of his life when Lara's father pulled a silver credit card from his breast pocket at the end of the meal and insisted he pay.

It was obvious they were becoming close, so much so that they even remarked on it from time to time.

'I see you more than I see myself,' Lara said one Sunday lunchtime as they sat in a Chinatown restaurant sharing noodles.

'You should look in the mirror more,' Dove said, pointing at the peppery sauce dripping down her chin. She wiped it clean with a napkin, laughing. He asked her about life in America, teased her over the mean weight of her countrymen, listened enthralled when she told him all about the size of a ranch her uncle owned near Denver. And she seemed equally fascinated by his life too, his natural instinct to reveal little about himself eroding as the waves of her intrigue crashed against it.

'So you didn't ever try to find your parents?' she said.

'Len and Maud?'

'No, dummy.' She jiggled a fist like she was rolling dice, an instinctive gesture that their smitten tutor had half joked marked her out as a great journalist of the future. 'Your real parents.' It was difficult to know how to respond. The answer was no, but he knew she'd push for far greater explanation than that. So he reverted to garbling the reasoning he'd read in sociological studies of people like himself.

'It's quite common for adopted children not to want to find their parents.'

'It is?'

'Often they resent their parents for abandoning them. Often they can't overcome the guilt they feel towards their adopted parents. Like mine. All that love they gave me – it feels like kind of a betrayal.'

'Really?' He realized she was applying the intense focus on him he'd only seen her give to her writing.

'Really. It's just that those aren't the versions of the abandoned-child story you see in films or read in books. In those versions they are happily reunited with their real parents and answer for each other the questions they've had all their lives.'

'I guess.'

'Can you imagine the disappointment if it wasn't exactly like that?'

'Huh,' she shrugged. 'I never thought of it that way.' She slurped down what remained of the noodles and he was warmed by having opened her eyes to a new perspective, by having planted a flag in her consciousness that he knew, whatever happened between them from then on, would always remain, flapping in the breeze of her thoughts. That part of him was part of her, forever. He'd never felt this way about anyone before, or even wanted to, but now it was happening he wanted more.

'Do you want to go for a drink tonight?' she asked, winding her fringe around a chopstick to curl it.

'Sure,' he said. He had a new shirt he'd been desperate to impress her with, unworn and not even to his taste (he'd overheard her remark favourably on one similar) but now hanging in his wardrobe, ready to go.

'It's me, you, Fiona, couple of the girls from netball club maybe and that French guy Aurélien from the news photography course.' Dove liked all of these people, particularly Aurélien, who was smart, charming and softly spoken enough that Dove had cast him as a handsome, highly evolved romantic, even though it was plainly little more than a broad Parisian caricature. This was why Dove, usually when drunk, enjoyed mining Aurélien for advice on how he might one day change his relationship with Lara from best friend to girlfriend. Aurélien gamely encouraged him with pearls of wisdom – like 'Tell her how you really feel' – that in retrospect seemed completely obvious. But in those moments, and in that accent, Dove considered them perfect distillations of old French wisdom he feared he'd never be able to enact.

'So,' Lara said, looking at the time on her phone, '8 p.m. at the student union bar?' Dove had already stopped listening and was mentally reassigning things he'd planned to do that evening. More research for his writing. Take a bath. Read a book. Call Maud. In light of her offer there was nothing that couldn't wait.

By midway through the third term he had an embryonic social life revolving entirely around the student union bar and a group of friends – Lara, Fiona and Aurélien – who were loyal, kind and constant. They enjoyed his company, and he enjoyed theirs. It was around then, and thanks largely to them, that he finally came to appreciate living in the city. What had seemed a dizzyingly complex and impenetrable metropolis had become, thanks to friendship, a patchwork of smaller, digestible pieces.

Maybe this was the night. With Aurélien's coaching, Dove was working up to revealing the extent of his feelings for Lara, a possibility that made every muscle in his body wriggle with nervousness. She was all he could think about. When he ate, he imagined it was with her. When he had a dream, she was in it. Everything he said, did and wore was precision-engineered to maximize the prospect of them one day having some kind of romance. Did love always feel so dangerous, so close to out of control? He wondered if he might ask Maud when he saw her next. He never got the chance.

Maud was alone when she died.

It was a peaceful passing, according to the care worker at the assisted living facility who called to tell Dove the news. It happened around midday. Maud had finished brunch, played cards with one of the other women residents and decided to go back to her room for a rest. There was nothing unusual about that. It was part of her routine. They found her body in her favourite armchair – the one that Len used to sit in at home and which Maud insisted stay with her when she moved. In her hand was a Polaroid photograph of Len, Dove and her, taken on the day Dove arrived in her life. The gloss had worn from it, she had held it so often.

Dove sat in the little bedroom he had in the tiny flat he shared with two other students he barely knew, and tried to cry. Instead, he looked out of the window at the people going about their day and got angry. How could they? Didn't they know she was gone? Hadn't they heard he wasn't there to hold her hand when she left? The guilt made him sick.

Eventually, and not wanting to sit on a train where other people could see him, Dove left home once night had fallen, hood drawn tight around his face. In amongst the shock, the sadness, the guilt, he felt lost. And now there was only one person in the world who might be able to find him. He needed to talk to her urgently and he knew where she'd be. The student union bar. Where she always was.

Fiona was the first person he saw, another American, her Californian accent more nasal than Lara's. She stood at her usual spot by the jukebox, pumping in the pound coins she still called fake money.

'Holy shit, Dove,' she said, 'you look totally terrible. Are you OK?'

'Where's Lara?' Fiona was so taken aback by his abruptness she waved her hand in the direction of the back room without saying another word.

It took a few seconds for him to fully comprehend what he was seeing, because initially it appeared to be one body. One giant amorphous body, with four arms and four legs and two conjoined heads that writhed together like twins in the womb. But eventually he was able to focus and discern its individual parts. Lara's hair. Aurélien's shoulders. Hands and fingers and lips. The two of them at the back of the room, kissing, in that side-on pose

228

only ever used by people kissing for the first time while seated. Dove's fury came instantly. He was not a person then. He was a collision of forces. He was speed and heat, weight and movement. And he was crossing the room towards them, fists fused to his instincts. Aurélien didn't even have a chance to open his eyes before Dove started to punch him, and if Dove had one clear thought as he unloaded this great, burning power through his hands, it was one that only enraged him more – he didn't know what Lara's lips felt like, but Aurélien did.

Dove knew then that the version of himself he had in that moment become – angry, jealous, devoid of reason – was so deeply engrained, so far from the values Maud and Len had instilled in him, that it could only be a terrible echo of his real parents, built into his code. He hit Aurélien like he didn't want his eyes to open again.

And this, Dove supposed, would be the last Lara saw of him. He'd be kicked out of university for sure. But she would never know that this figure being hoisted off by two security guards, kicking, screaming, from Aurélien's body (now rising from the ground, clutching his face but otherwise OK) was not Dove, but the shadow thrown by his father a long, long time ago.

Dove pushes Zachariah's wheelchair towards the Rose Garden so quickly Rita barely has time to gather what remains of the picnic. Beyond the entrance the path splits into seven smaller routes, each lined on either side by banks of rose bushes as far as the eye can see. Thousands of shy pinks and deathly reds, millions of petals applauding their arrival. And it is working. He can feel the headache coming, a gentle patter but growing like the first drops of rain landing inside his skull. Dove will remember. He'll remember what became of his mother.

'Slow down,' Rita says, holding her dress in a bunch at the front as though she might launch into a bold flamenco. But it is as though Dove is running into the memory and needs to reach the very core of it. So he pushes faster and faster, turning a corner so quickly the chair tilts onto one wheel, and the weight then is too much for him to balance. It tips. He digs his feet into the gravel, but they slip. Zachariah spills out into a bush of thorns that track bloody scratches down his face beneath his eye.

'What did I tell you?' Rita says, reaching them, out of breath. She is righting the wheelchair, lifting Zachariah back into it.

'I just need to know where he wants to go. I need him to remember.'

'Remember? I should box your head until you remember nothing. This is over.' But Zachariah's finger is still pointing ahead, up the path towards the far wall of the Rose Garden, and the ache in Dove's head is thrumming, stronger and harder.

'Look at him,' she says, stabbing at the air around Dove's chest. 'He's an old man. You could have killed him!' A young couple, who'd been struggling to take a picture of themselves in front of a tall, graceful Atlas cedar, pretend they haven't stopped to watch, and Rita's voice is carried by the wind towards a busload of tourists fresh from seeing the azaleas.

'You don't understand,' Dove says, desperate now, a hot sword of pain in his eyeball, through his skull.

'Oh, I understand perfectly.'

'I need him to remember, then I'll know who I am.'

'And I need to get him back to the . . .' And that's when she stops dead, and all sound falls away, but for the gasps of the couple by the cedar tree and the crunch of Zachariah's feet on the gravel. 'Oh my. Oh goodness me.'

Dove's not sure what he's expecting to see beyond the blinding sunlight bouncing off the arc of the glasshouse. But not the old man, some fifteen feet away, walking completely unaided down the path that slinks between the rose bushes, his feet still bare, now bloody.

'Zachariah,' Rita says, 'you're walking.' He doesn't respond to anything but the lure of what's pulling him onward, his finger then his hands then his arms then his whole body set a-tremor as he nears it.

He comes to a stop at the furthest end of the garden, where a small, bespoke glass dome houses a bloom set apart from the other camellias; for its rarity and fragility, its splendour, the best of them all, gifted a place of its own. And Dove knows it because the old man knows it. A mesmeric squad of pink petals, tightly bunched and shaped like a heart. Beguiling, beautiful, utterly unique, upside down in the tears that search his cheek. The Middlemist's Red.

And Dove remembers. He remembers because the old man remembers. He knows then because the old man knows. Dove knows what became of his mother, and who he really is.

SIXTEEN

Two days after arriving in Sumatra, Peter sat on the uppermost of four steps leading into the small tin-roofed house he and Harum had hired from a distant cousin of hers on the outskirts of Bukittinggi, and watched a turquoise haze twist above the gaunt horizon. Black smoke rising from rainforest fires took on a pearly lustre, forming a thick cloud of pollution that hung above the land like a guillotine over a traitor's neck. It ran from east to west, bleeding out into the curve of the earth.

'We can't go until it lifts,' Harum said. 'It'll choke us in the mountains. We won't see the Rafflesia like this even if we are standing beside it.'

'You sure?' he asked.

'I'm sure. Besides, I need to rest. I still feel a little sick.' She'd been feeling nauseous and tired for a week or more, a fact she attributed to the constant travelling and the inconsistent diet of a flower hunter. 'But it'll pass soon, I'm sure.'

Harum had been inside washing her clothes in a small metal bucket since first light, tingeing the air with the babyish scent of fabric softener. At 930 metres above sea level, the climate was cooler than he'd expected it to be, and he could hear Harum laughing when he sighed with relief. She had no idea it was less for the temperature than to be 6,000 miles from Hens Berg.

Their plans scuppered by the mesmeric bank of smog, he wrote a short letter to Susan. He'd never been one for penning lengthy letters, and was as sure his brevity would infuriate her as he was that he'd receive thirty-odd pages in reply.

Dear Susan,

I'm in Sumatra. With Harum. I'm pretty sure you're looking for a map of the world right now (if you go to my apartment there is a spare one in the drawer beneath my bed), but when you find one, the first thing you'll notice is that Sumatra is nowhere near Namibia. In fact, it's pretty much on the other side of the world.

You probably noticed I didn't say Hens was here. I know you've a pretty keen eye for the details. You'd be right. We left him in Namibia. Things got a little ugly. Let's just say you were right not to trust him.

Boring answers to boring questions you're definitely asking:

1. No, it's cooler here than you'd expect.

2. Yes, a lot of people speak English.

3. Yes, I cleaned the house where we're staying the minute I arrived.

Which brings me to Angelica! Go see her, make friends, tell her I miss her and that I hope business is OK. Tell her I have complete faith in her and I'll see her when I return. I guess 'when' is the operative word! But it'll be soon. We're going to go trekking – yes, in the jungle, the actual jungle – see if we can find the corpse flower (you don't want to know, but if you do, look up Rafflesia arnoldii – there are a dozen textbooks in my apartment, it'll be in one of them). It's the last flower in the love letter, and now that I've come all this way, well, it'd be a real shame to leave before we found it. Easier said than done.

One last thing . . . I'm really happy that we got to spend time together in Mexico, Susan. I'm only sorry it was in a tent beside a field. I'm pretty sure you'd have preferred that stupid hotel on Fifth Avenue with the chandeliers. Or that place that does the ribs on Twenty-Eighth, the one that always makes me feel like I'm gonna have a heart attack. But I can't really tell you how much I loved it, and love you. Maybe that's why I'm writing it down on the other side of the world. Pathetic, I know.

I'll see you very soon. And I hope more than anything I won't be alone when I come.

*Maybe choose a wedding hat, but don't buy it
just yet.*

Yours, Peter

*PS. I don't think this will happen, but if you hear
from Hens, just say you haven't heard from me.
It's best that way.*

He wrote a return address at the bottom, knowing
she'd respond immediately.

That afternoon, the haze refusing to lift, Harum and Peter
walked to the centre of town, swerving tourists who
meandered through the narrow streets in traditional Bendi
horse carriages. Most were drawn to the area by the
Lubang Jepang, a hive of underground tunnels built by the
Japanese during World War II that suffused the area with
the mystery of a hidden, second life. Pasar Bawah market
throbbed with noise and colour. Over Sianok Canyon,
despite the blurred sky, loomed hints of volcanoes Mount
Singgalang and Mount Marapi. Only one was active, but
Harum could never remember which, declaring with a
smile that if Mother Nature saw fit to rise from the earth's
core and remind her, then it'd probably be too late to run
far enough away. They drank spiced teas in a restaurant,
its balcony lurching over the roadside, and watched with
some amusement as an exasperated bus driver kicked his
smoking engine, hurling profanities that Harum delighted
in translating at length.

'Is it as you remember it?' Peter asked. She dabbed a tea leaf from her front teeth.

'Even noisier, maybe. It's impossible for me to say.'

He examined the menu, but the foreign lettering wriggled on the card. He could feel her eyes set on him.

'There is one thing I can be sure of. It is better for having you here with me.'

'I'm glad,' he said.

'But I feel guilty.'

'For what?'

'That I didn't tell you about Hens and me before.' He'd tried to forget about it. He didn't like to feel jealous. He didn't like to feel sad. He couldn't admit to her that the thought of them together made him feel both.

'Hens?' He pretended he didn't know exactly what she was talking about, which she seemed to appreciate.

'I wish it never happened,' she said. 'I believed the things he told me. I guess I didn't know who he really was. How else would I have ended up in bed with him?'

'You don't have to feel bad about that,' Peter said, and as jealous and as sad as he was, he meant it.

'But isn't that why he behaved the way he did?' she said.

'The way he behaves is his problem. Not yours.'

Harum sighed, partly through relief, but Peter could tell she still blamed herself for something.

'I find it odd you were ever friends in the first place.'

'I was lonely,' Peter said slowly. The words left him lighter, as if he'd confessed.

The restaurant slowly filled with lunchtime diners. Peter was wondering how he might recreate that moment in Harum's hotel room in Windhoek, when just for a second he felt sure he'd seen his desire mirrored. He was tired, though, and prone to convincing himself he could only have imagined it.

'Harum? Harum, is that you?' A woman approached, black hair scraped into two symmetrical buns. Harum stood cautiously. Peter found himself rising too.

'Asoka,' Harum said, 'good to see you.' The woman began to speak in Minangkabau, but with a polite flick of the eyes, Harum had her revert to English for Peter's benefit, and they embraced.

'Your cousin Jayakatong said you were in town.'

'He has a big mouth.' They both laughed in near-identical pitch, a delightful stereophonic trill.

'But a good heart. I had to come and see for myself. And this is your . . .' Asoka scanned Harum's fingers for jewellery.

'Friend,' Harum said. Peter retook his seat. 'His name is Peter.' Asoka pushed her lips against his cheek, leaving two greasy red slugs on his skin.

'Any friend of yours is a friend of mine.'

'That's nice to hear,' Peter said. Asoka waggled her gold-painted two-inch fingernails in the air as though she might cast a magic spell and the two women spent half an hour reminiscing over schooldays. Peter insisted they use whichever language they wished, and he happily whiled away the time watching the bus driver be harangued by his increasingly irate passengers. Eventually he heard Asoka lapse back into a tongue he understood.

'I hear you are a famous natural scientist these days?'

'You're getting your facts from all the wrong places,' Harum said, blushing.

'It's what Jayakatong tells me. He says that there is nobody in all Sumatra who knows more about flowers than his cousin Harum. He is very proud. We all are.'

'Like I said, he has a big mouth.'

'And his big mouth tells me you're here for the corpse flower.' As she finished the sentence, a hush descended briefly over the other diners. Peter noticed a waiter pause before delivering a plate of vivid greens. Clinks in the background; plates in a kitchen. Harum dipped her head close to the table and whispered.

'That's right.' Down on the road the bus driver gave up on his engine and threw his hat to the ground.

'If you know so much about flowers, why would you do such a thing?'

'It's an urban myth, Asoka.' Whatever it was Harum hadn't told Peter, he wanted to hear it now, but she reluctantly clamped her lips together, apparently content for her tea to go cold. He turned his eyes to the awning above them.

'An urban myth? In the rainforest?' Asoka swung her legs to face Peter. She folded her hands tightly around his and spoke quietly. 'Harum must have a very short memory.'

'Oh, come on, Asoka . . .'

'Everybody around here knows about the corpse flower. We even knew about it when we were children. When the corpse flower blooms it is because evil is coming. It is a warning. That is why it smells like rotten meat and is swarming with flies.'

'Actually,' Peter said, clearing his throat, 'I think that's more an evolutionary thing, to help it attract insects for pollination.'

'But it is not, I promise you. It is a precursor to evil.' A group of four men beckoned the waiter and asked to be moved to a table inside. Peter didn't know what else to say. Harum shook her head, the two birds on her necklace jangling. The waiter dithered for a while, as if he'd prefer they find another restaurant, then disappeared into a dark stairwell.

'Asoka,' Harum said, 'the world might turn more peacefully if people stopped believing in such fanciful things.'

They left then, Harum feeling too sick to eat.

Peter woke to the fury of a thunderstorm. The sofa was too short, and his right leg, over the armrest, stiff with cramp. He couldn't remember what his nightmare entailed, only that he'd had one. Scratching at the cold sweat dried in salt flecks on his skin, he was calmed by the familiar odour of furniture polish trapped in the ceiling cavity, and to remember that Harum was sleeping four feet away on a thin mattress behind a translucent partition. But only by checking that the front door remained locked could he find a sense of stillness. It was dark but he could still see the haze, softly focused through the blurred wet glass of the window. He did press-ups until his arms tired, sit-ups so his gut ached. Turning an iron poker in his hand, the one they used for the firepit in the yard, he felt embarrassed still to be thinking of Hens Berg. Finally he slept again, the poker's cold, hard handle pressed into his palm.

'You stoke fires in your sleep?' Harum stood by the concertinaed partition in a yellow silk dressing gown, pleasing in the way it caught the warm light of early afternoon. He sat up and gave his eyes time to adjust to what seemed a new reality lifted straight from his fantasies. Pushing the poker beneath the sofa, he let the matter vanish.

'Can't believe we slept that long.'

'Jet lag. Waits for no man. But we'd better hurry and get going.'

'You have more awkward conversations about hoodoo with old classmates lined up?'

'You would like that, huh?'

'Can't wait.'

'Well, you're out of luck.' She smiled. 'We're going flower hunting.'

She pointed out of the window, and through the glass now washed by the storm he saw a clear and dazzling sky.

A neighbour drove them to the entrance of Palupu Reserve, its awesome scale only now apparent. It felt like arriving at the shore of a new and undiscovered continent, trees stretching forever in every direction, a vast,

uninterrupted wilderness. They checked each other's rucksacks, then checked them again. Her cousin had kindly
supplied them with everything they might need; some of it
Peter could only guess at how to use. Apparently they'd
be able to last over two weeks if they rationed their food
and collected rainwater for drinking, but Harum enjoyed
loading Peter with bigger concerns.

'You're not scared of Sumatran tigers, are you?' she
asked. He searched her face for signs she was joking.

'Do we know where we're headed?'

She pointed to the mountains, so distant they could
have been painted on the horizon.

He swilled his cheeks with air. 'Should have guessed.'

The first eight miles were simpler than expected.
Sub-alpine low forest scrub and shrub thickets surren-
dered easily to their machetes. They hacked and walked,
and as they progressed he became keenly aware of how
vegetation changed at altitude; how he could feel ecosystems shifting in his body temperature's spasmodic
fluctuations on a spectrum topped by fire, tailed by ice.
They kept close. Though the vegetation was too thick to
sustain large animal life on the ground, the darkness of the
inner jungle promised to make possible any threat they
could imagine. They had the sense of being watched by
something inhuman, something dangerous, though Peter
was slowly realizing he'd felt that way for some time. He
vowed to himself that when they found the corpse flower
he would tell Harum how he felt about her – a notion he
conceded didn't sound so romantic. He had a bottle of

vaguely minty aftershave in his bag. Perhaps he could spray that in the air first.

They reached the entrance to a cave system, a glittering waterfall like a curtain over the opening. Above the water, where the canopy cleared, the moon's silvery clock face rose. Fumaroles spewed plumes of steam across it. This would be where they'd build camp.

Harum's clothes were discoloured with sweat. He watched, amazed, as she unpeeled them from her body until all that was left was the necklace and her underwear, washed them in the chute, then hung them over a rock to dry. She dived into the water, which seemed to part in acceptance of her form, reappearing ten feet away to find Peter still gazing at the point where she'd entered. Knowing he'd never see anything quite as exquisite as that again, he tore himself out of his boots, disrobed as quickly as he ever had and leapt into the water. They swam for close to an hour, accompanied by a choir of animal calls, before emerging slippery and new. As they lay on the bank under the stars, their breathing found a steady unison.

Day two was tougher from the outset. Though the thick shrub subsided on the gradual ascent, a fierce morning sun warmed the air beneath the leaves. Sweat clung to his body like a needy child, but they marched with impressive pace. Eventually they came to the face of a rock, where the forest split in two directions. Both pressed their backs against the coldness of the stone.

'We should climb it,' she said, 'see what we can see.'

'We'll see trees.'

'You're so American.' She removed a jumble of ropes and hinged mechanisms from her bag. He assembled them, remembering how they'd looked in his hands as he dangled from a Gibraltan clifftop, and they climbed.

The rock's peak emerged above the canopy, where they rested and tried to comprehend what they saw. To the west, beyond flocks of white-winged wood ducks bombing the treetops, the oily smoke of machinery swirled, and the noise of diggers building palm oil plantations. He'd never thought much about offspring. He hadn't had the cause. But here, above the jungle, with Harum beside him, he was struck by a sudden prescience. What would the world look like for his children, if he had any? What would be left? If there was a sign that preceded evil, it was more likely the whirr of machinery in the rainforest than the corpse flower in bloom.

'Which way do we go?' he asked. She nodded towards an amber sun.

They descended the rock face, shouldered their rucksacks, and hiked. The land was steep, the jungle thinning with the air. To stand a better chance of finding the corpse flower in bloom they'd need to reach the lowland forest on the other side of a vast ridge, where the vegetation was thicker. They arrived at a high-altitude glacial lake, a replica sky captured in it, and decided to swim across and set up camp on the far side, so that on the third morning – when all around them was lit a glorious fiery orange by the sunrise – they could begin the hunt proper with a gradual descent, just as exhaustion set in.

They'd trekked half a day into the rainforest's heart and Peter's machete blade was blunting when he noticed the scuffed metal of a stub pistol's snout peeking from the pocket on Harum's bag.

'Where the hell did you get that?'

'My cousin gave it to me. Said it was dangerous this far west. There are loggers and poachers and militia.'

'Militia!?'

'You hear about it, sometimes.'

'So you'd shoot them?'

'Don't worry, the chances of us seeing anyone are very small.'

'I should hope so.'

'You complain too much.' She stopped, turned, kissed him – not full on the mouth, more neatly than that – somewhere just south, the bottom half of his lower lip. It took him by surprise, but he kissed her back: clumsily, which made her smile. Then they continued. And despite the gun, despite lawless jungle armies, despite this nagging feeling they were being followed by a tiger – despite Hens Berg – Peter felt a trickle of bliss run through every last smidgeon of his flesh.

Something in his mouth. Buzzing. Crawling. He spat, and then he saw them: a swarm of carrion flies, thronging on the trunk of the tree where he leant. It was huge, magnificent, no different from the millions around it, but this is where they'd collected, as if this one tree was erected in honour of a great insect deity. It was as Peter had read.

He took the machete and swung it over the cluster of

flies until they dispersed like a shower of raisins. Sure enough, beneath them was a plump, bruise-coloured bud. This was the genesis of the corpse flower, tiny at first, but what would become an example of the largest-known individual flower in the world. It was free of roots and leaves, and lived most of the time unobservable inside the wooden stem of its host. But this plump bud had exploded through the bark, and, in a prime example of parasitic existence, would soon fill the surrounds with its fruits and foetid funk. From death, came life.

He thought of the verse of 1877 he'd found in a book of poetry inspired by nature in Brooklyn Library one evening, as he tired of Hens's attempts to dazzle him with science and sought relief in art instead.

> *What strange gigantic flower is here*
> *That shows its lonesome pallid face*
> *Where neither stems nor leaves appear?*

'How long can we make the rations last if we really try?' he asked. Harum was distracted elsewhere. Peter couldn't draw his eyes from the bud. Its shape, the way it was opening, made him think of childbirth.

'What?'

'Perhaps we could stay here and watch it grow. I mean, if we go back, we might miss it. It only blooms for a few days.'

'I don't think we need to do that.'

He stabbed his blade into the mud. How could she be so nonchalant after they'd come this far?

'You're crazy if you think we'll find this spot again so easily.'

'You don't understand,' she said. 'We won't need to.' Peter felt her tug at his elbow. He turned, half expecting to see a tiger. But in the direction she was looking, twenty metres away, was a corpse flower in full bloom. Over a metre in diameter, mahogany skin speckled with splotches of white, five lobes arranged in a cup-like structure. And in the middle of the cup, a column with a disc, anthers in its open jaws, like a giant mouth carved from meat. Ugliness, beauty, putrid majesty. He breathed in deep and could smell it now. How could he not have done before? An abattoir in summer.

The final flower on the letter's list. He had done what the love-struck student who wrote it never could. He wished that he could find him and tell him. Maybe that could be his next, much less dangerous, adventure.

Asoka had at least been right about one thing. It looked like an entrance to hell. They approached it carefully, as if it might snarl. Every flower they'd ever seen claimed a unique stake in nature. But this was truly unlike any other. Harum produced lavender oil from her bag, which they took it in turns to waft under their noses.

'It's grotesque,' she said, 'it's incredible.' Nodding, he felt the first raindrops strike his brow. The shower fell suddenly, and hard, a deafening commotion slapping the leaves. They quickly set up camp downwind and took shelter, watching water collect in the bowl of the flower.

'Now the rain in the jungle is one thing I do remember,'

Harum said, a slight edge to her voice. He could see she was upset, the tears on her face somehow distinguishable from the droplets around them, so he held her beneath the tarpaulin. It was almost too loud to hear what she whispered. They kissed again, properly this time, fully. It felt glorious and warm. For the time it lasted they could have been anywhere in the world and they would still have been alone. Afterwards they sat and listened to the forest.

'Do you think about him?' Harum said.

'About who?' Peter asked.

'Hens.'

'I think we should forget about Hens.'

Harum caught a droplet of rain, let it roll around her palm.

'You think we can choose what we remember and what we forget?' she asked.

'I think, this time, we can.'

She slid her arms around his waist.

'Will you stay here with me in Sumatra, Peter? Not forever. Just for a while, so I can visit family, see old friends.'

'Of course,' he said.

'Go to where my parents are buried.'

'Whatever you need to do.'

'Then I'll come with you,' she said, 'to New York.' He wound her necklace around his fingers, and bound them together. Two little birds.

Forty hours later the rain stopped as suddenly as it had started. A clear sky poked through the canopy. From far away came animal hoots, cheering the change in the weather.

Harum shot six rolls of film, covering the corpse flower from every conceivable angle. It formed as comprehensive a study as he'd ever seen recorded. Peter sketched and soon they could no longer smell death. They were far too distracted by each other, as if it was they who had come into bloom. The long hike back passed as a pleasure. At their final camp they made love. The days were hard but the nights were clear.

When they arrived home, Jayakatong was waiting. He was a tall man with long legs. A perfect circle of grey hair on his head looked like a coin secreted in the dense black.

'Look at you, Peter!' he said. 'You're so thin!' Neither Harum nor Peter had noticed how much weight he'd lost on the trek. It had been ten days in total, and there were still rations left, but neither of them could remember feeling hungry.

'Stop fussing, Jayakatong. Are you saying I am not?' Harum said, rubbing the slight belly she had somehow retained. She ditched her rucksack at the foot of the steps. Jayakatong threw his arms around them both, apparently unfazed by how disgusting they seemed next to his clean, sweatless skin.

'I am glad you're back. I've had Asoka coming to my office every day to talk about the stupid corpse flower. She says you'll bring a curse back to the town if you're not careful.'

'She's a pain in the ass,' Peter said. Jayakatong twisted in laughter.

'Listen, Jay,' Harum said. 'I think that I . . . we are going to stay a little longer than expected. There are things I need to do, people I need to see.'

'Of course, stay here as long as you like. As long as you tell Asoka to leave me alone. I have a busy police station to run.'

Peter paused as he approached the house, its door swinging on a gentle breeze that after the stultifying heat of the forest felt like goose feathers tickling his face.

'Say, Jay . . . you don't need a cleaner, do you?'

That evening Peter and Harum lay together, bodies bent to a mutual echo. Time's relevance had ceased. Peter could rest. There was just the future, and this was its wonderful dawn.

Despite feeling nauseous again, Harum left to visit an aunt in South Sumatra the next morning. Peter felt the first pang of missing her the moment she walked through the door, but was thankful for having scant time to dwell. There was work to be done. He arrived at the address Jayakatong had written on the back of a torn airmail envelope, wondering how the police were meant to maintain order from a headquarters best suited to housing stray dogs. Entering the crumbling one-storey-high office building through a door comprised of a beaded curtain and a battered baby gate, he found the station consisted of five overcrowded desks. At the back was a solitary makeshift cell, its rear wall split into three by deep cracks. Jayakatong explained how his seniors had recently acquired the equally decrepit building next door, and offered Peter a small sum to clean out its basement in preparation for the extension. Peter agreed, ingratiating himself with the officers who assumed it to be an elaborate practical joke. An American, cleaning for a Sumatran cop? Ridiculous. Truth was, Peter felt excited to get his hands dirty, to be of use.

He took the keys and let himself into the building, provoking a brief riot from the roosting pests. The room was filthy, but nothing he wasn't used to. He illuminated it with his torch, scattered spiders that had grown fat and lazy on their webs. The walls were a murky, unpleasant brown, the air stale. Suddenly visible at the back of the room was the door to the basement, and behind that a rotted wooden staircase. He descended through a foul stench that seemed to have deterred the rats.

At the bottom was a large windowless room, twice the size of the floor above. Fingering the bullet holes peppering the walls he found numerous false panels, each revealing a hidden cavity stashed with yellowed papers and books banned in the purge. A rusted safe obscured a secret door to another, smaller room. He wondered how many people had hidden here in fear of their lives. Whether they'd made it.

Peter removed his shirt and began to clear the space of objects: children's toys, mouldy make-up, old clothes, unsmoked cigarettes; possessions grabbed in haste by desperate people. He heaved it all into bags, threw the bags outside on the street. After five days of heavy lifting the stack was high and the basement empty. The blood wasn't easily coaxed from the wood. He tried cocktails of bleach and disinfectant, but nothing worked no matter how hard he scrubbed. With Jayakatong's permission, he gutted the basement of floorboards, leaving only the essential cross-beams and stanchions. Depending on how long Harum wanted to stay, he'd try and see the work through to completion, even if it meant a crash course in carpentry. He stripped the walls, soaked the plaster, blasted the ceiling of stains with a jet washer.

Back in Brooklyn, in Queens, in Harlem, that had been the dirt of lonely people. The world had given up on them by forgetting they existed. But those who died here were only forgotten once they'd been denied the right to exist. Perhaps that's why the grime stuck faster, why he almost wore his fingers down, scrubbing dried blood from the sills.

After three weeks' hard work, the room was habitable again, even if its ghosts remained. He could hear them when he downed tools. Memories of them were ingrained in the walls, far deeper than could be cleaned. His back was sore, his shoulders knotted, but he was filled by a sense of achievement. Harum was due to arrive back that afternoon. He looked forward to seeing her, to discussing New York. They'd need to marry for her visa. The idea, which neither had yet floated, filled him with a joy so immense he could feel his pulse rush. And there was more.

In their last phone conversation, she'd told him she had news, and that she wanted to be in front of him when she said it.

The door to the house was open, which was unusual. Whether in or out, they always remembered to at least close the mosquito screen. It was possible she'd had a long journey and forgotten. Or that Jayakatong's wife, Merpati, had come by to launder the towels, which she'd insisted on doing in Harum's absence. As though Peter didn't know how to clean a towel. Whatever the reason, it still struck Peter as odd, as though the house had opened its mouth to reveal that a tooth had been punched out of its smile. Unless Harum hadn't arrived yet and he'd accidentally left the door open when he'd left for work? This too was possible. He had woken late – one of many frequent power cuts in the area having reset his alarm – and remembered leaving in a hurry, his mind on other things, like the welcome-home meal he'd planned for the evening. He stopped at the bottom of the steps to remove his boots.

'Harum?' No answer. 'Hello?' It occurred to him that Harum might be in the small garden at the back of the property. He walked down the thin alley that separated them from the neighbours. She wasn't there either, but he noticed that the back door was also open. This hadn't happened before. He didn't even know they had a key. Peering through the back window, hands hooped around his eyes, he called her name.

'Harum?' He didn't want to shout. The neighbours had

a newborn daughter. Last time he saw them they looked like they'd not slept since the turn of the century.

He slipped inside the back door. The kitchen tiles were sweating; water had been boiled recently, and he could smell jasmine, Harum's favourite tea. The tap was dripping, which wasn't unusual. He tightened it, succumbing to an act of futility. Within an hour that same drip drip drip would again be nudging him towards insanity.

That's when he noticed a piece of paper on the floor, about the size of a postage stamp, then a bigger piece, by his foot. He knelt down to read the words scrawled on them and blushed. How had it taken so long to recognize the writing as his own? On the first piece were the words: *Dear Susan.* On the second: *PS. I don't think this will happen, but if you hear from Hens, just say you haven't heard from me. It's best that way.* How had his letter got here? Why was it torn? Harum had promised him she'd mail it. He'd needed her help – the nuances of the Sumatran postal service were beyond his comprehension. And he distinctly remembered her telling him she'd done it while he'd searched for suntan lotion, before they met Asoka at the restaurant. Recalling it now, he could still feel how his skin had turned pink, though the day felt deceptively cool.

This was only the beginning of the trail. Ripped fragments of the letter were scattered across the hall, towards the door that opened out into the lounge, the one that was never closed. Until now. But it wouldn't open. There was something behind it, something heavy at the foot of it, that wouldn't budge when he pushed. Something of its weight made him think of a tiger, and how if he managed to get into the room it would pounce and gore him, claw him to shreds.

'Harum!' A response, but muffled. His name through closed lips. He started to panic and rammed his shoulder into the door, again, and then again. Harder. Harder. On the fifth burst it moved just an inch, the tiger giving in, or rearing to strike. Again. Harder.

'Harum!'

The door gave, toppling the chest of drawers propped behind it. He entered, and amid the mess, and the pieces of a letter to his sister, was Hens Berg.

Hens stood, slippery with sweat, his chest spread wide, over Harum, who was sitting in a chair and shivering. Peter looked at her, implicit in his eyes the question: *Has he laid a finger on you?* She shook her head. *Not yet.* But Peter's arrival couldn't have been timed any better. He'd seen Hens angry before. Over small things, usually, like women refusing to give him their number. But never like this. It was amplified. An anger that had compelled him to somehow find them, and then propelled him around the globe. But for what? To break into their house?

Peter struggled to stay focused. He saw them both only in details. Her hair. His hands. Her neck. His mouth. The light dimmed by the terror in her eyes. He looked back at Hens, his face contorted into a disgusting smile. Peter thought of the corpse flower.

'Peter!' Hens said. 'How nice of you to show up.'

'What are you doing here?' Peter asked.

'Visiting friends,' Hens said. 'That's not a crime, is it? You are my friends, aren't you? Harum? Weren't we friends once?'

Her face. Peter hadn't seen it like this before. A blankness to it, as though moved beyond feeling, to a different place.

'Please, Hens,' she said.

'You don't remember when we were friends?'

'We *are* friends.'

'Until you both betrayed me.' Hens cricked his neck sharply to the left.

'Relax, Hens,' Peter said, but he knew Hens wasn't listening.

'In fact, Harum, weren't we more than friends once?'

'Stop it,' she said.

'You're right,' Hens said, moving around the room now, agitated. 'Maybe we should spare your new boyfriend the gory detail.'

Peter shuffled from foot to foot. He knew he needed to concentrate. He knew he'd need to be fast and strong, though he wasn't sure exactly what for.

'Nobody betrayed you, Hens,' he said.

'You did.'

'I'm sorry you feel that way.' Peter hated himself for apologizing. Hens had broken in, was frightening Harum, and Peter had every right to his rage. 'I don't know what I did to upset you.'

Hens laughed, like it was all so obvious.

256

'You took Harum.'

'No,' Harum said. 'I went with him. I wasn't yours to take.'

Hens stroked her hair.

'I remember you saying something very different back in Chile when you were on top of me.'

Peter thought about the discussions he and Hens once had about memory. How people remember. How the night Harum and Hens spent together now meant two entirely different things. For her, regret. For him, vengeance. Peter redoubled his efforts to remain calm, to focus. What was happening here? How could he get Harum out? He needed to distract Hens.

'How did you find us?'

'Went to visit your sister. Thought she might know where you were. Needless to say she wasn't too keen on letting me in, but . . .' Peter froze. He could think only of the horror on Susan's face as she opened the door to Hens, the thud it made as she slammed it on the metal toecaps of the boots he was wearing now. Peter started to tremble.

'You'd better not have hurt her.'

'Let's just say I found the delightful letter you sent her in the house.' Hens smiled. Whatever he was about to reveal, he considered it his coup de grâce – a devastating display of his superiority over Peter.

'What were you doing in her house?'

'Looking for you, of course,' Hens said. 'Don't worry, I didn't open the letter. It was already open. I found it on her bedside table.'

Suddenly, Peter exploded, grabbing Hens's right leg, lifting it from the ground and with all his strength wrenching him across the room. Hens tumbled through the partition screen, slicing his brow open on the drawers. He yelped loudly, which took Peter aback.

Then everything fell quiet.

Hens stood, now expanding to fill the room, the veins in his neck swollen, shifting.

'Oh dear, Peter,' he said.

'Now, Hens, calm down . . .' Peter found himself backing away, and was soon against the wall. Hens spat into his hand.

'You shouldn't start fights you won't be around to clean up after.'

Hens came towards him. Peter knew that if he took one hit he'd be flattened. If he was going to beat Hens then he had no choice but to do something about it now, and fast, because Hens moved with purpose and speed and one aim. To put Peter out of action; he wouldn't leave until Harum was his, however that might be.

In one smooth motion, almost as though it had been rehearsed all his life in preparation for this moment, Peter picked up the metal poker from the floor and held it above his head. He was quaking now, his skin burning.

'Get out!' he screamed.

Hens smiled. Blood from his forehead dripped down over his teeth, then his chin, and the long fall to the floor. He pulled his fist back to strike. Peter knew he'd missed his moment.

He had failed.

And then, from nowhere, movement. Harum snatched the poker from Peter and held it in the air like a sword.

'Get out,' she said, a cold distance to the words.

Hens began to laugh.

'Why?' he said, his hands coming forward, clamping round her hips.

With accuracy as devastating as it was forceful, Harum speared the poker right through Hens's neck.

Seeing how his cousin shook, Jayakatong didn't hesitate to assist Peter with their plan. After all, he was a man who knew how to clean. He warned they should leave as soon as possible and enlisted two of his most trusted lieutenants, who parked the police truck out the front by nightfall, and asked the neighbours to stay indoors firmly enough that they obliged.

They swaddled Hens's body in old dust sheets. It took all their might to lift him and turn him, and they wrapped until the blood stopped soaking through. Peter told Harum not to help, but she insisted with a vehemence he dared not counter. She hadn't said a word. Her eyes refused tears.

It was heavy and difficult to manoeuvre, but they loaded the body into the truck without being seen. Jayakatong filled two rucksacks with equipment. Harum sharpened machetes until their blades shone. Peter opened his bag of cleaning fluids and went to work on the floor with a stiff brush, pulverizing the blood that had clotted in the wood. The stains vanished under the bristles. It wasn't until he'd finished, and the air hummed with the smell of disinfectant, that he realized he hadn't worn gloves, and the bleach had burned white speckles on his hands. He felt no pain. The room was spotless. He only wished he'd killed Hens himself.

He found Harum by the truck staring at the road like it was floodwater rising to her knees. She flinched as he caressed her back.

'You don't have to come with us,' he said. She collected spit in the well of her tongue, fired it hard at the ground.

Jayakatong drove the truck into Palupu Reserve, further than before, with the authority his badge allowed. It was night-time. The jungle was alive with insects ticking. They donned head torches, took Hens's body from the van and dragged it into the cloak of the trees. Nobody spoke.

They moved as one into the black. Peter hacked a path through the undergrowth, the three policemen carried the body – trussed to a long pole like a hog – and Harum walked behind, the rearguard of an eerie carnival parade across the forest floor. The haze had unexpectedly lifted, and what prevailed were the fledgling steps of the year's hottest day so far. Harum still hadn't said a word.

He led them over the ridge, and they came to a stop at the edge of the glacial lake, where Peter washed. There was a certain calm in the way the lake rippled out into eternity, but only that which befalls a hen house after the fox has left.

They began the descent into the thick relict lowland

forest. Still nobody complained of tired legs. Harum scythed through the undergrowth. The others moved in her wake. Her reliance on instinct proved fruitful, and despite slow passage they came across the cloud of carrion flies before nightfall. There, on the flaking bark of its host tree, the bud whose infancy they'd witnessed before had bloomed to an adult corpse flower. It smelled exactly like the death they'd brought to it, so nobody would know, even those that came close, that this was the last resting place of Dr Hens Berg.

They each took a spade. Though the ground was hard and difficult to reach, they made short work of digging a hole beneath the flower, where if it didn't live parasitically its roots would have grown. Not one of them took any visible pleasure in lowering Hens into the ground. But Peter smiled as he slung the first spadeful of dirt across the body. Why? He wasn't sure. Perhaps through exhaustion alone. Perhaps because Hens's eyes were open, so that he saw above him, when the ground came in, the very final flower on the list.

Peter and Harum took their time. They not only needed to recover, but they also wanted to enjoy falling in love, to experience each of the many levels of it. It was as if they were learning it together, how to fall in love slowly, and as the days passed, becoming more proficient in one another. More knowledgeable. The way Peter saw it, they had forever, and Harum agreed. Everything that had happened to them so far had happened so quickly, so brutally, that falling in love had to be savoured. They wanted to feel it growing within them. And yet, it seemed important they did something to separate the past from the future.

The small, informal blessing ceremony that took place in their garden a month later wasn't quite a wedding. It lasted less than ten minutes, and passed so quickly that all Peter could remember of it afterwards was Harum struggling to tie a cotton bracelet to his wrist, and wishing Susan could have been there to witness it. His sister loved weddings. He'd written to her to tell her it was taking place, but hadn't mentioned Hens, just in case the letters ever became evidence. As if sensing something was afoot, Susan hadn't mentioned Hens's visit in her reply either. Both could read between the lines. They'd wait until they met again in New York to tie up the loose ends. It'd happen within a year. Peter and Harum would have liked to have gone sooner, but worried that it might seem suspicious if they went so soon after Hens's disappearance. And anyway, Harum had promised her late father that if she ever had a child, it would be born right here. Once she'd discovered she was pregnant, it made sense to stay put.

Watching Harum's belly expand, like a petal unfurling in slow motion, Peter began to appreciate what the human body shares with rare blooms. Both depend on an alignment of infinite possibilities. Life is little more than a seedling on the wind. The Udumbara had taught him that. How wonderful it seemed now, this collision of circumstance, gestating in the bowl of her belly as she slept. All it needed was nurturing, like the campion, in a nook on the harsh rock of a cliff face. Sun on its stalk. Rain to its roots. He resolved to be both, no matter what.

How consuming the pregnancy was too. Like the sheep-eater, the child inside Harum took the goodness it needed. But it would be worth it, for when it came it would be as beautiful as the Kadupul. And it was he and Harum that were most like the Welwitschia. Despite everything, they'd survived.

The months after that ceremony, as they waited for the baby to arrive, the pain of what they'd been through subsiding, were the happiest of both of their lives.

'Sumatra in the summer's no place to be pregnant,' she said, squeezing his hand until the shape of her fingertips stayed pressed in the flesh. It was a busy time for the Bukittinggi police force in the last two weeks of her final trimester, and Jayakatong had confessed to Peter that he hadn't been around as much as he'd have liked to help with Harum's sickness, which had grown as the birth neared, and which the doctors said was not entirely un-usual, but wanted to monitor regardless. Peter forgave him with a long embrace, both men enjoying the close-ness. He knew that assisting detectives from the New York Police Department with their investigation into the disappearance of a Danish flower hunter was a time-consuming preoccupation, and so appreciated any effort Jayakatong could spare. Lots of inexperienced trekkers go missing in the rainforests around Bukittinggi, he told the detectives, and they confirmed that the missing gentleman had, by all accounts, been quite an inexperienced trekker. The same had been said by the Namibian hotelier they'd tracked down in Windhoek (Jayakatong pretended never to have heard of such a place), and a Gibraltan pensioner had responded to a plea for information on a missing person by reporting that he'd seen Hens Berg on one of his flower expeditions. He said that the Dane was an ignoramus and a foolhardy climber, and it wouldn't have surprised him if he'd accidentally abseiled down a cliff without tying the rope at the top. Peter told himself, yeah, that sounds like the Hens I knew. Today, though, Jayakatong paced the floor of the lounge, where Harum's pregnant belly seemed to take up half the room.

'They're not leaving town anytime soon,' he said. Harum closed the door. It had creaked since they had it replaced, and Peter promised himself he'd have it oiled. He was surprised not to have remembered by now, given that he spent most days staring at it, waiting for it to be kicked open by cops coming to arrest him.

'Can we keep our voices down?'

'They're not leaving town anytime soon,' he said again, this time so quietly Peter had to lean in to hear. 'They're sure this was the last place Berg was seen. They've got witnesses from the town. Asoka . . .'

'Asoka?' Peter said.

'Asoka told them she saw him eating bebek goreng when she went to the market in Guguk Panjang.'

'She's a snake.'

'Be fair,' Jayakatong said, running his fingers through his hair. Despite everything that had happened, Peter hadn't seen him so visibly anxious. Until now he wasn't even sure Jayakatong had the ability to sweat. But the room sure was hot.

'Fair?' Harum said, fanning herself with a rag.

'A giant white Scandinavian guy eating duck at the market? It's the kind of thing you remember. She was only telling them what she was asked to tell them.'

'Well, she's still got a big mouth.'

'What are they going to do?' Peter said. His voice wavered and he swallowed to bring it under control.

'Search. They're not going home without a clue as to where he went next.'

'We shouldn't even be talking about this,' Harum said, slicing open a soursop to unveil the pulpy flesh inside. Peter had noticed her eating these when in discomfort, their sourness an excellent temporary distraction if eaten quickly and at just the right moment in their ripening.

'We have to talk about it,' he said. 'Not talking about it won't make it go away.'

'I'm fully aware of that,' Harum barked, apologizing immediately for her short temper. He didn't mind.

'I've got an idea,' Jayakatong said, standing still for the first time since he arrived. 'They're looking for guides to take them into the jungle. I could set them up with a few of my men. I'm sure for a little money they'd agree to walk the Americans around until they can't walk any more.'

'You think missing persons will be forgotten just because a few cops are too tired?' Peter asked. Jayakatong shrugged.

'I've seen missing persons forgotten about just because it's easier to forget.'

Harum groaned; a new wave of nausea. The two men helped her back into bed, where she fell asleep on her side, posed almost as though she was running.

Jayakatong waited on the porch while Peter prepared a cold towel for Harum. Peter found him later, occasionally glancing down the street towards the town, but it was a quiet day, most of the neighbours out at work.

'I need to talk to you,' he said to Peter, pushing his policeman's cap to a tilt at his hairline, exposing its dirtied hem.

'Didn't we just talk?' Peter drained half a beer bottle with one gulp. Though he appreciated Jayakatong's help, he was looking forward to having time alone with Harum before the birth.

'I don't want to worry Harum any more than is necessary. Not in her condition.'

'That's understandable.'

'There is more I didn't say. My sources believe Asoka might have mentioned you to the Americans.'

'Me?'

'Yes. Not that you were connected to Mr Berg. But that there was another American in town.'

'You think they'll look for me?' Peter finished the beer with a second swift flick of his wrist.

'It's possible. I would. We don't get enough Americans around here for it to be struck off as coincidence.'

'So what do we do?'

'Well.' Jayakatong rifled through a satchel, the cloth worn and smooth, its pockets hanging loose like the lips of an old beagle. 'I think we need to take, how you say . . . precautions. It might be a good idea, as soon as the baby is born, to go away from here. Not too far away. Just until everything is calm again.'

'I don't know, Jay. The last thing Harum will need is to start moving around Sumatra with a brand-new child.'

'I was thinking further than that.' He produced a tattered purple passport. 'To be safe.'

'That isn't my passport.'

'No. It's the passport of a tourist who, shall we say, mislaid it last week. Young man about your age, maybe younger. Looks like you. Same type of face and hair.'

'American passports are blue.'

'So fake an accent.'

Peter suddenly craved the eye-watering flesh of the soursop. Now he too was checking the road for traffic. He saw a couple of kids playing cricket with a frying pan, and a stray dog sleeping in the shade. Beyond that was a black car he'd not seen before, parked with its tyres at an awkward angle, perpendicular to the chassis, as though prepared to make a quick break. He retreated to the shadow beneath the awning.

'I don't know about this.' He opened the passport to the final page, where he was greeted with a photograph of a man he'd never seen before, who, he had to admit, would hold a certain similarity if it wasn't for one key detail. Jayakatong reached into his satchel and pulled out an eyepatch.

'Here. Put this on. One minute you're Peter Many-weathers. The next you're . . .'

'Zachariah Temple.'

'Precisely.'

Jayakatong straightened his cap and checked the road a final time – the car was gone now, though neither man had heard its engine.

'Hopefully it won't come to this,' he said, leaving. 'I'll see what I can do to make the Americans go away first.'

Peter pushed his finger into the beer bottle until it strangled the flesh. Only then did he notice how dirty the porch had become, the mucky fingerprints on the handrail and the weeds growing on the steps. He hid the passport in a crack behind the door frame. It'd be just his luck to get arrested for having stolen property, given what sins already stained his soul. A cricket ball bounced past, unenthusiastically followed by the dog.

Until he watched Harum go through labour, pride was a feeling Peter associated with work. Pride for a wall scrubbed, for a floor shined. So it was curious to be experiencing a far more intense version of the same thing while remaining so completely useless, as he had for the past nineteen hours at Harum's bedside. He was holding her hand, yes, but ultimately he was no more effectual than the spider watching from the lampshade. This situation would unfold with him powerless to affect its outcome, or the time it took to get there. All he could do was tell Harum that he loved her, over and over again. It was a task he set about with vigour.

The ward was small and crowded. Three beds down a woman screamed at perfectly timed four-minute intervals, while directly across the aisle another seemed intent on giving birth in complete silence, as if it were a vow she'd taken. Later that morning Peter glimpsed her daughter, squirming and waxy white. He watched another two women come and go before Harum neared the end.

'You should leave, Mr Manyweathers,' the midwife said. Compared to the others she was a tall woman. Her arms were long, as though she'd evolved to extract babies from birth canals.

'He's not leaving,' Harum said, with a determination that briefly hushed the ward. The midwife whispered to a doctor, who looked too tired to argue the finer points of hospital protocol. He sighed as the doors opened to admit another woman, this one with a belly big enough to contain a litter.

There was nothing Peter could say to ease the pain for Harum, who'd lost enough blood now to be locked in an unstoppable, protracted shiver. Concealing a fresh surge of fear that dried his throat, he looked at the monitors, each with their own electronic heartbeat. Not one of them had turned red, or flatlined, or any of the things he'd seen in movies that meant a patient was in trouble. Yet when he leaned over to kiss Harum he saw the bluish tinge of her lips, and in her wrist as he gripped it her pulse was faint, buried deep in the flesh, almost undetectable, a maggot in an apple. Maybe she was just exhausted.

'*Bersetubuh! Bersetubuh!*' she screamed. By now he'd learned a little of the local profanity. He smiled awkwardly at the other mothers, who were already bothered by his presence.

Out of the third-floor window he watched a group of young men in the square below smoking cigarettes around two of their number playing chess. He was briefly overcome by a daydream of a simpler time, when it was just him and Angelica, and Hens Berg was only a man he knew who pretended to appreciate rare flowers. Despite everything, he wouldn't have swapped it for this. A black car drove slowly around the edge of the square. Peter closed the bent plastic blinds.

'Peter,' Harum said through clenched teeth. He brought his ear close to her mouth and, as though she had willed it, it came to rest on her chest, where her heart thumped to reach him. 'Promise me when this is over, life will be calm.'

'I promise you life will be calm.'

'And we'll do all the things we want to do.'

'I promise, we'll do all the things we want to do.'

'I won't let you forget.'

'I shall never forget.'

One of the midwives walked away. Peter noticed that when she reached the doors of the maternity ward, she started to run. Minutes later she returned a little out of breath and with two doctors he hadn't seen before. They stood between Harum's legs, stroking their chins as though coming to some telepathic consensus. Peter spoke softly, slowly, so that Harum turned towards him.

'You won't be sick any more. You won't be frightened. You'll be perfect. *We'll* be perfect.'

'*Bersetubuh! Sialan bajingan!*' she screamed.

Peter heard a shift in the doctor's tone, and, for Harum's sake, did his best to stay calm. But he was in no doubt. They were near the end. This baby would be born soon, Harum would get better, and he'd keep the promise he had made. She'd bring into the world not just a new life, but a new future for them all.

'Talk to me,' she said.

'We'll take our baby to find the Middlemist's Red, in a glasshouse in England, the only one in the world.'

'Tell me what it'll look like.'

'As pink as your heart, and with so many petals you'll think it's a hundred camellias in one.'

A shorter midwife took Peter's arm. It was coming. He turned to kiss Harum again, left his lips against hers a second just to warm them.

'I love you,' she said, and in no time at all he was out on the ward, watching through a thin gap in the curtain around the bed as the medical team moved in a synchronized flurry. The beeps of machinery sped. The sound of Harum's screaming grew so urgent the other birthing women stopped to listen.

For all the wait and the patience and the pain that came before it, the arrival of the baby itself was swift. A miracle made in blood. He was prouder of her now than ever. The little boy Harum named Dove in memory of her father was new, and like no one else before.

Peter held the child's perfect form in his arms, and knew that though Dove was Hens's son and not his, he would always be his father. Always.

If it had been possible to describe to Harum how it felt to hold him, he could not have, for she was no longer there.

'Can I get you anything to drink, sir?' Peter stared at the back of the seat in front of him until the woman noticed the baby, swaddled in canary-yellow cloth, swinging punches at the abstract shapes in his dreams. 'Oh my! What a cutie! What's his name?' He tapped the handle of the Moses basket, where it was written. 'Dove,' she said, continuing to the back of the plane where another passenger had switched on a light to get her attention. 'Cute name.' Peter was relieved. The last thing he wanted was to repeat the rigmarole of explaining through inadequate hand gestures alone that he couldn't talk without crying, though he was too exhausted to find it humiliating any longer. It was more an inconvenience. Everything, his own grief included, was insignificant next to the boy.

He placed his nose against the baby's neck and inhaled the sweet honeyed scent of his skin. This usually worked to stop the sadness from overwhelming him, and it worked again now. What magic ingredient ran through the blood of a newborn? What instant salve?

Whether all babies slept this much he wasn't sure, but it was a stroke of good luck he accepted, for sleep had evaded him almost as much as language these last few weeks. Foremost on his mind was the transfer at London Heathrow to New York JFK. Sumatran airport security was famously lax. He was sure the British and American equivalents would be more stringent. But what man would have the gall to lift an eyepatch and check behind it for an eye?

Dove had pudgy baby cheeks and a tiny nose, but there wasn't one specific feature that reminded Peter of Harum. It was everything. She peered out through his eyes. Peter felt an unparalleled tenderness. The moment the seat belt light was switched off he lifted the boy onto his chest, over his heart, so that Dove might feel it for himself.

Jayakatong had filled his rucksack with herbal sleeping remedies and sandwiches. Peter's appetite was sated by a nibble of the crust, and he washed down a tiny blue pill with what remained of his water. Night had fallen outside. Droplets of rain on the window began to freeze into bullets of ice. He felt sure that, though at a shallow gradient, the aircraft was still in the ascent a full half-hour after take off.

'Crazy, huh?' The man in the aisle seat had gelled his hair into a smooth wave, hardened to the point of indestructibility. He wore a pinstripe suit, and had the ability some young, poorly suited men do to exude a confidence underpinned by nothing that came out of his mouth. 'Flying, I mean. They reckon one day it'll be so cheap everyone will be able to do it. I'm not sure that's a good idea.' Peter shrugged, and the man only imagined he'd asked why. 'It's a social contract. If you get in a tin can with a couple of rockets strapped to it and fly through the sky for twelve hours and you have to share it with other people, you want to be sure those people can be trusted, know what I mean? They could be criminals.' Peter stayed perfectly still, but even without encouragement the stranger proved his dogged capacity to not be dissuaded. 'I'm a great judge of character. They should give me that job. I could vet people, tell you whether they should be able to fly or not.' It sounded exactly like something Hens Berg might have said in a fit of arrogance, and Peter thought of his corpse feeding the foul-smelling flower above it. He watched the man drain his glass of red wine, imagined him choking on a pretzel, then closed his eyes and pretended to sleep.

As happened every time he closed his eyes, he saw Harum's face so vividly he could map the atoms of her construction. Her arms were shaped like a cradle that she rocked gently to and fro, though there was no baby in it. Peter desperately wanted to pass the baby to her, but he had no arms of his own. When she opened her mouth to speak she didn't make a sound. She was neither alive nor dead, but trapped in a third state of presence in his mind, where she'd remain forever, his love and grief for her one and the same thing. Still she said nothing as he slipped into a sleep that was needed, real and deep.

The stranger was asleep, a wine stain on his shirt blooming to the twist of a cackling purple mouth. It was the motion that had woken Peter, a rocking from side to side that reminded him more of steam trains than aeroplanes, though he'd never been on one. He briefly imagined himself holding Dove as they crossed the Potomac Creek Bridge, Stafford County, Virginia, sometime just before the Civil War, so vividly that it in fact became a brief, colourful hallucination. The potency of Jayakatong's medicines had surprised him again, even after he'd vowed never to let it. He'd caught flu when Harum was seven months pregnant, and after Peter had been bed-bound for three days Jayakatong slipped him a drug that, within an hour, had him on the roof convinced he was in a fit state to scrub all the dirt from the tin. The hallucination faded and he gradually became alert to the fact he'd experienced turbulence before, but never for as sustained, or as violent, a spell as this. The cabin lights were switched off, and from his seat at the front of the compartment he couldn't quite make out whether the hostess was still loitering in the shadows at the back. The only other person he could see who appeared to be awake was a young woman in the row behind, her hair black and tousled, mouth frozen into a grimace. It troubled Peter to witness the natural toffee hue in her cheeks fading, closer to the pale of nougat.

'*Bagaimana menurutmu yang terjadi?*' she asked, of

which Peter now knew enough to understand. *What do you think is happening?* He shook his head and pulled Dove tighter to his chest. '*Bagaimana menurutmu yang terjadi? Bagaimana menurutmu yang terjadi!?*'

The hostess appeared from behind the curtain of the compartment in front, dragging herself up the aisle by the seat tops, knees locked at doe angles. He yearned for her to spout the name of a weather system he'd never heard of, some phenomenon which might explain a lurch in the plane's altitude that made him feel as though he were floating and falling simultaneously, for it was simpler to pin fate to the inexplicable – it was why people believe in God, a folly in which he briefly allowed himself to see merit.

'The seat belt! Put the seat belt on!' He showed her the belt, already fastened around his waist. 'Not yours,' she said, 'the baby's.'

'*Bagaimana menurutmu yang terjadi? Kita akan jatuh? Kita akan mati!?*' the Indonesian woman screamed. Peter looked at the stranger, who still hadn't woken. He poked the man's shoulder with a stiff index finger and he fell forward, the dead weight of his head only kept from his lap by the belt round the tub of his paunch. Peter could hear his own heart above the screaming, and the roar of air cut in two by the wings.

He removed the eyepatch and used it to tie Dove into the Moses basket, then threaded the seat belt through the handles to secure it to the base of the seat. Finally, after kissing the baby's head once more, he fastened Harum's necklace around the handle of the basket, taking the silver ring from his finger and threading it through. He wasn't superstitious and didn't believe in ghosts, but in that moment truly believed Harum would keep Dove safe, that this was the reason she had died, so that Dove would not.

The plane nosedived, firing the hostess and anything not tied down into the ceiling. She fell back to the floor like a stringless marionette. There was more screaming from the back of the compartment, but still the stranger remained unconscious. From the cockpit, the hiss of a radio, its button depressed but no one talking, as though the limp weight of the pilot's body had come to rest against it. Peter turned to see the woman clambering over the seats behind her, the heel of her shoe piercing the soft flesh above a man's collarbone. Oxygen masks fell like stirred tree snakes. Peter attached his own, and then Dove's, surprised by how vividly he'd remembered the safety procedure. As he became aware that only the belt and not gravity held him to his seat, the woman flew over his head backwards, or forwards, and crashed through the curtain. Peter lowered his face – or was he moving sideways now? – so that it was close to the baby's head and inhaled a final time before slipping into unconsciousness, thinking of Harum.

He was underwater. The stranger clawed at his seat belt. The floor lights of the aisle remained on, and for a moment they all seemed to concentrate on the man's face.

His eyes dulled. Peter watched as the man stopped flailing and drowned where he sat.

Just before the lights were extinguished, Peter turned and saw through a field of belongings – handbags, dolls, wallets, passports, airline meal trays – that the Moses basket was still tied to the bottom of the seat. But the seat had come loose and, acting as a flotation device, was carrying both Dove and the basket towards a pocket of air in the far corner of the cabin that, even through the gloom of ice-cold water, Peter could see diminishing. He reached out to grab it but was seconds too late. His belt would unlock no more easily than the stranger's. Dove was gone.

There was a great clunk, and the cabin was cast into a sinewy blackness. All Peter could see as water filled his lungs was the glint of Harum's necklace, two small silver birds above him, moving further away, as though in flight towards the sun.

As the plane sank, it was pulled in two like a huge metal cracker. Unsure what was up, what was down, Peter used all that remained of his will to squeeze the clip of the seat belt a final time. It came undone in his hands and the seat sank into the dark with only enough time for him to grab the life jacket beneath it. He was free, floating and spinning through the water, to see below him flight PS570, halved, taking all that had travelled aboard it into the dark far beneath. He'd seen death at close quarters more than once, but few would witness it on such an unfathomable scale as this. He might have remained numb forever, given up and died himself, were he not overtaken in that moment by a powerful urge to live and find the boy. He frisked the life jacket for the emergency buoyancy cord and pulled. It inflated in his arms and he shot upwards, towards whatever was above. Life, or a semblance of it. This would remain to be seen.

He broke the surface and was welcomed by a generous morning as he emptied his lungs into a gentle sea. Somewhere nearby he heard a baby crying, a noise as beautiful as any. He swam towards it to find Dove, wet and cold but warming in the sun, and, above all else, alive. He could still smell the scent of his skin. Of her.

There was debris floating all around them. Seat bottoms, metal sheets, the plastic doors of the luggage holds. Peter hoisted himself across the biggest piece of it he could find and held on to the basket, drifting aimlessly until he found enough strength to kick his legs, while the sun dried his shirt. Dove quickly fell asleep again and Peter wrapped him in the warm cloth. He had no perception of where in the world he was, or in which direction he should head, only that the sun would go down before long. How cruel an irony it seemed that where a plane crash could not kill them, the spinning of the planet might. Paramount now was getting Dove to land, and he rubbed dry the birds on the necklace between his thumb and forefinger for the strength he'd need to start swimming.

Lowering his right leg into the water he tore an inch-long gash in his thigh. It was only then he noticed what it was he'd climbed atop. A sheet of metal from the plane's fuselage, about the diameter of a school desk. The metal was layered and sandwiched around a hollow, hence its buoyancy. Engineering wasn't Peter's forte, but he knew enough to see that this wasn't a part of the plane's wing or belly. When he turned the metal over he found, bolted to the other side, the black box recorder of flight PS570. It was floating, and that was all that mattered. He could use it. They could try to live.

He kicked and swam, the basket strapped to his back, and, if only to keep himself awake, he decided to tell Dove a story. The story of how he came to meet his mother. It all started with the day he found a small purple flower in a dirt-caked bathroom. And from there he told him about the Udumbara and the campion. He told him about the sheep-eater and the Kadupul. He told him about the Welwitschia and the corpse flower. He told him how he'd fallen for the most beautiful woman he'd ever seen, and what became of Dr Hens Berg.

He told him the story from the beginning, hoping for nothing more than to make it to the end. And as the words left his mouth, it was as though they were being deleted from his memory. In the shock and the grief and the pain, he was vanishing. It didn't matter that the child wouldn't understand the meaning of the words being said. By hearing them, they'd be recorded, embossed on his soul. Nothing there can be forgotten.

It was two hours until he saw land, over four until he reached it. When he sensed a mass beneath him, he abandoned the large chunk of fuselage with the black box attached to it, which he figured would wash up close behind him, and allowed the waves to nudge him onto the sand, where for a minute or so – long enough to dream for a final time of Harum breathing air from her lungs into his – he lost consciousness.

When he woke again, he remembered nothing of his life or what had gone before.

Dove was hungry, but otherwise alive as Peter dragged the basket up the beach.

Peter was now so exhausted that the density of his bones tripled. He was aware, and then not aware, that he was entering a state of some delirium – the combined effect of exhaustion, blood loss and shock had not only robbed him of the power of speech, but had also convinced him he was little more than a ship made of flesh, that he was being captained by another who'd failed to keep him from careering into rocks. Was he hallucinating the little girl, face white and round and smooth, a bucket full of shells in her arms?

'Hello,' she said, and wary of sirens he ignored her and carried on walking.

Dusk was setting in, and it was just the right time of year to wash the sky a pale purple. Peter made out a thin strip of twinkling lights in the distance, a village or town. But by now he could hardly walk and the lights moved further away the nearer he came. So he said it, actually said the words.

'I am going to die.' And then he sat down by a wall of

rocks with the baby beside him, screaming. He was absent from his mind and body. The world was an assembly of ochre shadows. But the cry was fuel. He knew not who he was, or even who the baby was, but on a level of basest instinct, that the baby must be taken to safety. That was all there was left. So he was walking. Carrying Dove. Moving towards the light. Dying.

After a while he found himself in a town square. One of the lights was blue. He set the boy down. And then, unable to remember the basket by his feet, the child in it or any of their past, he started to walk again.

He slept and walked for three weeks straight. When they found him he couldn't speak. He was alive but not alive, how he would always be without her.

'Zachariah Temple?' the man said, a battered passport in his hand.

SEVENTEEN

Professor Cole despises beaches, always has, always will. Quite why anyone would willingly spend precious leisure time on or around sand is a source of endless bafflement to him. It's a displeasure that goes largely unvoiced these days, mainly because it annoys his wife enough that she says it brings her out in hives. For as much as she's prone to exaggeration, she loves the sun and nothing pleases her more than a fortnight's beach holiday in southern Spain. Apparently it dampens her excitement to have him remind her of his reason for hating beaches. Sand is death.

So to be standing on a beach in his best suit and shoes is almost the exact opposite of what he wants to be doing – playing with his granddaughter in the garden – at this precise moment in time. However, he promised Dr Dash he wouldn't complain, at least until they were back in her car, driving up the motorway towards home. That, how-ever, seems ages away.

Another thing Professor Cole doesn't enjoy – though ultimately no one does – is memorial services, but he nods solemnly as the priest reads a eulogy, shouting over the rumble of the tide.

An old lady shuffles to the front of the small congregation to lay a wreath on the sand. She is crying. Cole is glad he'd worn sunglasses this bright morning, their lenses big enough to hide the wetness in his eyes. His own father died in a car accident months before his birth, and even now he experiences what he terms phantom pangs in the middle of the night: a longing for a man he's never met. Who is he to judge the extent of her grief? For a husband perhaps? A son? Remarkable, really, that she still hears the echoes of her loss thirty years on. Maybe that's why people worship the beach, he reasons. Billions of years of the past between your toes is a nice reminder of a lifetime's wider insignificance. To know we're grains of sand on the beach of history is to grieve a little less for life's end.

The woman is on her knees. Two young men try to lift her to her feet. No pain greater than a memory, he supposes. Cole can't watch. He thrusts his hands into the pockets of his coat, takes a few measured steps back and looks further down the beach, to where he sees a small group of people climbing out of a car. He assumes they are embarrassingly late for the service. And they'll be later still. With the large lady in the overbearing jewellery is a young, sick-looking man, charged with pushing an older gentleman in a wheelchair out onto the beach at which he points. What a ludicrous thing to attempt. Still, with some persistence and a considerable amount of effort, the young man manages it, positioning the wheelchair at the lip of the ocean. Good job my wife isn't here, Cole thinks. He'd not hear the end of this if she was. Age is the only excuse she deems acceptable for Cole despising beach holidays, and yet here is a man as old as the earth's crust, content to be pushed onto the sand in a wheelchair.

'So you'll still say a few words?' Dr Dash stands beside him, scarf wound twice around her neck.

'What?' he whispers.

'You agreed, remember?'

'That doesn't sound like me. I don't agree to things.'

'You agreed to speak at the end of the service.'

'Must have been under duress.'

'I think everyone would like to hear what you've got to say, Professor Cole. You're the hero of the piece, after all.'

'Hero?' he says, a little too loudly. A man in front, tall and broad-shouldered enough to resemble a wardrobe in silhouette, turns around and shushes them both with a serious brow. Dash lowers her voice to a level Cole can barely discern over the heckle of a passing seabird.

'You know what I mean.'

'There are heroes greater than I.'

'I'm sure there are,' she says. 'But it's you whose words we want to hear.'

Cole has even less time for public speaking than he does for picking loose sand out of his underwear. But events have aligned in such a way that delivering a short eulogy is a civic duty only he can fulfil. He turns away again, hoping that not looking into the crying eyes of the relatives of those lost on The Long Forgotten may help him find a few words of tribute that won't be considered overly sentimental. Sentimentality gets civilization nowhere, as any true scientist knows. That said, sentimentality has a time and a place, and when he remembers his and his wife's courtship, he comes over all gooey, as though his bones are as soft as his heart. Those were happy times, studying in New York City, writing silly little love letters to the botany student he had fallen for and leaving them in books for her to find, feigning knowledge of flowers in the hope she'd be impressed.

The young man who had been pushing the wheelchair lies on the beach where the dry sand turns to wet. He seems peaceful enough, gently cajoled by the nudge of the waves like a beam from an ancient shipwreck washed ashore. The woman watches as the old man stands from the wheelchair, takes the few steps towards the young man and kneels to cradle him in the ocean. As the waves burst around them, Cole thinks of his favourite sub-aquatic creature, the seahorse. Most of his peers pay little attention to its study, but for Cole, the humble seahorse is that most special of living creatures. Not for its unusual shape – the prehensile tail for clinging to underwater vegetation, the tube-like mouth for sucking in tiny crustaceans, the protective bony plates in the skin – but for a trait unique to the family Syngnathidae, and indeed natural life. The seahorse is the only creature in which the male of the species becomes pregnant and carries the young. Births them out into the depths of the sea to try their luck on life's capricious currents.

What led him down this train of thought? Ah yes. The man and the boy. Father and son, he's no doubt. And with that, it is time to speak.

EIGHTEEN

Peter holds Dove in the water as if in baptism, and sure enough says his name: 'Dove', as though it is being given. For the first time in Dove's life, it feels right. It is his.

He sees a flicker in Peter's eyes, and knows that now they both remember. This is where they once made it to land.

'Dove,' Peter says again, smiling this time, and his arms coil around Dove's chest so tightly that Dove feels as if he'll never be let go of again.

'You're Peter Manyweathers,' he says, and Peter nods, lost in reminiscence of a time long forgotten, thirty years before, when he was a cleaner and a flower hunter from Brooklyn, New York. In his hands, a piece of Harum. In his hands his son. 'You're my father.'

Rita waits further up the beach. She is crying. Beyond her, a crowd of people, apparently gathered in mourning, their sobs also carried on the wind: sounds that seem to Dove so entirely misplaced. This isn't an ending. It is a beginning.

'You'll freeze out here,' Rita says. 'I'll go and heat up

the car.' But Dove hasn't noticed the cold. The drum of the waves soothes the ache in his head until finally it is gone. He knows it will not return. There is nothing else to remember. Everything is complete.

The thin, silvering man finishes speaking to the people, who break into a ripple of applause. This moves the man so much that he too starts to cry. The woman who'd been accompanying him comes to his side and stands on tiptoes to wrap her arms around his shoulders. They step aside so that another woman in a black hat and veil can lay a wreath made of roses where the man had stood.

Two red petals are plucked free by a stiff and sudden breeze. The petals tumble and joust in mid-air, carried high above Dove and Peter's heads as Dove stands, takes Peter's hand, helps him to his feet and walks with him over the sand towards home.

ACKNOWLEDGEMENTS

My friend and editor Francesca Main is perfect. No book without her. Thank you. Thanks to Paul Baggaley, Kish Widyaratna, Laura Carr, Katie Tooke, Lucie Cuthbertson-Twiggs and everyone at Picador.

Thank you to Cathryn Summerhayes, brilliant and indefatigable friend and agent. Thanks to Irene Magrelli, Katie McGowan, Amanda Davis, Hannah Young, Melissa Myers and Siobhan O'Neill.

Onwards, occasional partners in writing crime and crime writing, Michael Holden, Michael Gillard and Rebecca Lucy Taylor.

Team Bon Volks.

Love to Jill and Keith Whitehouse, mum and dad. Love to Alison, Darren, William and Oliver Munro. Love to Glenn, Alex, Thomas, Anna and Jonathan Whitehouse.

Love to all the Jakemans, Mark, Elaine, Edward, Sam, Evie, Grace, Rob, Amy, Betsy and Buddy.

Love to my friends.

Without Lou and Douglas, nothing. A love beyond expression.